The Emerald Prairie

The Emerald Prairie

by

Harold G. Ross

Sunflower University Press®
1531 Yuma • P.O. Box 1009 • Manhattan, Kansas 66505-1009 USA

Printed in the United States of America on acid-free paper.

Cover by Tom Bookwalter, Olsburg, Kansas.
Line graphics by Rodney Hoover, Manhattan, Kansas.
Edited by Carol A. Williams.

ISBN 0-89745-274-7

Sunflower University Press is a wholly-owned subsidiary
of the non-profit 501(c)3 Journal of the West, Inc.

For My Father
Herbert Thomas Cleveland Ross

One

I WOULD GUESS that God-fearing men know that everything began in the Garden of Eden in that first light of God's golden glow. My destiny was sealed there, my blueprint cataloged for the future with all mankind, when I, Bruce Jacob Ross, became a descendent of Adam and Eve. My ancestors down to Noah are listed in the book of Genesis of the King James Bible.

But after the great flood, my forebears remain unknown, for Noah's prodigy soon scattered across the earth. Yet, millenniums later, I can see another dawning, from out of arctic snows — the dauntless beginning of my lineage on the wheel of time.

Along the pristine shores of Norway, a bold young Viking warrior peered into an endless North Sea to far horizons. A week later he stood at the bow of a ship that plowed waves, with rough seas running and wet winds blowing . . . a ship of many warriors, dressed in skins and armed for battle. The young Viking assessed the distant shoreline of Scotland as thirty oarsman pulled for land, along with ten other ships. He waited for the grating of the hull to hit the beach. His muscular body was tense, his long blond hair whipping in the wind, his determined hawkish face anticipating the battle.

The engagement would be fierce, for he had fought the Gaelic before, only to be defeated and pushed back into the sea. He'd been one of the few to escape and return to his homeland.

With his sword gleaming red from the light of the setting sun, the Viking and his fellow warriors spilled over the sides of their ship to ravage and plunder the nearby village. They took the land, then stayed and intermarried, their offspring becoming my forefathers, the Highlanders of Scotland.

In 1774, my Great-Grandfather John Ross shipped from Tain, Scotland, to the eastern shores of America, and settled in Virginia. Seventy-eight years later, at the spreading feet of the Blue Ridge Mountains, I was born, and when I was going on eighteen, my family moved West, to the still-new state of Kansas. Though thrilled with the endless horizons and magnificent vistas from the rolling plains and uplands, in time I had a yearning for adventure, a desire that ran heavy in my blood, passed down in the seed of Ross men.

It was 1870 when Ma, Pa, my three sisters, one brother, and I left Virginia and came West. We'd taken the train to what seemed to be at the heart of the American continent, a town called Junction City, and homesteaded nearby, amidst the rolling hills of prairie grass above the rimrock east of Upper Humboldt Creek. Where we lived was Upper McDowell Creek, our home only a few hundred feet from the divide that separated McDowell from Humboldt. But after we'd built the house, I began to think I might want to see more country before I set my hand to a life of farming.

By the middle of the following year, I'd become restless. In my bedroom, in the glow of a kerosene lamp, and before walking down the steps and outside into the gray of dawn, I looked at my image in the mirror. The dim light reflected a young man with sandy brown hair and ruddy complexion. I carried a solid one hundred-eighty pounds on a five-foot, ten-inch frame, and felt older than my eighteen years. Almost everyone called me B.J. Only when she was angry with me did Ma call me Bruce Jacob.

Ma worried that I was still a lad, but when I was eight, I'd temporarily become the man of the house, doing man's work while Pa was away fighting for the Confederacy.

That warm June day when I left Kansas, Pa and I shook hands and Ma was teary-eyed as I mounted my black stallion, Dandy. Flashing a white blaze and stockings, there wasn't a faster horse around. He'd been named after his grandsire, who was then in the hands of Civil War General George Armstrong Custer.

The Ross men were horse people, and had been since the Revolutionary War. We'd raised some of the best quarter horses in the country back in Loudoun County, Virginia, near Snickers Gap. Not only were we horse people, but our entire part of the state was noted for raising horses. Pa had told me almost all the boys that went off to the war from our county were horsemen with the cavalry, or were with the teamsters, using mules to haul wagonloads of supplies for the Army.

I was riding a horse by the time I was three, and at eight I could race with anybody. I'll not forget Pa's advice soon after I'd started on horseback.

"Son," he'd said, "take good care of your animal and he'll take care of you; and be gentle with your horse." He'd paused, then hastened to add, "Never beat a horse; there are kinder ways to make him mind."

At the time, I wondered why he'd made the point between good care and gentle care, thinking they were the same; but after watching Pa handle his mounts, I could see the difference. His gentleness conveyed a kind of love the animals understood.

I recalled how on a warm day in May of 1868, Pa had asked me to go to the barn with him. In a box stall, a mare had just given birth to a foal, and standing on wobbly feet was the prettiest black colt I'd ever seen.

"It's yours," Pa'd said, as we stood by in admiration.

I ran to the foal, and could see that his coloring and markings were the same as his grandsire, Dandy, who'd been one of my favorite horses. With my arm around the colt, I asked Pa if I might call him Dandy too.

A soft breeze was rustling the leaves of a nearby oak tree, and summer lay green across the land when I rode away from our Kansas homestead. I think it was in all young men those days to take wing to see what was beyond the next bluff. Curiosity for the unknown had been part of me for years. When a lad in Virginia, I'd lay abed at night listening to the eleven o'clock train as it whistled from Manassas Gap some ten miles away. The lonely echoing blasts coming across the grasslands started me to wondering who it might be that rode those railcars, even in the night. Who were these people? And where were they going? To some desired destination . . . or nowhere? Those were the nights the seed was planted to ride the mysterious rails.

Pa was all for my seeing the world beyond the fences of my youth, but Ma was none too happy about my leaving. Although I'd be nineteen in October, it'd be the first time I'd ever been away from family, except for a winter at Washington College.

I couldn't remember, looking into my past, when responsibility hadn't laid heavy upon my shoulders. When Pa went off to fight with Stonewall Jackson, it was left for me to care for the livestock and plant the row crops. Ma helped me at first with the milking, and in the early part of the war, Pa managed to get home to do the spring plowing and planting, but I carried the biggest share.

I furnished most of the table meat while Pa was gone. Game was fairly plentiful in the mountains where we lived, but I'd usually hunt afar, with my .44 Henry rifle and .44 Remington handgun, leaving the game close to home for emergencies. Ammunition was scarce in wartime, and I made every shot count. By the time I was nine, I rarely missed bringing down whatever I was aiming at on the first shot. Those were the years I learned to handle guns and to track game. Mostly I'd hunt deer, rabbit, squirrel, and beaver. By early summer, we always had plenty of chicken to eat; and we raised a few pigs on the place, so that by harvest moon I'd butcher a hog.

I handled butchering the same way I'd seen Pa do it. Under a tree limb rigged with block and tackle I'd heat a barrel of water to boiling. Ma and the girls would herd the hog close to the barrel, where I'd shoot it with my rifle; then with my hunting knife I'd quickly stick the jugular and gut it. After latching the tackle to the hog's hind feet, I'd hoist the animal up over the barrel and drop it into the boiling water, then lift it up and back down again. I'd repeat that process until the hog could be easily scraped. Then, after moving the barrel, I'd drop the hog to a tarp, and following upon a thorough scraping, Ma and I'd set to butchering.

I was twelve when Pa came home, in April of 1865, after the Confederate surrender at Appomattox. Our farm had been destroyed during the last days of the war by Union cavalry, and all the family pitched in to rebuild.

In 1870, Pa sold the farm, and it was in July of that year that we moved to Kansas. By the next spring, we'd finished our homesteading requirements to clear and improve the land, and that was when I told Pa I'd like to see some more of the world before I settled down. Pa approved the idea, acknowledging he'd want to do the same were he my age.

I knew there were risks and that I'd have to be wary, for those were dangerous times. The West was still untamed, and the law was most often enforced at the barrel of a gun. My thoughts rambled off in many directions as I readied Dandy and strapped down my bedroll.

I kissed Ma goodbye, and she reminded me not to forget my Bible. I told her, "Don't be worryin', Ma, I have it in my saddlebags."

Pa never had much to say, but we shook hands as he simply advised me, "Take care, son." To my surprise, he handed me his twelve-inch dirk, an heirloom passed down from my Great-Great-Grandfather James.

"This is yours now, " he added. "I won't have to tell ya of the dangers you'll face in your travels; and don't be gone long, for what's here is yours too."

The sun was at my back and barely peeking over the far horizon when I stopped Dandy along the bluffs above Humboldt Creek. Except for the long dark shadows, a lemon sunlight owned the prairie grass as far as I could see. At the place where the rimrock was split wide enough, I reined Dandy gingerly down through the fracture and slope to Humboldt Road.

When Dandy breasted the Clarks Creek hills that June day of 1871, I paused along the bluff and looked down upon a view of the lonesome prairie and valley.

In 1871 another eighteen-year-old, named Riley, in Newton, Kansas, had killed four Texans in a gunfight at a local bar and dancehall. When the smoke cleared, the kid was gone, and no one ever saw him again.

James Butler Hickok — "Wild Bill" they called him — was the Marshal at Abilene then, some twenty miles west of Junction City, and at around the same time of my leaving home, Jesse and Frank James rode into Abilene. Not more than two weeks earlier, they'd robbed the bank at Corydon, Iowa, word had it, escaping with $6,000. Hickok, hearing that the James boys were around, became concerned and met with the outlaws. They soon came to an agreement. Hickok would not bother them while they were in town, if they caused no trouble. But I can only imagine that Hickok had the banks closely watched. The James boys kept their word, however; they were not a problem, and two days later they left Abilene and returned to Missouri.

That was also the year gunfighter Clay Allison, from Tennessee, had moved onto his newly purchased ranch in Colfax County, New Mexico. And it was the summer that eighteen-year-old John Wesley Hardin paid a visit to Abilene, coming in with a herd of Texas longhorns. At fifteen, he'd killed his first man, and at twenty-one, his thirty-ninth. One of his victims had died in Abilene.

Hardin had checked in at a hotel there, and the story's told that when a cowboy in the next room was snoring, Hardin shot through the wall to shut him up. He did quiet the wrangler — his second shot killed him. In the excitement that followed the shooting, Hardin realized that Marshal Hickok would be coming to arrest him. Only partially dressed, he jumped out of his bedroom window, scampered out of town, and by morning was on his way back to Texas.

That same year, 1871, General Custer was on extended leave from the Indian Wars, spending most of his time vacationing in New York. And earlier in the spring, Union General William Tecumseh Sherman, traveling northeast across Texas to Fort Richardson, had barely escaped disaster in the first train of wagons on the trail. One hundred Kiowa warriors would attack the second train, in the vicinity of Trinity River, killing seven men and capturing all of the train's supplies.

All through the 1870s, the U.S. Army had been fighting two fronts. Some twenty-five thousand soldiers tried to control two hundred-fifty thousand Indians in the West and a frugal Congress in the East. And 1871 was the year that Ben Thompson was elected Marshal in Austin, Texas, and the year William Barclay "Bat" Masterson, also eighteen, with his four brothers, sons of a homesteader, settled in on a farm near Wichita, Kansas. Masterson would later become known for his gambling ways and as Sheriff of Ford County, in southwest Kansas.

When I crossed Clarks Creek at a humming riffle, excitement rose up inside me. I was now on my own in the world. I had with me but one change of clothes, and what I carried on my horse. My protection was my

.44 Winchester and my .44 Remington, and Pa's dirk, and I had $80 in my pocket, a sizable traveling stake — some three months of wages. I thought to myself whatever situation or problem that came along it was on me to take care of, and I felt ready for the challenge.

A short time later I topped out on the Grandview hills. Reflecting off my eyes was the breathtaking view of the Smoky River valley. And in the distance, near the outskirts of southeast Junction City, the river made a sharp curve from the south then looped east. Flanked by cottonwood and willow, it ran long to the cliffs of Grandview, where I sat my horse, then made a sharp bend north, coursing along eroded rocky ledges. At the foot of the distant town slope, a golden sunlight gleamed off the depot roof. On west, a finger of smoke lifted into a noontime sky, from the blacksmith shop north of the stables.

To the northwest above the plains on a plateau was Fort Riley, one of the U.S. government frontier outposts that had been built in '53 to protect the early settlers, travelers, and commerce as they all crossed the territory. From the bluffs I heard two sharp blasts of a train whistle and the chugging of a steam engine. As the train came into view, it raced across the trussed bridge over the Republican River like a miniature toy, with its dark stack billowing smoke a few feet into the air before streaming back along the cars behind.

I reined Dandy down the bluestem slope of the Grandview hills near a flour mill and dropped into the Smoky River at a low-water crossing. I took the wagon road into Junction City, then urged my gelding north on the main street of town.

Spencer Jones was sitting in front of the stable, on an old kitchen chair next to the opened double doors, when I dismounted and loose-tied Dandy to the hitching rail. I smiled as I peered over and asked the skeptic, "How's business?"

Spencer predictably frowned. "It's awright, but it could be better."

"I'd like to stall my horse overnight, Spencer; I'm headin' West, maybe to Fort Dodge."

"Business or pleasure?" he asked.

"I want to look the country over before settlin' down, but it won't be all pleasure. I'll be needin' to find work wherever I go."

Spencer reminisced. "I had the wanderlust my ownself at your age, but after a time I was ready to settle. Watch yourself, and don't get caught up with the wrong crowd. I rode with the James boys at one time —

thankfully not long — then I left 'em. Far as I know, the law's not after me.

"Frank and Jesse were through here a few days ago headin' for Abilene, but they'd told me it was a pleasure trip for a little rest. I always liked the James boys. I guess what I'm tryin' to tell ya is even if some outlaws are likeable, stay away from 'em and from breakin' the law. It can make for a short life. Who wants to end up hangin' from a tree in some Godforsaken place?"

"I get your meanin', Spencer. . . . I'll watch the company I keep."

Spencer pointed inside the stable. "Pick the stall ya want. The prairie hay's in the loft. The corn and oats're in the stockroom in barrels."

I took Dandy inside the barn and let him drink from the tank. I picked the stall closest to the door, crawled the ladder to the hayloft, and pitched down some hay.

It was dark in the loft, and I almost ran the tongs of the fork into a man nestled in the loose prairie hay fast asleep. He didn't wake, nor did I bother him. Back down on the ground I said to Spencer, "Ya got a disheveled-lookin' hombre up there; he's either asleep or dead."

"Yeah," he affirmed. "I forgot he was there. That's Reginald Kempthorne. Most folks call him Slim, but I call him Reggie. When ya see him in the daylight, you'll see where he gets his name. He spends his time in the area hereabouts, but he never hangs one place very long. He's from back East, educated in the best schools, and from a well-to-do family; but he has a serious problem. He's a drunk."

I learned that Reggie received a stipend of $60 a month from Baltimore — twice the money earned by a cowhand — money mailed to him at Junction City from his father's estate. His check would be at the post office around the fifteenth of each month. But Reggie had no incentives, so each month he'd carouse and drink until the money was gone.

Spencer told me though, that a drunk or not, Reggie was a good man. Spencer let him sleep in the loft whenever he wanted, as usually by the first of each month he'd be broke. I was planning to stay at the hotel, but Spencer told me I could sleep in the loft, too, if I wanted.

It was starting to turn light when I rolled out of the sweet-smelling hay the next morning. Reggie was sitting up looking at me as I slung my gunbelt around my hips. He stood, staggering slightly as he put out his hand and introduced himself.

"Nice to meet ya. I'm B.J. Ross. Ya mind if I call ya Reggie?"

"No," he declared. "I'd like that."

Down below, Spencer motioned to a bowl of water setting on a bench, near a broken piece of mirror on the wall. "Clean up if you want; there's soap 'n towels on the shelf by the water. Help yourself to what ya need."

I thanked him and after I'd washed up and shaved, Reggie dropped down the ladder. Then the three of us ambled over to the cafe for a breakfast. Earlier I'd taken Spencer and Reggie to be older than they were, but as it turned out, Spencer was just twenty-three and Reggie thirty-nine. Reggie was having trouble drinking his coffee, the way his hands were shaking, but by the time we'd finished our meal he'd settled down.

Later that morning I told Spencer I'd be leaving for Abilene come light the following day. Reggie overheard me, and wanted to ride along.

Two

THE SUN WAS above the rimrock when we hit the Smoky Hill Trail as it followed the river. Reggie was riding a roan quarter horse that had seen better days, but you could tell the gelding had been a good animal; it was just getting on in years.

We rode a lonely country, in dawn's gentle light, and in three-foot-tall prairie grass brushing our legs as we kept the southern hills and river over our left shoulder. The breeze-blown grass looked like an endless, shifting, silver-green carpet with purple stars. The bluestem was woven with spiderwort, a comely purple-blossomed wildflower that waved on spindly three-foot stems and sheathed with long narrow leaves.

We were five miles out when we'd reached the Smoky. Rain hadn't fallen for a week, and we were leaving such a dust in the air it was certain someone was on the trail. Wary of renegade Indians and outlaws, we veered off the traveled way and made our own path in the rich bluestem grass.

As we rode the wilderness, Reggie told me a little of his past. He had wandered West back in 1857, depressed and lonely, for but a year earlier, in '56, his wife, four-year-old daughter, and two-year-old son had died in a fire. He'd been at a meeting until the late hours that day, at his father's bank. He'd heard the clang of the fire wagons, but thought nothing of it until he'd gotten home and found smoldering wood and ashes. He had tried for a year to carry on, he said, but the wanting to run away from it all and drink got the best of him. That had been fourteen years past, and the only person he could really call a friend was Spencer.

Reggie had stopped first in Council Grove for a time, some thirty or so miles to the southeast, and then in 1858 he traveled to California to prospect for gold. But what gold he found he'd squandered, and in '64 he'd returned to Kansas, moving between Council Grove, Abilene, Junction City, and Manhattan ever since, living off the allotment he'd receive from Baltimore.

Though slight in body, Reggie was six-foot tall, and you could tell he'd been a strong man at one time. If he'd stay off the demon liquor, he could be again. There were times, he'd said, that he'd do no drinking for as long as six months, and then something would happen to start him off again. As we made our way westward to Abilene, Reggie determined he was going to stay away from the booze, and maybe find him a job to keep busy. I wished him well, but from what Spencer had told me, I wondered if he could keep to it. Yet he seemed too good a man to be in the clutches of alcohol. I had tasted whiskey one time back in Virginia, when a neighbor boy had sneaked a part of a bottle. But I didn't like it, and decided I wanted no part of something that I'd heard could ruin my life.

It was June the 25th, 1871, and my second day in Abilene, a busy, exciting town. My curious eyes took in all the people on Texas Street. I'd had a bath and was wearing the clothes I'd just bought — a pair of black denim pants, white shirt, blue kerchief, and a dark gray, flat-crowned hat. I felt like a new man, with the world in my hip pocket.

At noon I ate at the Merchant's Hotel, and afterward stepped outside to where a crowd of people had gathered at a fight down the street, near Texas and Cedar. I could see a local gunfighter beating up a defenseless older man, then realized it was Reggie, and nobody was helping the poor soul. From the looks of the gunman, Reggie seemed for a time to have held his own. Reggie was stronger than I'd thought, for his foe had a couple bruises to his face; but Reggie was out of shape, and the gunman had him down, unmercifully kicking him with pointed boots. Reggie lay moaning and in pain, and when the gunman pulled his .44 Colt to shoot him, I drew my handgun and shouted.

"*Hold it!* "

The man turned to peer at me and saw my drawn six-shooter. Snake eyes burned at me with evil hatred as he angrily swore, ordering me, "Stay out of this fight, it's none of yer business!"

Staring into that dark-eyed nest of hatred, I calmly told him, "It became my business when you took it upon yourself to shoot an unarmed man!"

The gunman hesitated for a moment then growled, "Maybe you're right; let's forget it!"

But something back in my mind made me wary, and when I put my gun back in its holster I never fastened the thong, staying alert. Two men volunteered to carry Reggie off to the doctor, and I began to turn away, to walk to my hotel. When I moved, the gunfighter drew. From the corner of my eye, I caught the blur of his hand and instinctively I fast-pulled my six-gun and shot from under my left arm, without completely turning around. I only fired one bullet, but it was all that was necessary as the coward lay choking on his own blood. Shortly he was dead.

Two renegade friends of the gunman stood opened-mouthed for a short moment, and then the taller of the two thugs sneered at me.

"I wouldn't give ya two cents for yer life, kid, when Dirk Kennedy hears of what's happened. . . . Yer a dead man."

I called back to them, "Well, he'd better hurry, for I'm leavin' town tomorrow!" My eyes carefully followed the men across the street and watched them mount their horses and ride off.

After the shooting, Marshal Bill Hickok, the law in Abilene, showed up, and I told him what'd happened. He explained I'd have no problem with him, for the hoodlum had gotten what he deserved; but if Kennedy came looking for me, Hickok advised, I might want to think about leaving town. Kennedy was known to be fast with a gun — maybe the fastest around with a six-shooter.

Later that afternoon when I entered the hotel, the desk clerk handed me a note. It requested I meet Kennedy at eight the next morning in front of the Open Door Saloon.

"Be there," it threatened, "or I'll hunt ya down like a yellow dog."

My first inclination was fear, but then the note angered me, for it had been a fair shooting. I felt a calmness that, for some reason or another, always came over me in critical situations. I'd just killed my first man that morning, and now I wanted to shed myself of the incident, to go and spend time on the trail, alone with God and Nature. But I couldn't walk away. Pa'd always told me to face my problems or I'd have 'em all my life.

I wasn't going to run, for I hadn't done anything to Kennedy; but I'd find out what he had to say. And I had a pretty good idea he'd want a shoot-out.

I went to see Marshal Hickok again, and he allowed it was up to me as to what I wanted to do. If I decided to meet Kennedy, he'd be around to make sure it was a fair fight. Hickok didn't seem to mind a gunfight in town; as a matter of fact, I think he was somewhat taken with the idea. He was a lawman that lived on the edge I'd heard, and as near as I could tell, the rush of excitement hadn't bothered him a bit.

The news of a shoot-out gunfight traveled fast, and later that day the town was abuzz with talk about Kennedy. As I stepped down the boardwalk, folks moved out of my way, as if I had a contagious disease. Although anxious, I went to bed around ten. I wanted to be rested and alert the next morning.

It was daylight when I dressed. I poured some water from a white porcelain pitcher and bowl setting on the dresser, then washed and shaved. The mirror reflected a plain-looking young man, not much different from most others of the time. Satisfied with what I saw, I went over to the chair where I'd hung my handgun and threw the cartridge belt around my hips. I checked the loads and spun the cylinder, then dropped the gun into its holster.

At seven I went downstairs and ate a hearty breakfast — bacon along with two eggs. I had finished by half past seven, so I sat back to relax and enjoy my hot cup of coffee.

I believed in promptness, or maybe being a bit early, and watched the big clock in the room slowly tick off the minutes. I studied my hands, and they were steady when I stepped out of the hotel door at five minutes before eight. Outside, I paused to look around. The street was empty except for Hickok, who was standing across from me, leaning against a store-way post. He lifted his hand to wave when I looked his way, as though to tell me he was on the job.

I moved into the street, where I'd be clear of any obstructions. The morning was one of the most beautiful I'd ever seen, a golden sunlight playing with the dark shadows along the boardwalk. Purple shade filled the narrow walkway between two buildings across the street. Through that shaded passage between the structures, I could see gleaming in sunlight the Kansas Pacific tracks and part of the depot. To the west down the street my eyes moved out into an empty landscape that I knew traveled to endless horizons. I remembered that landscape had struck me when I first saw Kansas; the horizons appeared to have no end.

A finger of smoke lifted in the far distance, and I wondered what it was, hoping it might not be Indians, for the Kiowa were never far away and looking for goods. I took a deep breath of the refreshing morning air. It was a great day to be alive, yet the thought flew through my mind of the possibility that I might be dead within the hour.

"*No!*" I heard myself whisper aloud. "*Get away from me Satan!*" I would not let my thoughts to be tempted to self-doubt.

I walked down the street, tugging my hat brim down closer to my eyes, thinking I'd always honored my father and mother, and God had promised me a long life.

But that life raced before me as I thought of God and family, and of all the beautiful things I wanted to see before I died. I believe all decent men think of God, Nature, home, and family when faced with death.

After I'd walked the dust-packed street to the front of the saloon, four armed men stepped out onto the boardwalk. From the description I'd heard, Kennedy would be the one in front, a tall man, probably around two hundred pounds. He carried a .44 Colt handgun in a tied-down holster, and as he walked toward me he released the thong holding his gun in place. He came up to me and asked, "Are you B.J. Ross?"

"I am."

"You killed Bob Steele, a friend of mine, and you're gonna pay."

I held his angry eyes and calmly replied, "He wasn't much of a man. Anyone who'd beat up someone unarmed and helpless, and attempt to shoot 'im in the back, is not my idea of a person I'd want as a friend."

Kennedy sneered. "That old fool's nothin' but a drunken bum, and he needed killin'."

"No, he's a human bein' who accidentally bumped into your ill-tempered friend. A witness told me he'd tried to apologize, but Steele wouldn't hear of it."

I don't think Kennedy had heard a word I'd said. He just wanted to kill me and put another notch on his gun. With a scowl on his weather-beaten face, he suddenly made his proposition.

"You go to Cedar Street, I'll go to Buckeye. We walk toward each other, and when I stop, draw."

What he proposed would put the sun in my eyes, and not only that, his knowing when he'd stop gave him another advantage. But I wanted him to be the one to draw first; he was the aggressor, not me. I shouted, "No! Draw now!"

Kennedy was completely shocked. His reflex drew his hand away from his gun. He had thought I'd be begging for mercy, but instead my call for a draw was so close that neither of us could miss, and we both might die. I'd taken a chance, and it'd put him off balance and on the defensive.

Pa had told me most gunfighters that pressed a fight always wanted an edge. Kennedy was fast, but he was no dummy, for he knew that at close range, he'd be hit. I'd surely get a slug into him.

It had scared him for a moment. He thought I might draw, and he quickly shouted, "No! Not now!" moving away from me, backing toward Buckeye Street. His rejection of my challenge shocked his friends, for they'd never seen him back off from a provocation before. Kennedy noticed their surprise, and it appeared to shake his confidence as his eyes darted from them to me.

The clock had now passed well after eight, and the summer morning sun had raised itself into a higher sky, to a level of peaceful beauty. I pulled my hat brim lower, to shade my eyes from the glare.

Hickok was close by on the boardwalk, and when I looked his way he had a smile on his face. But I could also tell that Kennedy's confidence had returned, and there was now a good fifty feet between us. His three henchmen started to scatter, so they could get in the act and draw if necessary.

Hickok shouted at the men. "You hombres stay right where you are, where I can keep an eye on ya. This is a warnin'! Stay out of the fight or you'll be facin' me!"

The three renegades did as they were told when they saw that the Marshal had his six-gun in hand.

At best, a handgun could be erratic at fifty feet, and I had practiced at that distance many times. But to hit my target, I'd have to aim about two inches high and to the right. I wasn't the fastest draw in the world, but years of practice had made me accurate.

The sun was now high enough in the sky that it would no longer be a problem, and I stood waiting in the sunlight with its warmth on my shoulder. It felt like Ma's hand as she'd lovingly rest it there at times when I was a lad.

In my mind I practiced my draw as I waited, thinking how many times I had actually rehearsed that move — the reach and grasp of the handle, the cock of the hammer as I raised the weapon, the pull on the trigger as the barrel came in line with my target. I had done it so many times I knew I needn't worry; it'd be automatic.

Kennedy drew, and shouted angrily, "*Die you bastard*!"

He was fast — too fast — and I felt the tug of his bullet as I fired. It ripped my shirt and left a deep bloody scratch along the fleshy part of my left arm. My shot was a bit slower, but I put two bullets not an inch apart through his left-front shirt pocket. He slumped to the ground, tried to get up, then fell back as his eyes glazed over and froze. Pa always told me it was better to be accurate in a gunfight than fast. And whenever Pa told me anything about guns and their use, I listened.

I closed the door to my hotel room, and as I walked to the stairway I became wary. I felt for the Remington in my holster. It was there in place, the bone handle and cold steel reassuring to my touch.

At the top of the open staircase I paused and looked down into the large foyer at the desk clerk talking to a lady checking in and signing the register. Two well-dressed men sat in easy chairs, one of 'em reading the newspaper. A lady holding the arm of her gentleman friend walked into the dining room.

I looked at my watch. It was six o'clock and suppertime when I stepped slowly down the stairs. A buzz of conversation turned silent when the patrons looked up and saw me entering the room. A lone table was empty in the far corner. I sat down with my back to the wall, where I could see anyone who might enter.

The buzz of conversation picked up again when the waitress took my order. As I was eating, Marshal Hickok came in, walked over, and sat down in the chair next to me where he, too, could see everyone in the room. He may have lived on the edge, but he lived cautious. He gave me warning.

"B.J., I'd be careful leavin' town. I don't think those hombres'll be layin' for ya, as I gave 'em a talkin' to; but I'd ride wary."

I thanked him and said I'd be setting out for Fort Harker, near Ellsworth, in the morning. I'd thought about going back home after the shooting, but that'd be kind of like running from life. So I was heading on westward. I believed that the solitude of the rolling hills and prairie grass wilderness would be a balm for my soul.

Three

I WENT TO BED around ten that night, and when I woke up it was still dark. As I walked through the lobby of the hotel, the clock ticked away into the stillness of morning; it showed half past four.

The hostler was up and stirring around when I stepped into the stable to pick up Dandy. The gelding was glad to see me, and raring to go. It'd been three days since I'd ridden him into Abilene, and he didn't care where we went as long as we were together and he could poke his nose toward another horizon.

After saddling up and tying down my pack that the hostler had purchased and fixed for me, I stepped into the stirrup, threw my right leg over the cantle, and settled down into the familiar squeaking leather. I'd hardly got set before Dandy rushed out of the barn, like he was in a hurry. He wanted to run, so I let him go. After a mile or so he settled down into a pace-eating walk. I didn't have to rein him right or left, he just took off into the purple maze of darkness like he knew I wanted him to find a trail west.

With Abilene at my back in the distance, the dark sky started yielding to gray and the landscape took on its daylight shape. I reined

Dandy onto a dark trail north of the Smoky Hill River and then the sun rose up, looking like a giant red ball through the blue haze. The crimson orb soon turned gold, its morning light charging across the prairie grass and pursuing its enemy of reluctant purple shadows into a veil of woods along the river.

It'd been only a week since I left home, but it seemed an eternity with all that'd happened. Pa was right; these were dangerous times, and I hoped things turned more peaceful.

Some sixty troopers were at Fort Harker when I rode into the Army post. The remaining two hundred or so had been sent to protect travelers along the Smoky Hill Trail and the nearby homesteaders. While at Harker, I could see I'd need more supplies than I could carry on one horse, and so I purchased a roan gelding for $20 from one of the teamsters. From the well-fed storekeeper at the commissary, I stocked up with necessities.

The next morning I mounted Dandy, leading a pack horse, and left Fort Harker behind. I reined Dandy around south, heading for Fort Zarah on the Arkansas River and the Santa Fe Trail near Walnut Creek, not far from the reputedly dangerous area settlers called Pawnee Rock.

Daylight had lit up the countryside when I splashed across the Smoky Hill River at a low-water crossing. I hadn't seen a soul, but I rode wary, for being alone made one vulnerable to the lawlessness of the land. The country lay wide and empty, untouched by plow or civilization as far as I could see. I rode through a lonesome, silent, but beautiful gray-green rolling grassland that wished only to be loved by man.

The morning haze lifted and once again the crimson sun slowly turned itself gold as it painted a cloudless sky a brilliant blue. To the south, two buzzards swung wide loops high in the sky, hovering patiently for a victim. All life must end, something the buzzards knew well, and they never waited long for dinner.

Though it didn't appear so then, I knew that the peaceful scene I was looking at could inflame into violence at a moment's notice. Before topping each rise, I held Dandy back before skylining myself, only slowly advancing into the next arroyo. You'd think you might see for miles on the plains, but the intermittent valleys were cruelly deceptive and could hide a whole village of angry Indians. A rider wouldn't know his danger until he was in the midst of a horde of warriors.

I rode a careful saddle all that day, and in the afterglow of twilight I reached Fort Zarah. The next morning I crossed Walnut Creek, and two days later I rode into Fort Dodge along the Arkansas River where some two hundred troops were stationed, with a few civilians.

I'd already spent $35 of the money I'd left home with, and figured I'd better find a job. I checked my horses at the livery and asked the hostler, David Carlson, if he knew of anyone hiring. He didn't, but he thought he could use me now and again, and so I went to work for him. Before long, however, the work and the hours increased, and I was making $30 a month.

I'd fixed up a bunk in Carlson's storeroom, and saved most of the money I'd earned. When time allowed, I rode Dandy into the plains for exercise. I stayed away from the card games and drink that working men found so enticing, for after meeting Reggie I was no stranger to the effects of liquor on a man. And once each week, on a Saturday, I'd go to the Fort Dodge commissary to catch up on the news.

By September, I'd decided to go to Texas. Word was out that the Double Bar Z, near Uvalde, was wanting hands. The ranch went all the way to border at the Rio Grande, some fifty miles to the west.

I thought it'd be prudent to ride with some other men through the lawless and warrior-infested territory I'd be traveling, but when I asked around, no one was wanting to head south.

It looked like I'd once more be on my own.

It was a dark and frosty October morning the day I left Fort Dodge for Texas. I had sold the roan, deciding to forsake a pack horse on the trip so that I could travel faster. The way things turned out, it was a good decision. But I'd need to live off the land for meat, as the meager foodstuffs and jerky I carried in my saddlebags wouldn't be adequate for the trip.

Some five miles west of the fort, I rode by a lonely sod house that a year later I learned would be inside the new town of Dodge City, a town that would spring up almost overnight. In the fall 1873, the Atchison, Topeka and Santa Fe Railroad would arrive in town, and with it would come the

Texas trail herds, turning Dodge City, Kansas, into one of the toughest gun-shooting towns in the West.

But that day, as I left for Texas, the sun was coming up in the east when I crossed the sands and mountain water of the Arkansas River. The brilliant golden sunlight danced with the purple shadows among the rustling cottonwood leaves that shimmered like golden Spanish doubloons. A soft breeze blew in the cool fall air, taking down several of the leaves onto the water, while a few others fell onto Dandy's mane. The countryside was ablaze with the reds and yellows of autumn.

That night I camped within view of the Cimarron River, its waters twisting through the plains, like a blue necklace, on its long journey to the sea. Darkness came fast, and I lay on my prairie sheet, listening for a familiar sound; but all I heard was Dandy cropping grass. Then, gradually, from a distance, came the faint chorus of what I feared to be howling Indians. As the sound became clearer, and closer, I hoped they might pass me by, unseen. My eyes searched the moonlit sky, and soon I found the silhouettes of the night callers just above the horizon. Long dark lines of geese flying south on slow easy wings, in formation, were soon above me. They called, with strident honkings, a beautiful throaty cry heard by all the country. On determined, proud, and noble wings they flew south, in the light of a harvest moon, like pointed spears, toward marsh flats and golden dawns. Far to the south again came their muffled cry that dissipated in autumn winds, no longer mistaken for the warrior's call. Straining to hear more, I listened, but was engulfed in only a primitive silence that lulled me to sleep.

Two days later about all I'd seen on my journey were a few buffalo herds and jack rabbits, but I was still riding wary, for I was in Kiowa, Apache, Cheyenne, and Comanche country. Though some of the eastern Kansas tribes were friendly, I was amidst a treacherous land inhabited with the most hostile and ferocious warriors of the West. I knew that if they were to catch me I might be a cushion for arrows, or buried to my neck in an ant hill, wishing I was dead.

When I crossed the Canadian River down into the western part of Indian Territory, my intuition was nagging at me. Something wasn't right. It felt as if a thousand eyes were watching me. Yet I scanned the horizon beneath my hat brim, without seeing a thing. Nothing moved in the way of life, except for a lone hawk and an owl perched on a cottonwood limb, waiting for darkness. Ahead, in the veil of twilight maybe a half mile, I could see a coyote slyly moving in the grass, only to disappear again, like a ghost. I heard nothing but my horse's footfalls and the creak of my leather saddle. Even the songbirds had rushed to their secret places, and out of the encroaching darkness came the steady drone of silence. It was so ghostly, it made a body wish he'd stayed at home.

I camped along the Washita, not by the stream, but across the river and on the highest ground I could find to the south. I wasn't about to be caught in that tangle of a river bottom fenced in with brush, willow, and cottonwood. It was near there, three years earlier, in '68, that General Custer had tracked a Cheyenne raiding party to a small Indian village, which turned out to belong to Chief Black Kettle. Custer attacked the village — the upper of four other campsites that included Arapahoe, Kiowa, Comanche, and Apache along ten miles of the Washita. Black Kettle had escaped the Sand Creek massacre in '64, but this time he was not so fortunate, and he and his wife lay dead, next to the river's edge.

I pondered the bloodshed that had taken place there. It was an area of beauty and grace, and I could see why the Indians were drawn to that part of the country.

The purple of dusk was settling in when I curried Dandy. I gave him a bait of corn where I had picketed him close by, near a seep of spring water. I fixed no fire and ate a cold supper of jack rabbit that I'd shot and cooked earlier.

In the darkness I surveyed the countryside and peered into the mystery of night. The sky seemed a little lighter off to the northwest along the Washita, a night sky that lay like a blanket of deep purple satin stitched with hundreds of tiny scattered diamonds. The light could have been from a campfire in the distance, but I wasn't sure. My imagination even began creating footsteps where there were none.

I lay on my blanket listening to Dandy crop grass and thinking of family. I could not have asked for better parents, and a pang of sorrow raced through me as I thought of the poor children raised in Godless and unloving households, and homeless children, with no family. I'd surely been lucky.

Virginia was on my mind that night, and my youthful days. Even with the War Between the States and all the struggles our family had gone through, mostly we'd shared happy times and fond memories. I knew that family ties could overcome all the difficulties life confronts, and those earlier days were years of close family bonds and assuring love. I didn't know what Pa's memories were of the four long years he was away, fighting for the Confederacy, but as for the rest of us, his love was always with us in spirit. And except for the war, I was sure Pa looked fondly upon our times together. The day we'd left Virginia for Kansas, I remember taking one last look at our home as we wagoned north to the main road, and it felt like there'd been a death in the family. A part of me will always be there in the foothills of the Blue Ridge Mountains.

I'd wanted to read the King James before retiring that night on my travels south, but my better judgment told me to avoid fires or lamplight, and instead I let my thoughts meditate on God's words before going to sleep. With my Remington pistol in hand, I rested comfortable with the thought that Dandy would wake me if anything, human or animal, came near.

It was still dark when I awoke, broke camp, and quietly rode south into a country of soft velvet black, so dark I could barely make out Dandy's nodding head. But I figured he could see better than I could, and let him pick his way south.

Daylight began to paint a gray on eastern horizons as I rode just below the rims of dark hills slowly coming to life. Mornings and evenings were when I liked to pray, so I beseeched the Almighty aloud amidst the silence of His creation.

Into the coming dawn I heard the lighthearted songbirds from the nearby brush, and their waking melodies helped lift my spirit. Suddenly the sunrise blossomed like a flower, shooting primrose petals of brilliant light into a countryside of darkness, escaping into crevices and hiding beneath foliage.

An hour later the sun was climbing into the sky, and I continued to ride wary. I considered that my intuition might have been wrong, or that maybe my extra precautions might have been sufficient, but I still had a feeling I was being watched. I checked the loads in my rifle and handgun, and when I felt for the dirk resting at my back I was reassured.

I rode in a land of sparse grass, but nonetheless a fair and beautiful place, empty of mankind. Then suddenly the songbirds stopped their harmonies and from behind the silence mounted Indians lifted up, as if out of the earth. Where they came from I never knew, but all at once Comanches appeared. A war party of some twenty warriors, no more than a mile away, were quickly hemming me in to the east, south, and west. No doubt they wanted me to run north, probably toward other hidden braves. But I wasn't going to fall for a ruse like that and continued walking my horse south, my mind transfixed and unaware of the sound of his footfalls in the soft earth. I held Dandy to a walk as we moved closer to the enemy. At maybe a half mile away, the Indians had scattered out to some hundred yards apart, and I was in the middle.

If there hadn't been the aroma of death in the air, the warriors dressed for battle would have been a magnificent sight to behold. I surely must have been a disappointment to the eager braves, as the only white man present to obliterate from the earth. Even so, they seemed determined to send me into my own otherworldly destiny. For a moment, the advancing warriors stopped to scan the countryside, as though they wondered if they had ridden into a trap and I was but a decoy. They grew wary and seemed baffled as to why I had made no attempt to run.

Their Chief was south of me when I rode directly toward him. At a hundred yards I was completely surrounded by impressively outfitted warriors closing in for the kill. Yet, still, they made no attempt to shoot me with gun or arrow, as I believe they wanted me alive, probably to torture, and by that time they knew they had conquered their quarry. Meanwhile, I'd made up my mind that when they had closed to within fifty feet I'd make my attempt to escape right through their strength, where they'd least expect it. As they approached, I could feel Dandy's muscles tense; he was ready to bolt to my slightest touch. That horse of mine knew one thing — he wanted no part of those Indians.

We were too close for rifles, and so I pulled my handgun, then loudly screamed, "*Ya-whee! . . . Ya-whee!*"

Dandy jumped like a shot toward the six-foot space between the Chief and another warrior, probably a sub-Chief. As Dandy was running at full speed, I shot the warrior on my right, and when others tried to fill the gap, I managed to shoot through about a four-foot opening between horses, slashing another warrior with my dirk. But deflecting his sharp lance away from my chest, I nevertheless felt it cutting a deep gash into my right leg.

I had run through them and was leading the pack south. Once Dandy was out in front of the fearsome savages, I ceased to worrying, for I had never seen a horse that could keep up with him. Two hours later, only two warriors were left in the chase, and they were some two miles behind.

I slowed Dandy to a walk; he was one horse I didn't want to ride to death. Around noon, there was still one lone Indian on my tail; he wasn't going to give up, and was on a horse that had all kinds of stamina. I knew I'd have to put a stop to him, for Dandy was looking tired; I didn't know how much more hard riding he could take.

Hidden in a coulee, I rubbed down Dandy with grass, then quickly cleaned and wrapped my leg wound. When the warrior breasted into view, he was coming fast and unaware of an ambush. As I shot him with my Remington, he rolled off the charging horse and lay unmoving. I knew he wasn't dead, for I had shot low, and the bullet went through his hip; but he wouldn't be following me again for some time, and I hoped never.

I removed his weapons and checked his wound. It didn't appear to be fatal, so I cleaned and bandaged it as best I could. I saw hate in his eyes, and I knew he still wished he could kill me. And I knew, too, that the Comanche would have taken me down on the spot if he could have, yet I was not able to kill him. I'd been raised a Christian, and forgiveness was part of my culture, deeply imbedded in my nature. The Indians just had a different view of things. Theirs was a culture handed down over the centuries and, I could see, not too different from my ancestral Vikings. The Indians were a proud people, savage fighters by nature, but kind to their own. It was not a sin to take what they wanted by force — goods or life — from other tribes, or white men. I knew I liked my culture better, but I didn't despise them for their beliefs.

I rubbed down the Comanche's horse with fistfuls of grass. He was a fine animal, and I would have liked to have kept him, but the warrior would need him if he lived. I left the silent, but angry, Comanche and put his weapons near his horse. I had lightly tethered the mustang where he could reach water and break loose later if the brave died. I left him there with food at hand, not knowing whether he'd make it or not, but I had a suspicion he would.

I crossed the Red River at the Texas border before I made camp; I figured I must have traveled eighty miles that day.

A week later I signed on with the Double Bar Z.

Four

EARLY IN 1872 we started our drive from the Double Bar Z up the Chisholm Trail, from San Antonio to Wichita, Kansas, with two thousand head of Texas longhorns. Abilene was over as a trail-herd town. The town council was tired of the fights and the killings, and they'd fired Marshal Bill Hickok for taking down two men in a gunfight, accusing him of being too quick on the trigger. They drew up a document that requested Texans to find some other point to ship their cattle. The council's declaration was printed in the Texas newspapers, and the drovers obliged the Abilene townsfolk by taking their herds to Ellsworth, Newton, and Wichita.

That was also the year Bat Masterson convinced his brothers Tom and Ed into walking away from the drudgery of farm life for buffalo hunting in the southwest part of Kansas. After leaving home, Bat never looked back, nor did he ever return. He followed the buffalo herds south, through the Indian Territory, into the panhandle of Texas, and found himself at the sleepy little village of Adobe Walls, not far from where I had crossed the Canadian River in October of '71. The place had just two buildings — a blacksmith shop and a saloon.

Some two years later, in August of 1874, all of the West would hear of Bat Masterson's initiation into the Indian Wars. For five days, he and thirty-five other buffalo hunters would hold off five hundred Kiowa, Comanche, Cheyenne, and Apache warriors. After that battle, he would sign on with Colonel Nelson A. Miles as a scout in a campaign against the same warriors.

With a dust cloud a mile long, we reached the rail head at Wichita in late June of 1872. The town was but two years old, and the railroad from Newton had been only recently completed in May. Wichita lay at the confluence of the Little Arkansas and the Arkansas Rivers, and in 1870 the population was only one hundred-ten. By mid-1872, however, the fast-growing town had a population of two thousand.

That first evening I checked in at the Southern Hotel north on Main. The town hadn't seen rain for days when we rode in covered with trail dust and hitched our horses to the rail in front of the two-story frame hotel. The streets were layered in dust, but they could turn to mud, depending on the weather. Down the way a wagon train of some twenty Conestogas pulled by oxen were lined up along Main Street, in front of the General Store. The travelers were buying supplies for their trip West. The town was busy with the wagon-train people and others milling around and talking in front of the stores, along a street filled with local buckboards and wagons.

The next morning, after a hearty breakfast at the cafe beside the hotel, I found Clint Jefferies, the Double Bar Z trail boss, at the Drovers Cottage. He paid me $210 in gold for back wages, and he wanted me to stay on with the Double Bar Z. He'd make me *segundo* — the second in charge — at $50 a month. I thanked him kindly for the offer, but turned him down, explaining that I wanted to see some more country, like the Colorado plains and the Rocky Mountains.

After leaving Jeffries I started past the Keno Corner Saloon at Main and Douglas, then stopped and tied Dandy to the hitching rail. I went inside to talk to the bartender, knowing he'd be a wealth of information, and thought I'd catch up on the local news. After two cups of coffee and an hour on the clock, I decided to stay over another day in Wichita. I felt on top of the world with close to $250 in gold secure in my money belt, and I rented an upstairs room.

Darkness ruled the morning when I picked up Dandy at the livery and rode through the opened hinged door into a still-hidden world. The Arkansas River lay behind me as dawn cracked a silver light along the eastern horizon, dimly displaying a sleeping country.

Three days later I rode into Abilene. I'd been away from home for a year, and was planning on heading east for the Humboldt rim in a couple of days. I was anxious to see Ma, Pa, and the girls, as well as little James, who'd turned eight in January. I had intentions on going home — until some things happened that would delay me for a time.

The following morning, after a leisure breakfast, I took a walk down Texas Street. At the east end was the Great Western Stockyards. Farther on, and across the Kansas Pacific tracks, was the Twin Livery stable. And just east of that and connected to it was a corral and shed, with a sign on the sloped roof that advertised, "Quarter Horses for Sale."

From the distance I could see Reggie in the corral currying down a palomino. I walked across the tracks, and when he spotted me he was so happy he couldn't quit talking. He introduced me to the owner, Jeff Olson, a tall, angular man with a handlebar mustache, a kindly soul who told Reggie to take the afternoon off.

That night Reggie and I had our evening meal together at the American Hotel. Reggie told me he'd been laid up for two weeks after the fight a year earlier, with mostly broken ribs. It wasn't until later that he'd learned of my intervention on his behalf.

When he had fully recovered, it was fall, and he had tried to catch up with me, but lost my trail at Fort Dodge. He returned to Abilene, and had been working at the livery for the past nine months. He'd not had a drink in a year, and looked good — like a man that could take care of himself in most any situation, and not the broken-down soul he'd been the year before. After I'd related my own experiences over that year, Reggie leaned over and whispered that he had something important to relate. It was something I would find hard to believe.

Slowly, in a hushed voice, Reggie told me he knew where there was a hidden cache of gold bars, five miles south of Council Grove along Fourmile Creek, not far from the Neosho River. We were still sitting at the supper table enjoying a hot cup of coffee when he confided that I was the only trusted friend he had in the world, except for Spencer in Junction City.

"I want to share the gold," he told me. "I've never wanted it all for myself.

"I owe you for my life; putting yourself on the line for me is something I'll not forget. I've known no one who would have had the courage to stand up for an old broken-down bum like me."

I was taken back by Reggie's gratitude, and told him I appreciated his friendship and kind words. We decided to meet for breakfast the next morning, then ride out into the countryside where conversation couldn't fall on curious ears. In Nature's vast emptiness, he would tell me the story.

The clock had already struck eight that evening, and Reggie had gone back to the livery where he had fixed up a bunk room. It was close to my bedtime as well, but Reggie's story of the bullion — ten fifty-pound bars — had captured my interest, and I wasn't sleepy.

I stepped out of the hotel doorway onto Texas Street, pausing to look things over. A few people strolled peacefully along the boardwalk, though one never knew in a town like Abilene if that peace was permanent or not, for violence could swell up in a moment's notice. I'd found from experience that it paid to be watchful.

I walked down Texas Street to the Alamo Saloon. I knew better, but the night seemed innocent enough, an opportune time to catch up on the latest news. Though I'd discovered early in life that the best way to avoid trouble was to stay away from places where it can breed, where circumstance can pull you into problems you didn't ask for or want, I nevertheless walked through the saloon's swinging doors and into the smoke-filled room.

I stepped up to the bar and ordered a shot of whiskey to be sociable. The bartender was a big barrel of a man with thinning hair and a walrus mustache. Between his huge fingers the shot glass looked the size of a thimble. He sat the glass on the bar and poured me a drink. I sipped on the bitter brew as we visited; I could tell he was a gentle man in a tough world, and though kindly, he was the sort you'd not want to anger.

I looked around the dim-lit room. Ten to twelve patrons were sitting at nondescript tables. At one nearby, a yellow pallor hung in the dust-filled air, circling around two toughs in deep conversation and sharing a bottle of whiskey.

"That'll be five cents," the bartender said.

I felt in my pants pocket, but I had no change. I'd used it all for supper. The only cash I had was in my money belt, and so I went into the canvas as covertly as I could. The effort was almost impossible, but I finally managed to pull out a $20 gold piece. From the corner of my eye, I glanced at the two ruffians who were watching me with interest. Turning, I peered over at 'em, and they looked away. When the bartender gave me my change, he seemed concerned.

"You'd best watch yourself, son. The kind of money you're carrying could be dangerous in this part of town. There's not a man in here that wouldn't kill you for even the change you've put in your pocket."

I regretted not opening up an account at Wells Fargo like I had planned. I just hadn't gotten around to it.

I talked with the bartender for another ten minutes, thanked him, and turned to leave. The two thugs were nowhere in sight.

I stepped quickly outside into the blending darkness along the building, pausing there to accustom my eyes to the night. The street was empty of life, but I remained alert. I was only a few doors from the hotel and moved out, my footsteps echoing on the boardwalk.

It was from the alleyway next to the hotel that they jumped me. I managed to pull my handgun, but it was knocked away spinning by one of the thugs. In the struggle that I knew was for my very life, I reached back and pulled my dirk. Fighting desperately, I lunged into the tough facing me and felt the knife sink in, tearing flesh. The hoodlum screamed and fell away struggling for distance. I'd been hit over the head and was also struggling, not only against two assailants but to shake off the effects of the dizzying blow. When I turned to face the remaining combatant, he saw the gleam of my knife, and when I lunged, he ran off down the street. I looked around and both men were gone; only the night silence and my gasping breath remained. I found my handgun and somehow managed to get to my hotel room, putting a chair under the doorknob before I passed out.

Around noon the following day Reggie was pounding on my door, for he'd heard nothing from inside the room when he had called and knocked. He finally pushed the door open, dislodging the chair beneath the knob, and found me on the bed, barely conscious. Later, after he managed to get some coffee down me, I revived some, but my head throbbed with a deep, painful ache.

It was a good week before I felt anything like my old self again. That afternoon, I deposited $250 at Wells Fargo.

Ten days after the night attack, Reggie and I finally went on our ride. He confided to me that for the past year he'd been closely watched and followed by two men, Josh Allen and Luke Dillard, who also knew about the shipment of missing gold. Like Reggie, they had signed on with the Confederacy to be muleskinners on the wagon train that was carrying Confederate gold from California to Virginia, back in 1863–64. The Confederacy was in desperate need of the gold to buy armament and supplies at that time, for no country would accept Confederate currency. The legal tender of the South had become worthless as time went on in the desperate struggle with the Union.

It turned out that Allen and Dillard also were the two thugs who had attacked me, and they believed that Reggie could tell them the location of the missing Confederate gold. All they knew was that it was somewhere near Council Grove where the wagon had disappeared, and that Reggie was the muleskinner of that particular wagon. They had confronted Reggie many times about the bullion, but he had pleaded innocence. And now, he didn't know how long it might be before the ruffians became persuasively violent.

I had planned on going home to Humboldt for a few weeks, but things had become complicated and Reggie could be in danger. The two desperadoes would have to be taken seriously. If I ran into 'em again, I vowed to give 'em a sermon from the Old Testament. I figured what they needed was to find a job earning their money, instead of spending all their time trying to steal it.

The next day Reggie found another bed, and upon the hostler's agreement I moved in with him at the livery. We decided it'd be safer, and would give us time together to make plans for going after the gold. Reggie said it was located on the Kansa Reservation south of Council Grove, and the rumor was out that in the next year, 1873, the reservation land would be open for settlement, as the Kansa would be moved southwest to the Indian Territory. We determined we could wait until after the Kansa had gone; it would eliminate any Indian problem — one dilemma we didn't need. To travel with five hundred pounds of gold would be no small chore without being noticed. I'd found that most people are always seen by someone, and so we'd need to make our journey through that area look like two cowhands just moving across country. Two pack horses could handle the job, and that shouldn't look too suspicious, especially with two horsemen.

It was August of 1872 at that time, and I told Reggie I needed to be going to Humboldt in a few days, to see my family. I'd asked him to go along, but he declined, though he rode with me to Junction City to stay with Spencer. After my visit home, we planned to meet back at Spencer's livery and from there travel to Council Grove and retrieve the gold.

The sun had rolled halfway to its zenith, and it filled the sky like red-hot brass. Reggie and I had left Abilene at daylight, on our way east to Junction City. We swung our mounts out of the rolling countryside imprisoned by the bronze sunlight and rode into the intermittent shade of the Smoky Hill River. The summer air was still stifling hot, but it seemed cooler when we caught the breeze over the waters. We reined our horses out into a rushing riffle beneath a giant cottonwood along the shore to rest, and let them bury their noses into the fast-moving flow. Dandy loved the stream, and playfully splashed at the cool water with his hoof.

There in the shade and dappled sunlight along the bank of the Smoky, Reggie began his story of his trip from California nearly ten years before, and the passage of the lost gold.

Five

REGGIE TOLD the story of his travels, explaining how he'd spent the winter of 1857–58 in Leavenworth, hankering for the gold fields of California. In March of '58, he'd caught a wagon train heading for Sutters Fort on the Sacramento River.

"I traveled with a large train of covered wagons, and most of the Indian warriors we saw on the trip stayed their distance. I think they were leery to attack such a big caravan. However, one night in Wyoming they made an attempt to run off twenty of our horses pastured outside the wagons. I was helping guard the mustangs, but the Indians managed to get away with two of the herd.

"The wagon master took the Oregon Trail to the Hastings cutoff, in Nebraska Territory, and from there to the California Trail and to Sutters Fort. A year after leaving my home in Maryland, in September, I'd made it to the gold fields of California."

Reggie paused, checked our back trail, then went on with his story.

"I'd panned for gold until the spring of '59 without a lot of luck, but when I cashed in my nuggets, the clerk counted out three hundred-ninety dollars. My six months of prospecting amounted to a year's salary back East, and it spurred me on to look for a bonanza strike that waited in the California wilds.

"One summer day I decided to ride to the coast to look at the ocean. I'd seen oceans before, having lived in Baltimore most of my life, but I'd never seen the Pacific. The morning of the second day I topped a rise, and there in the distance was a most beautiful sight. From the high ground, I wove my horse through meadows of gold and purple wildflowers to a cliff some hundred feet above the sea. Peering at the Pacific from the heights, I could see unending blue water. I dismounted from my gelding and stood before the panorama. It came to me that there was something different about the Pacific — it hadn't the open hostility of the Atlantic, or maybe the Pacific was just more subtle.

"A mile south lay anchored ships, their dark masts pointing into the sky. The ships were set among shrouds of gray fog that rose slowly into the gleam of probing sunlight, and then the misty hazy-like fog disappeared into the Pacific winds.

"I found a break in the cliff, and through the opening a long sloping path twisted to the sea. I started my gelding down the narrow graveled way, but after a short distance I felt him tense. Ahead of me, about fifty feet, the edge of my six- to eight-foot path was sheer cliff. Too late to turn around, I slowly plodded the gelding on. The horse was nervous, as was I, but he stepped carefully, though gingerly, and we soon passed beyond the fluted edge."

As Reggie spun his tale of the Pacific West, I could feel excitement stirring within me. He was a man after my heart, a man who loved the land and all God's majesties. And he was a different man now, from what he'd been a year past.

He went on with his amazing story.

"On the shore there of the Pacific I dismounted and walked along the sea, across damp reflecting sands. I listened to the pounding surf, with its incessant waves rushing swells of water onto the shore, where it all hesitated then fell back, only to crash into another wave. A two-master at sea was riding the swells along the horizon, and I wondered what secrets that ship could tell about Neptune and Davy Jones's locker.

"By late afternoon, out where horizons and oceans meet, ashen clouds bulked high above the sea and grew festoons of blue shrouds like a fine mist. Then as I peered at the giant clouds, they mysteriously turned into a bright cathedral with glowing halls of golden light shining on wispy white mermaids, with their heads of golden locks bowed in prayer before the glowing light of God.

"Before returning inland, I rode a day north and camped in a forest of redwood trees. I couldn't believe what I was seeing. A local in the area told me that the trees were thousands of years old, some as wide as twenty feet and three hundred-fifty feet tall. I had never seen such a wonder in all my life."

Reggie's tale of California piqued my longing to see for myself the enchanting Land of Angels and the marvelous ocean he'd described. It convinced me there'd come a day when I, too, must travel to that grand state. Surely only God could produce such beauty as Reggie had described, and my thought was that we'd best tread lightly on this earth and leave it, much as possible, as we'd found it. Pa had always said that one who loves the land has been blessed of God and receives in return a book full of fond memories.

I thought of what Reggie had described and promised God I'd do everything I could to leave the land as it had been given to me — or better.

After leaving the riffle behind and while riding the river-bottom tangles of the Smoky, Reggie continued his story.

"In November of 1858, I was panning for gold north of Redding, along the streams of California's Trinity Mountains. Before I knew it, I'd gotten myself caught in a snowstorm — snowed in — and couldn't get out for supplies. I spent four months alone in a makeshift ten-by-twelve cabin that someone earlier had abandoned, and I almost starved to death. But somehow fortune smiled, and in late January I shot a deer. I had lost track of time, but I figured out later that it was in March that a warm spell had settled in, and I hustled down from the mountains as fast as my feet could plod through the deep snow. I learned a hard lesson, and was never again caught with winter coming on in the high country.

"In 1859, I traveled to all the gold camps in the Sierra Nevada Mountains, including the Comstock, which turned out to be a bonanza of silver.

"Then in 1861, north of Eagle Lake, in the gravel bar of a streambed, I made a good find on the inside bend of a deep gorge. After a week, I had prospected five pounds of high-grade gold nuggets worth well over a thousand dollars. It was a great find, and I staked my claim."

Reggie paused, almost sighing at the recollection, and my heart felt as if it was pounding against my chest.

"I tried to keep my diggings a secret, but miners were drifting by all the time. I don't know how, but the word was soon out of my strike, and the stream was overrun with prospectors.

"The biggest problem in gold country those days were the thieves and riffraff that would move in to steal your claim. It was a lawless country, and if you came against these interlopers, you were on your own. Gold mining was a treacherous business, for there were those whose only work was to prey on the honest and decent men who had struggled for the gold in their possession.

"And so it was that on a cool summer night, I lay in my pallet by my campfire listening to the rushing mountain stream. It had been a long day, from dawn to dusk, shoveling gravel down to rock, and I was tired. I'd had a good day, however, and I figured I had dug out at least a pound, some two hundred-fifty dollars worth, of pure nuggets. The streambed claim I was working would probably last another month before it played out, and I knew that would come to a good sum of money.

"Earlier that day, however, three claim jumpers had come by my diggings, but when they rode up, I had my Sharps rifle pointing at them. Looking across the polished barrel, they offered me fifty dollars for my claim. I, of course, refused. The burliest of the trio suggested I had better take it. I refused again. They sat their horses, staring at my Sharps for a moment, trying to decide if I would shoot, then they decided I was serious and reluctantly rode off.

"That night, I was on edge; it was good thing I hadn't gone to sleep. Across the stream I heard horses and the next instant the claim jumpers rushed me, overrunning my camp and firing gunshots into my bed pallet. I managed to get out as the bullets hit, but I still took a slug in my left arm. By the time they had turned their horses to come back, I was in the brush. They looked for me, but the dark of night and the recollection of my rifle no doubt discouraged them. By the break of dawn, I was miles away."

Reggie closed his eyes for a moment, as if picturing it all in his mind once again, and I could only imagine the terror of that night. "The bullet had gone through my arm. I cleaned the wound as best I could with water from a nearby stream. Two days later, the arm felt better and seemed to be healing without a problem. But it was a week before I returned to my diggings, by then angry and ready for action. At a safe distance I could see them working my claim, though now there were five men and two were standing guard. I moved away to a safer position, figuring there was no way I could take back the claim.

"Late that night I managed to get within a hundred yards of the camp, close enough to quietly dig up the gold I had mined and hidden. At least they had never found my cache. And then I fired eight rounds into their camp before I rode off to safety. I don't know if I killed any of the claim jumpers or not, but I did hear a scream from out of the darkness."

I learned that a couple years later, in September of 1863, Reggie was in Reno, Nevada, living it up after another winter of hardship. His recovered cache from the summer of '61 had come to nearly $2,000. And he was mostly sober those days, except when he'd gone to town. Reggie continued his story.

"I'd pass by a saloon, hear the tin-panny music, and go in for a couple drinks. The problem was, I could never stop drinking once I had started. Only when I ran out of money would I return to the gold fields.

"I was down to my last fifteen dollars when I met the Confederate at the Gold Mine Saloon, a nice-looking blond-haired man, taller than average, maybe five-foot eleven, and dressed as a frontiersman. His name was John Hampton, and I overheard him tell the bartender that he was from Frederick, Maryland. I hadn't come across someone from home for a while, and I was anxious to talk with the man.

"I introduced myself, and we spent the evening conversing about many matters. Then he suddenly brought up the War Between the States and wanted to know what I thought about it. He kind of caught me off guard, and I told him I hadn't given it much thought, being gone from the East for so long. All that just seemed like a long way from life out West. But I did tell him I was surprised that Maryland had stayed with the North, for I remembered that most of the sympathy of those I knew lay with the South.

"Hampton never responded to my comment. But he asked me if I wanted a job, and I told him it depended on what it was. He wanted our conversation kept confidential, and I agreed. It turned out he was a Colonel in the Confederate Army, and was looking for muleskinners. He had put together a mule train of fifty wagons and needed four or five more teamsters for the trip. The pay was forty dollars a month; their destination, Virginia.

"I wasn't a teamster, but I had worked a pair of mules for a time on the Comstock, clearing timber, so I told Hampton I had been wanting to leave California and I would take the job. And I knew of another man, and possibly two, who would jump at the chance to leave the gold fields, especially for those kind of wages.

"Colonel Hampton never told me what kind of freight they were hauling, but it didn't take a long sharp pencil to figure out some of it was gold — especially when the wagons were to be flanked by some twenty armed Confederate soldiers. Hampton tried to keep everything he was doing secret, but an operation that size was bound to find enemy ears.

"At the time, I didn't much care who won the war. It was a conflict that should have been settled in the halls of Congress and not on the battlefield. A war of brother fighting brother was nothing but the killing of good men."

Six

THE CALENDAR had turned to October of 1863 the day Reggie's wagon train pulled out of Sacramento. Lieutenant Colby, in charge of the wagon Reggie was on, told him they'd be taking the Royal Road to San Diego and then travel east to the Butterfield Stage Line, across the border states, because of the time of year. The Confederate wagons were less likely to be attacked by Union soldiers on the southern route, even though Arizona and New Mexico were then in Yankee hands. When they'd reach Texas, Reggie added, they believed they'd have safe traveling.

"I'd arrived an hour early in Sacramento, at the warehouse where the wagon train waited. The mules were already harnessed and ready for departure. Before the other teamsters got there, I watched the last of eleven wagons being loaded, with what appeared to be a heavy wooden box in each that took four men to carry. When the box was placed in the middle of that last wagon, somehow I knew they all contained gold.

"Tarps were placed over the boxes and tied down. I don't know if it was because I was there early or not, but the Lieutenant assigned me to one of those eleven wagons. All the others of the fifty were partially empty, to be filled with supplies when we reached San Francisco.

"The sun was a quarter high before the Colonel waved the wagon train south, with the eleven loaded wagons at the front. I don't recall the first few places we encamped, but on the fifth day we stopped just outside San Francisco, a beautiful and busy seaport surrounded by low mountains.

"Early the next morning we were at the waterfront. A three-masted ship was unloading, and our wagons were filled to capacity. Many were stacked with boxes that I thought, from their shape, probably contained rifles and ammunition. My wagon and the other ten already heavily weighted were further stacked with some light containers that I felt sure were full of clothing and shoes. After loading the supplies, the wagons were again covered with tarps.

"Later that day, our caravan was on the Butterfield Trail south of San Francisco, and on the 5th of November we crossed the Santa Margarita River below Los Angeles. Moving south, we traveled with the San Bernardino Mountains on our left shoulder.

"That Saturday evening we camped in a beautiful valley of grass along a crystal stream meandering west. We weren't far from the ocean, for I had seen the Pacific in the distance from the hills before we dropped into the valley.

"We never traveled the next day. We were on the move six days a week, but each Sunday the caravan stopped. Colonel Hampton was a religious man, and on the Sabbath we rested. He conducted services promptly at eight in the morning for those who wanted to attend, with readings from the King James.

"I had trailed my roan gelding behind the wagon and decided that Sunday I would make one last trip to the sea before we moved on. But it turned out that the ocean was farther away than it looked. Around noon, I finally topped out on high ground, and saw before me the Pacific, maybe a half mile distant.

"Along the bay was a village of Chumash Indians, and on the shore resting silently were many boats pulled up on the sand. There must have been a hundred small Indian lodges on the higher ground, some three hundred feet back of the beaching breakers. I didn't know the reception I might receive from the fishing village, so I stayed put and spent the afternoon, unseen by the Chumash, taking in the peaceful surroundings. The ocean waves made a plangent sound that I would compare to the night winds heard from inside a home, as you sat warm with a feeling of contentment. And, yet, mystery abounded amidst the incessant roar of wind and ocean.

"There was little movement in the village, and in the mellow light of late afternoon I decided to head back to camp. Taking one last look into the far beyond where the sun and water met, I watched the giant orange sphere seemingly drop into the sea.

"Suddenly, the Chumash exited their lodges and gathered near the largest of them. In single file they moved in the gray twilight, as clarion singing rose into the salty mist. Each bronzed native was lifting a flaming torch into the fading purple light. Then they disappeared into a foothills dingle, only to appear again, in minutes, on a winding hillside trail, where they moved slowly in torchlight up the slope of mesquite. They topped out on the hill, black silhouettes against the cobalt sky. Amidst a vagrant breeze, they formed a circle of golden guttering flames, all evenly spaced. From their dark promontory overlooking the sea came a lamented chorus, like an incantation of ancient rites, appeasing and paying homage to the gods. I was transfixed, watching their religious ceremony, but I felt like an intruder, and moved softly away into the darkness of night. The stars were gleaming from their midnight positions before I made it back to camp."

I watched Reggie's face as he unwound his tale. His eyes glistened in the heat of the August sunlight that bounced off the waters of the Smoky Hill. The rhythm of his voice and the faint breeze off the river had come near to hypnotizing me. He paused only briefly to draw in the refreshing summer air and continued with his story.

"I was up at four the next morning to harness the team and fix a light repast. A velvet black night had encompassed the countryside and gold and silver stars blinked on and off at me. I stopped what I was doing to peer back into the deep mystery of time and distance. The glowing celestial lights seemed to penetrate my wounded soul, and there came within my beating heart a pensive feeling, like the nostalgia that tugs at me whenever I think of Maryland as it was before the fire took away my family.

"Nevertheless, by five o'clock we were on the move again, and in a few days the trail turned east. On the 20th of November we reached Yuma, Arizona.

"Each of our wagons carried a supply of water, along with several wagonloads in barrels, with the foodstuffs in the middle of the caravan. Thus, as for food and water, we traversed the desert without a problem.

"When we crossed the Gila River south of Phoenix, we were struck by a band of twenty Apaches. They had been waiting for us, hidden in the brush and drift-logs along the meandering river, which was mostly sand and shallow water. They had held down their horses from sight, and then like ghosts appeared out of nowhere on horseback. We lost three men in the ambuscade, and one of the wagons that had been bringing up the rear. The confrontation turned into a moving fight as we continued east, but the Apaches were no match for the firepower of veteran Confederates, and in several miles they fell away.

"Yet the hostile warriors would have a party before the end of day, for Apaches loved mule meat, and they would not hesitate to eat one from that lost mule wagon when they stopped for the night.

"We rode our high seats in cactus country, surrounded by giant saguaro, cat claw, and cholla, which some called jumping cactus. It was said that all you had to do was stray close to the cholla spines, and they would spring at the slightest touch, latching deep into the skin.

"We continued by patches of the yellow-blossomed cholla that stretched for miles, as if they were waiting patiently for some unsuspecting victim. And it was prudent not to stray far off exploring from our traveled way.

"This was also sandy country . . . though that's not to say there wasn't plant life, for many survive in the desert — the creosote bush, yucca, Apache plume, seep willow, and mesquite. And wildflowers at times blanket the desert with blooms after an occasional shower.

"But day turns to night quickly in the desert, and unbearable heat in the daytime becomes an unpleasant cold in the night.

"The next day we traveled beneath a brassy sun through vistas of saguaro and cholla that appeared in uncertain depths, like scribbled images of dancing warriors, and watery shapes of heat waves shimmering in the distance.

"As I drove the wagon eastward I had a haunting feeling that I was a prisoner of the desolate region, as if it held me by the throat, and if I sinned it would drown me in the taunting mirage of its shimmering blue water. I soon found it to be harsh and unforgiving, yet a seductive place that lures with a mysterious potion. And once you have been in clutches of the desert's charm, you want to return again and again.

"It was ten days later that the outlying areas of Tucson appeared before our mile-long caravan of wagons.

"On the 12th of December, the Dos Cabezas Mountains peered indifferently at our slender strand of wagons as we passed by in the lowlands some twenty miles south. A hot bronze sun filled the sky, almost glowing off the dust cloud that followed our slow movement. Above the dust, buzzards were swinging wide loops against the sky. I wondered what they knew that we didn't.

"Around noon that day, in the stifling heat, we stopped for an hour to rest, and to give our mules and horses some needed water. Suddenly from out of the north the winds picked up and gently blew through the desert foothills and coulees. Along the escarpments of the distant Dos Cabezas, dark purple clouds, creased with intermittent lightning, came down into the canyons and veiled the peaks. As we traveled east, the clouds grew more somber, and more truculent. Out of the darkness miles away came flashes, darting spears of web-like lightning. Then came the booming of thunder, like far-off shots of artillery echoing off canyon walls, with a surprising crosswind, a comforting breeze that refreshed my dust-covered body.

"The sun blazed where we rode, but the air now was cooler and our caravan moved on, plodding east, to the labored pounding of tired hooves. An hour later, the storm clouds to the north had disappeared into a bright sky. About that time we came to an arroyo, some twelve feet deep, and two hundred yards wide. The wagon trail declined into the bottom of the ravine, crossed the dry stream bed, then traveled up the other side. You could tell that the channel had at times been full with run-off water, from the looks of the driftwood scattered along the top of the eroded wash.

"I could see six of the wagons ahead of me had dropped down the slope and were in the bottom crossing to the other side. But my four mules had stopped and wouldn't budge, even with the whip snapping about their ears. The officer in the arroyo was waving me on, but something was spooking the animals and they would not move. In an instant I heard the sound of a fast-moving train. I looked up the arroyo, and coming down the gully, maybe a mile away, completely filling the channel, was a wall of water over a dozen feet high. My heart fell — a flash flood, and it carried with it all the debris in its path.

"The disgruntled officer in the arroyo kept waving me across as I was frantically pointing north. He finally looked, and you could see the panic grab hold when he saw the wall rushing toward him. He shouted at the muleskinners in the bottom to hurry, as he too pointed north, then dashed on across and up the other bank. The frenzied teamsters and mules raced for the other side. All made it but one. He was partly into the upward slope when the avalanche of water hit, pulling him, mules, and wagon into the furious maelstrom like weightless straw. Then, in but minutes, only a few inches of water flowed in the arroyo.

"The Confederate horsemen found the wagon miles downstream. They brought back the drowned teamster and a heavy box, which I assumed was gold. An hour later, only puddles remained in the dry wash, and the rest of the wagon train crossed.

"Eight days later, we reached Stern's Peak Station just inside the New Mexico border. The Confederates rode alert through New Mexico Territory, for it was no secret that Union troops were stationed throughout. The Colonel issued orders that the wagon train was to travel only at night. Confederate scouts would locate a stop where the caravan could camp out of sight from the trail in the daytime.

"At first light, on the last day of December 1863, we made camp some thirty miles west of Las Cruces, in the foothills of the Florida Mountains. A day earlier, one of the muleskinners was found to be missing, along with a horse, and the Colonel was concerned that he might be a spy. It wasn't until later that I learned he was, indeed, a Union agent.

"From our campsite near the Floridas, we had planned to swing southeast through the Potrillo Mountains, missing Las Cruces, for Lieutenant Colby had been informed that a large contingent of Union troops was stationed nearby. In three days we would be in El Paso, Texas, in the security of Confederate territory."

Seven

I WAS ENGULFED in visions of the Western mountains and desert that Reggie was painting in his story. He continued on, but I could tell he was feeling the sorrow of his life's tale, while I was hanging on every word of the adventure.

"The New Mexico twilight closed in with the sounds of low conversation amongst the men and the rustling of harness being thrown on the mules. I loved the desert evenings, and the mystery of the far blue mountains half buried in sand. There was a kind of tranquility in the air that I had not found anywhere else in my travels. Nights reposed as if the entire countryside was absorbed in peacefulness after a day of blazing hostility.

"The camp had been on alert all day, and in the fading light we prepared to move out. We were breathing a sigh of relief, having made it through without being discovered by the enemy; with darkness coming, we felt safe from attack. But that sense of security was soon shattered when federal troops assaulted. All hell broke loose, and we were caught unprepared. In less than thirty minutes, the Battle of the Florida Mountains was history.

"Some two hundred Union soldiers overran our position, killing six

Confederates, including Colonel Hampton. Lieutenant Colby was one of ten wounded. His injury was serious, but I had heard sometime later that he had pulled through, was part of a prisoner exchange between the forces, and was back in Virginia. The remaining fourteen Confederate soldiers were Union prisoners.

"Along with the other teamsters, I was interrogated and released. The Yankees held little interest in us. The Union Colonel in charge had decided that since the muleskinners had only been hired by the Confederates to work, we would not be imprisoned. He offered to hire us, at the same pay we received from the Confederates. The only thing lost was our back wages. But a few of the skinners were sympathetic to the South and left, though I and most of the others stayed on. I was assigned by the Union Captain in charge of the expedition to stay with my same wagon and team.

"Two days passed before the wagon train was on the trail again, only this time our destination was north, to Topeka, Kansas, where the supplies would then be shipped by rail to the Union Army in the East. We lumbered into Las Cruces on the 5th of January, 1864.

"A warm sunlit day ruled the heavens when we tooled our wagons into line. I snapped the reins, shouted *"Gee! . . . HAW!"* and the wagon jolted to a roll. We were moving north on the Rio Grande Trail and heading for Santa Fe, with some forty cavalry troops accompanying the caravan.

"The officer in charge was Captain Jeffrey Culberson. Back home I had known his family, and remembered him slightly from school, though he hadn't recognized me until I had told him I was from Baltimore. After that we visited frequently, and he told me he would be in charge of the wagons as far as Topeka. Then, after turning over the captured supplies to Union authorities, he would return to his garrison in New Mexico.

"Culberson made no mention of the gold. He seemed to trust me and another teamster called Post. He left us each on a wagon carrying gold, and on the other nine he put his own men. Apparently he didn't trust any of the other muleskinners. But I figured he was right, for I wouldn't have trusted them either. Many would steal from their own mother.

"The Rio Grande valley made traveling easy on the eye. It was a beautiful remote region of wildflowers and cacti, framed by the backdrop of mountains. We traveled seven days a week; it was as if Culberston couldn't get to his destination fast enough.

"I believe you're attuned to this too, B.J., knowing you as I do, when

I say that from the beginning of time, man has had an instinct within himself — an inner system — that warns him he's being watched. As we moved north, my instincts were warning me, for I felt the presence of peering eyes. It wasn't long before I saw an occasional Indian in the distance, but they left us alone; they either were friendly, or thought we were too strong to attack.

"The sky was an amazing blue when the sun peeked over the lava of the Jornada del Muerto — called the Journey of the Dead, for what had been the most treacherous part of the early desert route between Mexico City and Santa Fe. Our wagons rumbled through the sleepy village of Socorro, and we camped in a meadow just north of town, along the Rio Grande. Near the river were the colorful serviceberry trees with their white flowers and deep purple fruit, loved by songbirds. And graceful willows edged up close to and intermittently patched along the lazy-moving water. Culberston told me we would spend the rest of the day there and move out the next morning.

"The meadow where we camped was plush with grass, and we didn't have to forage for hay. I picketed my mules, then decided to ride my gelding into the foothills behind the town. A half hour later I topped out on a promontory, dismounted, and walked over to the rim where I could see the village and valley below. It was a magnificent panorama, with the town nestled far beneath me, along the gleaming waters of the Rio Grande. Upstream from camp a gambel oak stood out among patches of other smaller trees and brush.

"The village was just waking up, but a few early risers were on the street, and at least ten horses were tied to hitching rails. My eyes followed a couple that had entered the small adobe church next to the cemetery.

"When I peered at the countryside and canvassed the scene, a strange feeling came over me — like somewhere in my past I had been there before. The sight was so familiar, but I knew that it was impossible. Yet, why had I so easily chosen that particular pathway to take me to that overlook? I had ridden directly to the almost obscure trail leading to the summit. How did I know it was there?"

I understood what Reggie was getting at, as I mulled it over in my own mind, for I realized there were things in life man cannot fully know.

Reggie had thought that maybe his spirit had been there on that hillside many years before. I knew how he felt. But he'd shrugged it off, and aimed to enjoy the magnificent view before he rode back to camp.

"Around noon, I decided to walk up to Socorro, just a half mile away, and look at the village close hand. When I took the way to town, two of the muleskinners, Joshua Allen and Luke Dillard, caught up with me and invited themselves along. I had noticed them before, usually together in camp during the trip, and decided they were two characters to stay away from. I had managed until then to keep distant from their likes, so that this was the first time I'd even spoken to them. I wasn't too pleased they decided to tag along, but figured it wouldn't hurt to be polite.

"As I moved across the gravel walkways of the small village, once again I had that feeling of familiarity, but I ignored it and thought no more of such coincidences. The two skinners had a thirst, and so we walked into the Casa del Gato. I hadn't been drinking for some time; it hadn't been available. But I took one, and quickly relaxed. The pair immediately asked me about the gold, but I pleaded ignorance and told them I knew nothing about it.

"Well, I could tell they didn't believe me, and just to get away from them, I excused myself and left the cantina. They followed me out, and as we walked back to camp, they asked me to help them steal the bullion. I refused, and told them I doubted there was any gold. They quickly became angry, calling me a liar. We reached the camp and I told them I'd not be a party to any scheme, then walked away from them. From that time on, I determined to stay away from the two renegades.

"That evening I was fixing a bite of supper when I noticed storm clouds beginning to build along the San Mateo Mountains. The sky darkened and then a blackened overcast rolled into the canyons. The soft wind turned cool and blew down into camp in brisk, sharp gusts. The San Mateo peaks were soon veiled in clouds that had become restless and foreboding. From the threatening cumulus came the intermittent flash of lightning, and out of the turbulence a thunderous declaration like booming shots of cannon, echoing down out of dark canyons. I had expected a downpour, but we got only a few sprinkles. An hour later, as the angry clouds cleared, the sun came out, as if to apologize to man and countryside.

"We had moved, and north of Albuquerque we ran into a snow shower, which slowed us down; but the next day the temperature rose and, with a mere swipe of God's hand, the snow melted.

"It was February when we topped a rise, and you could see Santa Fe in the distance, the surrounding mountains capped in snow. Around noon we pulled into the town and the cold I'd felt earlier now had a soothing warmth.

"Santa Fe was a place of adobe structures and narrow streets that centered around a plaza, a village mostly inhabited by Spanish decendents and friendly Indians from the surrounding area.

"We leisured about the town and resupplied our wagons with foodstuffs and blankets for our remaining trip into what we knew would be the grips of a Plains winter. The next day, Sunday, I attended church at the chapel of San Miguel Mission, said to be the oldest church in America, dating back to Santa Fe's settlement by the Spanish in 1609. Two days later, we left town with a rumble of wheels and hooves on the Santa Fe Trail. It wasn't long — the following day — before the weather turned bad, and about then I was wishing I had an inside job. But we continued on into blowing snowflakes from out of the north.

"In late February, somewhere near the line of Colorado Territory and what would later become the Oklahoma part of Indian Territory, we ran into a blizzard. There must have already been six inches of snow on the ground, and the mules were continually slipping on the slick trail. The day had started out calm and cold, with great flakes softly falling into a cushion of silence. But by noon, from my perch atop the wagon, I could see only a few hundred feet ahead, as the bitter, sharp-cutting wind was blowing out of the north through what appeared as a wall of falling snow. It was drifting across the landscape and howling dreary tones through the leafless trees along the frozen waters of the Cimarron River.

"We moved cautiously along the flank of a ridged extremity. The mules were having a hard time staying on their feet. The day passed slowly with many of the animals at times on the ground, and it was a struggle to get them back up again.

"After an hour stop at noon, we moved on, quartering into the winds of blowing snow. I was hunched down into my greatcoat, sitting high in the wagon box, and fighting my own war of survival. We traveled only some four miles that day, then camped in a timber of cottonwood partially protected from the wind. I built a large blazing campfire from a downed tree, and after a time, from the warmth, I felt as if my bones began to thaw. After cooking an evening meal, I made my bed near the fire, as did others.

It was a night of roasting warmth, facing the flames and covering my backside against the cold.

"The next morning brought in a cold southern sun amidst a country buried in snow. We moved out around noon and slowly pushed through the deep white landscape. The land lay frozen as we plodded by the shoulders of rolling hills hibernating beneath a white blanket.

"Three days later, we punched out of the white depths and traveled a rumbling frozen trail that the winds had swept clean. Forty-five days after leaving Santa Fe, and after miles of tough going, we crossed the Arkansas River, with a bitter tailwind pushing us swiftly over the ice-covered water. West of the corssing we stopped at the trail's campgrounds . . . grounds that in two years would become Fort Dodge.

Reggie paused to look around at the running Smoky Hill next to us, and wiped the sweat of the August heat from his forehead. I could tell he was thinking, as was I, how the climate's extremes seemed to direct everything we do. But I was anxious to hear of the rest of the trip, and encouraged him to go on about their stop at the encampment.

"Well," he continued, "you've been there, so you know that area is out in the middle of nowhere on the Kansas plains, and in the throes of winter it made for a dreary place. Two days later, we left the camp. It was the 25th of March.

"The days and nights began a slight warming, but then fierce spring winds began blowing across the open plains, cutting us to the bone. We were traveling a countryside with no natural windbreaks, and we took the brunt of the blasts. Although the temperature was above freezing, it felt like sub-zero. Our saving grace was that the gusts were out of the south-west and at our backs. We rode the days and part of the nights sitting high on our wagons, hunched down in heavy coats, and praying for warm weather.

"Five days from the encampment, we rode into a protected area of timber, and it felt like a reprieve from chaos. While the winds raged outside the barrier of trees, the interior of the woods felt almost calm, with only intermittent weak bursts. But in the tops of the trees, limbs were tossed about relentlessly as the currents roared and passed overhead with the sound of a fast-moving train.

"On the sixth day of April we crossed the Little Arkansas River, and like a theater curtain being raised, the winds died down and the temperature rose into the seventies. Sixty miles later, rolling along the Santa Fe Trail, the land was awash with early spring. The tawny prairie grass had been colored a light pastel green. Along Diamond Creek, west-southwest of Council Grove, the riffles seemed to sing joyfully, as you often describe them. Their banks of wild thickets had shed their winter gloom and were bursting in pink and white blossoms, along with the willow and cottonwood that were misted with a fine chartreuse along their gray branches. That night we camped near the headwaters of Fourmile Creek some ten miles west of Council Grove.

"Earlier that day, the scouts had spotted a group of some thirty Kiowa warriors about ten miles to the south. Captain Culberson came by my wagon and told me he wasn't concerned, thinking they'd not risk going on the warpath against thirty military men and fifty teamsters. I had my Sharps rifle and handgun at the ready, however, and in any kind of a scrap I knew I'd be in the middle of it, as would the other teamsters. But I figured Culberson was probably right; the Kiowa never would attack a body of eighty well-armed men — though you never knew for sure, as we had what they wanted in the goods we carried."

Eight

I WAS TAKING in every word of Reggie's story, recollecting the Comanches that had ambushed me in October of '71. Reggie was right in his suspicions of the Kiowa, no matter what the Captain had said, for he went on to tell of the following morning and the fight for their lives.

"I awoke and looked at my pocketwatch; it was half past four. Captain Culberson had us up and on the trail by six. Straight ahead over the mules' ears, gray daylight was breaking through the darkness as we lumbered east. Then just as the sun was peeking over the hills, my wagon hit a rock and cracked my right front wheel. I fell out of the moving column to put on a spare.

"The Captain left two of his men to help, with orders to hurry and catch up with the caravan when we were finished. But by the time we had put on the new wheel, the last of the wagons had disappeared from sight.

"This was rolling hill country, and you could ride into trouble before you knew it. I quickly crawled into the wagon box, and with the snap of the reins we moved out. It was then that we heard the volleys of gunfire. One of the soldiers rode ahead to see what was happening, then stopped at the top of the hill for a moment and raced back. The wagon train had run into an ambush, and a moving firefight was taking place. But the wagons were continuing on, and we were left behind to fend for ourselves.

"I quickly snapped the reins and took off along Fourmile Creek. I hoped we could distance ourselves from trouble and get into Council Grove from the south. The two soldiers followed and tried to cover our track. If it fooled the Kiowas, only time would tell. In the distance we still could hear intermittent rifle fire for some twenty minutes; then came silence.

"We were moving through the prairie grass as fast as the mules could run, without killing them. The valley was getting narrower and the hills steeper as we drove east, with the creek on our right shoulder. The morning was coming onto nine o'clock, and feeling like we had escaped disaster, we slowed down for the mules' sake. But I soon learned that as isolated as we were and with hostiles nearby, it was no time to breathe easier.

"A half hour later ten warriors flew out of the prairie grass hills like a nest of angry hornets. I snapped the whip over the head of the mules and they took off through the bluestem as if their food lay over the next rise. It was beautiful country I was passing through, but I had no time to look — especially with my thoughts on how to save my skin. I was no match for the mounted warriors, nor were the two soldiers who by then were both down behind me, and probably dead.

"The warriors were shortly alongside the wagon, leaning from their horses and grabbing hold of the sides and reins to stop me. I was fighting them off as best I could, when I felt the sting of an arrow hit my back; and then a bullet jarred me to the bone. I felt myself falling from the wagon, and heard my own thud as I hit the ground. The last thing I remember was the runaway mules and wagon disappearing from sight and being chased by the warriors, just before everything turned black."

Reggie woke up the next day in Council Grove in the doctor's office, who practiced out of his house. He lay abed between clean sheets, next to an open window, he'd said, and could feel the soothing spring air, coming in through the fluttering laced curtains and passing over his fiercely hurting body. I pictured the scene in my mind — it brought back to me gentle thoughts of Ma's bedroom curtains at home. Reggie continued on with his story.

"Captain Culberson came by to see me the following day and told me they had lost three men, including the two with me. After they had driven off the renegades, he had sent twenty of his troops to find us. They found the two soldiers dead, full of arrows, about a mile west from where they found me. They had searched for the wagon and mules, but found no sign, and reasoned the Indians had made off with them.

"Captain Culberson was moving on to Topeka, so he paid me my $160 in wages and wished me well as he left the room. I lay in bed for some fourteen days from two broken ribs, one bullet wound, and three arrow wounds. The doctor told me I had lost a lot of blood and was within two shakes of being dead when the troopers had carried me into his office.

"But as I lay recovering, I thought that there was something strange about the Captain not finding the wagon, for I couldn't imagine those warriors carting it off. I was sure they would be in a hurry to escape, and it would be too slow for them. Usually the Indians burned what they left behind, but Culberson had told me they found no signs of fire.

"It was almost May when I left the doctor's home and walked to the stable just north of Main Street, which was also part of the Santa Fe Trail. I was in need of a horse, and Jeff McConnell, the hostler, soon had me fixed up with a fine palomino gelding. McConnell gave me a good deal, and I happily parted with the $50.

"That night I checked in at the Hays House, with the idea I might be staying a while, for I wanted to do some looking along Fourmile Creek. . . .Two days later I closed the door to my room and walked down the hall to the stairway steps. As I reached the main floor I could see that the large dining room was almost empty of patrons. But by the time the waitress brought me my bacon and eggs, the room was starting to fill.

"The waitress, Katy Payne, was a slight, beautiful young lady. I could tell she liked me, and for the first time since my wife and children had died, I had feelings for a woman again — not that I didn't still love my wife who lay in the grave . . . but I thought it might just be time to turn a new corner. In the end, it came to be one of those things that just didn't work out — but that's another story.

"By seven that morning I was in the saddle and taking the trail south out of town. Within minutes I was crossing Elm Creek and moving up the slope of the hill overlooking Council Grove. Topping out above the rimrock maybe a half mile were the rugged bluffs overlooking the Neosho River.

"A short time later I stopped my gelding to let my eyes canvas the Fourmile valley. The beauty of the narrow lowland and steep surrounding hills almost took my breath away.

"I vaguely remembered falling from my wagon after crossing a trail that went north into the hills, and I was sure it was the trail I then rode. Yet, surveying the countryside below, nothing seemed familiar. There had been no rains, so I thought that maybe when I reached the creek bottom I would find a sign, or landmark, that might jog my memory.

"I rode cautiously, for this was Kansa Indian land, though from everything I had heard, they were mostly friendly. I knew, however, that if there was any loot nearby, they would find it sooner or later.

"From atop my palomino, I looked around, in every direction, but no one was in sight, and I preferred it that way. I decided after further observation that Fourmile Creek was about the most twisting stream of water I had ever seen, and spent the next three hours along the creek looking for signs of that wagon, all the way to the Neosho River.

"The creek was a streambed of deep pools with straight earth banks, some as high as fifteen feet. I found nothing, no sign of anything. Then I realized that the wagon would have been higher up the slope and unhindered from all the twists and turns of the creek. I backtrailed past the road that went north. It was there that I found my first sign.

"The ground had been torn up a bit, and dried blood lay in the grass. That would have been from one of the troopers. An hour later, I found where I had fallen from the wagon, maybe a mile east of the north trail, and some two miles from the Neosho. The grass was thick and heavy, but I followed the runaway wagon as best I could, occasionally picking up a wheel track. After a half mile, the tracks ran out, but occasional horse and mule tracks could be seen moving east and then crossing the creek south. Yet the Indians took no wagon with them. I scoured the creek banks, thinking I would find the wagon somewhere in the deep water, but had no luck.

"It was coming onto dark when I made camp and fixed myself a bite to eat. I built a small fire of dried wood, for I wanted no smoke to be lifting into the atmosphere. After heating some beans, frying ham, and making coffee, I doused the fire. For a time I lay there listening to a nearby riffle playing its music, and that was the last I remember.

"Daylight had just emerged when I stood by the last wagon-wheel tracks I had found the day before. What seemed peculiar to me was the mule tracks I saw farther on didn't line up. The wagon would have had to veer sharply north, and I could see no sign of tracks in that direction. Sighting down the last of the wheel tracks I had found would take the wagon into a shallow ravine that ran into the creek some hundred yards downstream.

"And so I rode to the ravine and dismounted. I could see some disturbance of the brush nearby, but I couldn't at first see the wagon. I walked through the brush, and there below in the shadows it lay, shattered, in the bottom of the gully. I could barely make out the broken mass to be a wagon. And what I had thought to be simply a shallow ravine was in reality a deep chasm choked with briars and undergrowth. As near as I could figure, the wagon tongue had broken off, freeing the mules. The wagon then traveled straight on into the abyss. I could see now why Captain Culberson had failed to find it.

"By that time it was about ten o'clock. I hid the gelding from sight and worked my way down to the broken-up wagon. It looked like the Kiowa had managed to confiscate some of the supplies and rifles, but amazingly, buried in the bottom of the debris, was the crated box of gold bullion.

"That evening I was back in Council Grove. When I entered the lobby of the hotel, the desk clerk handed me a telegraph. The wire was from my mother, answering mine from the day before. My father had died. He had left me a trust of $60 a month. With grief in my heart, I sent my return telegram, arranging for the checks to be sent to Council Grove."

The afternoon was in its shadows and Junction City lay in the far distance when Reggie finished his story of the hidden gold. We continued our ride along the Smoky, listening to the music of the low-water riffles, and keeping to the shade as best we could. Mostly I listened to Reggie's tales of adventure as I took in the comely sights of cottonwood, walnut, oak, and willow edged along the sandy slopes, with their delicate leaves hanging out and brushing lightly along the current of flowing water. Two insignificant figures in a vast prairie, we pushed our mounts on into the grass of a fair and lonesome land, as my eyes surveyed our wide valley of far-shouldered bluffs resting silently against a blue sky.

We talked little, with the only sounds a clarion tinkling of our horses bridles, the plodding hoof-falls in the grass, and the creaking of our saddles. Pushing at our backs a complacent wind blew, shifting the waving green bluestem into a silver sheen, and I felt a peacefulness within as our horses breasted through the tall grass.

We rode our trail throughout the day with an awareness, but we'd not been followed.

That evening, Spencer, the feisty hostler at Junction City, was so happy to see us he took us to supper. Later, Reggie and I once again made bed at Spencer's livery stable. We opened the loft door to allow in a breeze, and the night was halfway comfortable. Lying in the hay, deep in thought, I bluntly asked Reggie, "What makes you think the gold would still be there? Surely someone would've come across it by now."

I could see Reggie's brief smile in the dusk.

"Because," he said, "I moved it. . . . I moved it that day. It took me ten hours to find a safe place and cache it away."

Before we slept, Reggie continued his story.

"It was by accident that Josh Allen and Luke Dillard had spotted me in Abilene. I had heard they thought I'd been killed along with the two troopers in the battle with the Kiowa. They knew the wagon carrying the gold was missing, but figured the warriors had taken it. But when they had found that I was alive, they became suspicious, and then were convinced that I had hidden the gold somewhere — especially since I seemed to have plenty of money and had no job. Even my going to work at the livery hadn't changed their minds.

I nodded to Reggie's account and asked, "What happened to Katy?"

Reggie paused for a moment, took a deep breath, and slowly began his narrative.

"I stayed in Council Grove until the fall of 1865. We courted regularly, and it was the happiest I'd been for nine years. I even quit drinking altogether, and things were looking bright for the future. I was thirty-four, and decided I should marry again and have children.

"But I had been away from home for eight years. My mother, now alone, was getting on in years, and I decided if I was to see her again I should do it before I married.

"In October I boarded the train in Junction City and headed back East. When I arrived in Baltimore, I found that my mother was sick, and so I stayed by her bed for many hours caring for her, until suddenly, and for some unknown reason — even the doctors had no answer — she was over her malady. Time passed, and it was May of 1866. I had been away from Katy and Council Grove for seven months. I had written to her religiously, but I hadn't received a response for some time. I was concerned that all was not well.

The day I returned to Council Grove by train, I walked into the Hays House dining room around noon. Katy was serving at the tables. Though she was busy, I thought it strange she didn't hurry over to me, but I sat down and waited. It seemed as if she was avoiding me, for she rarely looked my way. When she finally walked over, she took my order, then nervously struggled to tell me she was married.

"Well, I had known something was wrong, but I was stunned. I barely managed to speak. I left Council Grove the next day, and I've not been back."

I could sense Reggie's sadness. "I'm sorry it didn't work out," I told him.

"Well, I am too," Reggie smiled, "for that was when I took to drinking again — though I've thought about it lately, and I believe I should have cherished the memory we had, let it go, and moved on. Our marriage for some reason just wasn't meant to be. Our separation should have made her affection stronger. I think mine had. . . . But from a lack of faith, her commitment had failed."

I asked Reggie then why he'd decided to get the gold now. "Why not years ago?"

"I had no reason to get it. I would have, had I married, and maybe bought a ranch somewhere. But that kind of money is meant to share with someone you care for, or value. I'd not want it for myself; and after Katy, I had no one else to share it with until I met you. You had put your life on the line for me, worthless as I am."

I was sorry for Reggie's disappointment, but had to tell him, "Reggie, I look on you as one of God's children; you're sure not worthless."

The next morning I rode home to the Humboldt farmstead. Reggie and I had decided we'd meet again around the first of October. We would plan our next move in bringing back the gold.

Nine

IN EARLY OCTOBER 1872, after some pleasant eight weeks at home, eating Ma's cooking and helping Pa on the farm, I saddled Dandy and was heading for Junction City. Ma had a smile on her face when we said goodbye, and was not nearly as upset as when I'd left home a year and a half earlier.

Blue was the sky, golden was the sun, and purple were the long shadows along the barn when I mounted the stallion. I noticed that not only the day but the entire countryside was a blaze of color when I rode off the rimrock into the Humboldt Creek valley. Junction City and Reggie were on my mind when I hit Clarks Creek. The water was softly humming complacent tunes when I reined Dandy through the riffles. Below the crossing I frightened a flock of ducks, and the water exploded into waves and flapping wings that lifted off the stream into flight. They soared low down the waterway, then suddenly rose above the trees, flashing dark, wide wings, only to disappear into the glow of the rising sun.

Two days later, Reggie and I rode into Council Grove. We sat by the fireplace at the Hays House, along the far wall, the flames warding off the chill in the air.

To Reggie's surprise, Katy was still waiting tables. Her marriage hadn't worked out, and a year later, we learned, with cuts and bruises on her face, she'd left her brute of a husband.

Reggie introduced me, and I could see why he had been smitten with the charming lass. Her pretty face and slight but curvaceous figure could set a man to passionate thoughts. I'd spent a few evenings with young ladies in my travels, but nothing serious had come about, and I'd figured sooner or later to meet the right girl.

The next morning Reggie and I mounted our horses to head for Fourmile Creek. We rode easy, but watched our backtrail to make sure we weren't followed. It was a day of sun, with a hint of the coolness of winter in the air . . . a day when God had fully dressed His foliage in rich and varied colors.

We never went down to the creek, where the gold was buried. Reggie just pointed from the hilltop overlooking the valley, and explained where it was hidden.

That night back at the hotel, at our evening meal, the dreaded Josh and Luke walked in and sat down across the room. But they weren't alone. With 'em was Johnny Slater, the Texas gunfighter, lately from Deadwood, South Dakota. They eyed us with hasty, but threatening glares. I knew we had trouble looking at us.

The outlaws would turn away from our direction, to hunker down in what appeared to be serious talk, and then would glance our way again. They were still eating when we finished our meal. We left the room and went upstairs to bed, a cloud of uncertainty now over our heads. I sat a chair back under the knob of the door, as I didn't want any surprises waking me in the night.

We stayed on at the Hays House, but saw the outlaws no more that week. I was certain that we hadn't seen the end of 'em, however, for they'd be even more suspicious of Reggie's knowing the whereabouts of the gold bullion after seeing him back in Council Grove — and but a few miles from where the bullion had disappeared.

It seemed too dangerous to go after the gold at that time, with the troublemakers lurking about the area, and with the Kansa still nearby, so we kept to our earlier decision to wait until spring. I tried to get Reggie to go back home to Humboldt Creek with me, but he turned down my invitation, staying on at Council Grove. Reggie and Katy were seeing each other again and, as Pa always said, he seemed as happy as a raccoon in a watermelon patch.

Earlier in the week I'd been in the dining room when Reggie was off somewhere taking care of business. It was the middle of the afternoon, and Katy wasn't busy. She came over, pulled up a chair, and sat down. I could tell she had something on her mind she felt she needed to explain to me.

"B.J., I made a bad mistake when I married. I think you know Reggie and I were to be wedded when he returned from Baltimore. I can't make excuses . . . but he'd been away nearly eight months, and the man I met here swept me off my feet. I thought I was in love, but he changed almost overnight after we were married, and many times I was beaten. I left him, and a month after that he was dead; he'd picked a fight with the wrong man.

"I felt bad for him, yet I breathed relief at the news, for he had threatened to kill me, too, and I believe, sure as the world, he would have sooner or later. Many a night I've not slept thinking about the wrong I did Reggie."

I shook my head. "We all make mistakes at one time or another, Katy, things we regret. You've learned from yours and, like my Pa says, that's important."

Katy seemed to appreciate my words, but was still bothered. "Do you think he can truly forgive me after what I did? I believe I was confused, and know now it was him I loved."

Knowing Reggie's feelings, and what he'd told me in our private talks, I was sure he would, but I told Katy I couldn't be certain and speak for him, though I knew he still had a mind for her.

"He's a keen man of compassion, Katy, and it wouldn't surprise me if he had the same feelings you do."

It was the next week that Katy and Reggie were once more an item.

When I rode into the yard at home, frost was on the trees east of the rimrock causing leaves to drop, like golden rain, to the cold dark earth. The winter months of 1873 then settled in on the Kansas prairie, and the winds blew harsh, insensitive to man or beast. January was frigid, with snow and drifts. The only thing not white were the trunks and limbs of trees peeking out where the unceasing wind hadn't allowed snow to stick to them.

This was the year that Jesse James and his gang had pulled off what was said to be their first train robbery, near Adair, Iowa, some seventy miles east of Council Bluffs, and the year Custer would be stationed at Fort Abraham Lincoln, in Dakota Territory. And 1873 was when the Colt .45 Peacemaker and the .44-.40 Winchester rifle, with its extra rear sight, became the best-selling guns in the West.

One early Sunday that winter, with the cold wind howling outside the house, I was up and building a fire out of the few embers still glowing in the kitchen stove. Ma and Pa were abed, and I was dressing warm to venture out to do chores. I scraped ice off the kitchen window to look outside, and visibility was clear as far as horizons, if you could figure out what was drifted snow and what was the horizon. I opened the door to the porch, but before I could get outside and shut it, a skiff of blowing flakes came into the house. Off to the east I looked at a peaceful white scene, but the cantankerous winds would flurry into gusts, which veiled the distance by picking up fine surface snow and carrying it long down the hillside. Then suddenly the wind would die down and drop its ghostly veil.

Outside I was greeted with a bright and glaring four-foot-high drift at the steps off the porch. Pushing through it, I plodded amidst two feet of snow into a world that at times had shrunk to a few feet distant when a gust of blowing ice crystals would twirl along with me. The wind tore at my clothes, as if frantically searching for a way to get at my body heat, and tried to steal what little breath I had in my lungs.

When I reached the barn, I found a huge drift pile swirled upward before the door. After tunneling through about ten feet of snow, I was able to get into the frozen and empty building, a cold tomb of dust-filled air. Thankfully our horses were inside, away from the wind, where I could pitch 'em some hay from the loft and give 'em a drink after breaking ice in the tank. But the cattle were held outside near the spring, and I'd need to find my way to them to break the ice so that they could get to the water. The chores shouldn't have taken an hour, but three had passed before I could return to the warm house.

The next day's sky was calm, clear, and frigid. In the hue of afternoon, the far southern sun angled a path of pastel blue and pink onto a crusty white world to where I stood by the barn. Something about that cold, snowy, January day, when we were imprisoned in its grasp, made a body wonder if you'd ever see humans again.

But winters pass, and in early April the spring winds of Kansas again came blowing from the southwest, melting all the snow in our country world and surely blessing our home with the birth of the new season.

From the rimrock of the broken hills, Council Grove lay nestled serenely along the Neosho River with a backdrop of delicately colored springtime slopes surrounding the village. I rode a chestnut gelding into the town, and a mighty fine horse. I'd left Dandy at home to stud with some new mares Pa had purchased. And I thought I'd heard Pa tell that some of our close neighbors — as I recalled, it was the Pooles on Upper McDowell Creek, and the Barrys east on Deep Creek — wanted the use of Dandy for breeding.

The sun was high in the sky that Saturday morning when I rode down the slope and crossed the wagon bridge. Not only was the countryside blossoming into life, so was the town. People were out taking in the pleasant air from the hard winter of '73. Five geldings stood three-legged at the hitching rail in front of the saloon. Buckboards and spring wagons were parked all along the boardwalk, with their teams patiently waiting. The womenfolk were happily visiting, walking the boardwalks, and looking in the stores, while some of the menfolk, many in pairs along the street, were in deep conversation. The General Store was a buzz of excitement where small groups had gathered to visit.

It was a day when it felt good to be alive. I was in high spirits when I entered the Hays House to see if Reggie was there, and to catch up on the news.

Katy saw me enter the dining room and came rushing over to where I stood. Tears streamed from her eyes and her sobbing was uncontrolled. I put my arm around her shoulder until she'd settled down.

Something was terribly wrong; my morning's feelings of the joy of life were about to be cut out of my heart.

"Reggie's *dead*! . . . *Murdered!*" Katy cried. "Beaten to death . . . I don't know why! Why, B.J., would anyone want to kill Reggie?"

and rafters hung a grayish hue where an occasional pigeon flapped wings and flew through the dusty haze. Along the planked stalls and manger a ladder waited patiently for someone to crawl up to the hayloft. When I walked to the storeroom of the darkened barn, glaring brightness hit my eyes where slices of sunlight came through the splintered walls, stitching long golden threads through the floating dust motes.

I walked out of the storeroom and bridled a three-year-old gray gelding I called Prince, after his ancestral grandsire from Scotland. I lay on the blanket, threw on the leather saddle, and tightened the cinch.

I was leaving Dandy with Pa, for it seemed like all the ranchers around wanted him for service. Pa and I talked it over, and we decided we couldn't turn down the $50 fee; Pa could use the money.

I mounted the gelding and peered off into the rolling horizons where adventure lay. The excitement of breasting another hill into the unknown gave me a wonderful feeling. What I searched for I didn't know, but I knew that something or someone had to be out there waiting for me. Some time later I would learn that usually what a person was looking for was nearby and under his very nose.

Dandy looked longingly after me from the corral as I rode away from the house and down the lane. I knew how he felt, and I wanted to share with him my travels, but once he caught sight of those four-year-old fillies he'd be taking care of, I was sure he'd forgive me.

Prince had been born in the spring of '72. His sire was Dandy, his dam a white mare Pa'd bought at auction in Virginia. Like Dandy, the mare had bloodlines that dated back to eighteenth-century England. Prince had been a beauty, and I gave him many hours of attention. As Pa had heard it described by his grandfather, the colt's coloring was similar to his English grandsire, mostly white with just enough dark hair to give his coat a grayish-blue tint, accented with dark mane and tail.

We'd planned to use Prince for stud, but in '74 he'd caught himself astride the near pasture fence. How it'd happened, Pa never knew, but before he could get the young stallion loose, the horse had severely cut himself. Pa had to finish the castration and Prince was lost for any breeding.

As I rode along, I took in the mist of green covering the timber along the creek bottoms. The pink and white blossoms of the plum and redbud were nearly gone, scattered into the far winds.

Afternoon's curtain had fallen when I rode into Junction City, bringing down a purple twilight about the town. I walked into the fading light of the cafe, and sat down at a table along the far wall. The waitress came out of the kitchen, walked over to my table, and lifted the chimney of the kerosene lamp, striking a match that flashed into a golden flame as she lit the wick.

"What would you like?" she asked, and then added, "our special's fried chicken, with potatoes and gravy."

I ordered the special; it sounded good. The young woman was attractive, but a little on the heavy side. Then I wondered what was the matter with me. I needed to get over being so picky about young womenfolk.

Ten

A SILVER MOON rose above the hills when I rode into Abilene and checked in at the Merchant's Hotel. It was after six and the dining room was nearly full. A pretty young lady was sitting by herself at a table along the far wall, and one empty table remained in the middle of the room. But I was too cautious to sit there and walked over to the lass who'd been watching me ever since I'd entered.

I introduced myself and asked if she'd mind sharing her table.

She kindly invited me to have a seat. She had the most beautiful smile a body'd want to see.

The lady's name was Susannah Longstreet, from Georgia. She was heading for Denver to find her fiancé, Devon Hamilton.

I asked if she was related to the famous Confederate General James Longstreet, and learned he was her uncle.

I felt compelled to be polite in my praise of the General, but never qualified my remarks, for Pa'd always told me that Longstreet had been a "three-quarters" General, great on the defense, but only fair on the offense, and never the equal of Lee or Jackson.

The war had left Susannah's young fiancé destitute, and he'd gone

West to make his fortune. They'd planned to marry when he was a success, she told me, and for two years she'd received mail regularly from him. But six months ago it'd stopped, and she decided to go to Denver, his last address.

"Wait a minute," I cautioned. "He might not be there; then what would ya do?"

Susannah was determined. "Well, I've enough money for a couple weeks, and if I don't find him, I'll go to work."

I said no more, but I figured the poor bloke was dead. No one in his right mind would stop writing a lady like her if it was humanly possible.

The next morning after breakfast, around eight, I walked Susannah to the train and wished her well. I waited for the engine to pull away from the loading platform, as I sat on one of the benches placed beneath the depot windows. Through the open doorway, you could hear the teletype chattering. I waved to Susannah as the train slowly puffed out of the station, watching until the caboose became a speck on the horizon, fading out of sight.

From the depot I walked over to the Alamo Saloon. Whenever I was wanting local information I'd stop in, especially early in the day, when there might be few customers. When I walked through the swinging doors, the swamper was using all his energy attacking the wooden floor with his broom. I sidestepped out of his path as he swooshed dirt through the doorway, onto the boardwalk. Inside the room I smelled the odors of dust, stale beer, and cigarette smoke. A few feet away from the bar and coming through the fly-specked dirty window penetrated a stream of light beaming into the shadowy room, where it revealed a fallow atmosphere filled with dust motes. The bartender was washing glasses and cleaning up. I didn't know why, but bartenders always seemed to be big, tough men, and this one was no disappointment. The bruiser was bald as a post, and had a nose that had been flattened and broken more than once. I footed it up to the bar with a sociable "Howdy."

"Mornin'," he replied, without lookin' up from his tasks. "What can I get ya?"

"Well, it's too early for a drink . . . how about coffee?"

The bartender turned out to be friendly, despite my first impression, and we must have visited for a half hour before he answered the question I'd posed to him. He apparently had mulled it over and, willing to offer information, finally said, "Josh Allen and Luke Dillard were in Dodge City two weeks ago; and I'd heard earlier the gunman Johnny Slater was in Colorado." He continued, "Slaters's a mean hombre, and likes to hang around the bars if he has money. If he ain't in Denver, he'll be hangin' near the gold camps. I doubt he's ever done a hard day's work in his life, unless ya call stealin' hard work, and he don't mind murderin' someone to get what he wants. If ever a man needed killin', it's him."

I for certain agreed with that, and told him, "Slater killed a good friend of mine, Reggie Kempthorne."

The barkeep nodded. "So I'd heard. I knew Reggie well; served him many a drink. He was a good fella, . . . just drank too much."

I acknowledged he was right, but told him, "Reggie had straightened out and he'd been off the bottle for some time. At the time he was killed, I believe he'd quit for good."

"Well, that's what I mean," the bartender added. "Slater needs killin' . . . and I predict somebody'll do it in the not too distant future. If ya catch up with him, be careful; he's not stacked with a full deck. . . . I've heard tell that when he's ready to draw, his left eye'll twitch. The reason I want ya to know is he always tries to catch his victims off guard . . . 'n ya need to be watchin' his eye."

The sun had reached its highest arch in the sky when I told the bartender I'd be moseying on. I walked outside, mounted my gelding, and rode out of town.

That night I camped along the Smoky Hill River, and by daylight I was riding in an empty land still untouched by civilization. That day, the landscape changed from prairie to plains, for I'd left behind the tall grass and was riding in short-grass country. It was green, beautiful, and rolling, going on forever, but a deceiving land, where I knew I had to ride wary. It had a flat look to it, but shallow gullies and low hills abounded everywhere. Atop each rise could be hiding a passel of warriors, and that kind of trouble I didn't need.

My good sense was worrying my mind, so I dismounted and slowly topped the next hill where I led my gray into a small verdant copse. I canvassed the vast valley before me with searching eyes. Ships of sailing clouds moved across the sky, casting cloud shadows like purple islands in a sea of gold sunlit grass. Hours away to the north, storm clouds began their relentless march south with a steel-meshed curtain of blowing rain. I saw nothing to be wary of but the coming storm, yet my senses kept me from moving.

Prince began to swell his belly, and I quickly grabbed his nostrils to keep him from whinnying. Then below me, from the corner of my eye, I saw them upwind. Never looking directly at the Indians, I counted fifteen mounted Cheyenne warriors dressed for battle. They moved south in single file, and not over a hundred yards away. A beautiful sight that could turn deadly in a moment's notice moved slowly away from me, and had I been careless, who knows how things might have turned out.

For an hour I remained hidden, with the sunlight glowing her warm hands on my shoulders, the only sounds the humming of a bee working his way through a patch of wildflowers, and the occasional stamping of my gelding's hoof.

After the warriors had disappeared from sight I surveyed the countryside and felt it was safe to move. The restless storm still miles away to the north was flashing spears of lightning out of the dark clouds and rumbling an ominous warning. I rode beneath an unconcerned sun, and by the time it was setting I'd made my way southwest to where I could see the Arkansas River hidden in the distance behind a veil of willow and cottonwood. A purple darkness had invaded the woods below a fading sky when I made camp for the night. I determined I'd either outridden the storm or else it had veered off to other ports of call, for by morning, overhead hung a beautiful blue without a blemish.

Two days later, I rode into Dodge City, four hours short of the setting sun and two hours before suppertime.

Front Street was a busy place that afternoon. Smoke rose from the chimney of the blacksmith's shop, and out the double swinging doors came the ringing sound of his anvil. Two horses and a buckboard stood tied at the rail. On my left, a train waited patiently, along the Santa Fe depot, taking deep breaths while it panted steam. On down the street I stopped Prince, to pause and look things over. Dodge City was only three years old, but it was a booming fidgety town. Moving along Front Street on my right, to the north, was the Dodge House, and just past First Avenue across the tracks was the Great Western Hotel. Between First and Bridge Streets were the saloons on both sides of the tracks. North of the tracks were the Opera House, the Alamo, and the Long Branch, and south were the Lone Star and Lady Gay. At the end of the next block, Third Street, across the tracks was Ham Bell's huge stable. Called the Elephant Barn, it was said to be the largest structure in those parts of Kansas, and Bell had built it after he'd come to Dodge City in '74, to accommodate the wagon caravans and freighters. Bell was sitting outside the double doors on an old wooden bench when I rode up and dismounted. He got up to pat my horse.

"Nice lookin' animal you're ridin'."

I acknowledged, "Yeah, he's a good one, and royally bred . . . back to eighteenth-century England."

Bell nodded. "I know horse flesh, and I can see he has good bloodlines. I figured he was somethin' special. He looks like he'd be fast on the start and down the stretch."

"He's that all right. I know of only one other horse that can beat him."

Bell nodded again, affirmatively, and asked, "Well, what can I do for ya?"

"I'd like to stable him for a spell. . . . How much?"

Bell announced it was forty cents a day for care and keep, and if I wanted him to feed Prince some grain, it'd be an additional dime. I told him to include the grain. It gave a horse stamina, and one never knew when he might need it.

It was nearly five o'clock when I checked in at the Dodge House. The entryway was a spacious room with a large rising stairway to the second floor.

I carried my saddlebags up to my room. No lock was on the door, so I'd have to take with me anything of value. It was a large room, with a table and two chairs by the window above the street. On the table was an unlit kerosene lamp. The bed was along the west wall, and north of the bed, in the darkness of the corner, set a rocking chair. Along the east wall stood a dresser. On top, at the back of the dresser was an oval mirror, and in front of it a white porcelain bowl and pitcher filled with water. I poured out a goodly amount of water, washed up, and shaved off three days of beard.

Six o'clock chimed from the entryway clock when I walked into the dining room. I had beefsteak, canned beans, and mashed potatoes and gravy for supper.

When I finished eating and left the hotel, I hitched my gunbelt into place and the cold steel of my six-gun felt good. Kerosene lamps were being lit inside the buildings as I paced down the boardwalk, wading through squares of golden light spilling out of the doorways into the lurking darkness. Tin-pan music was coming from the Alamo and Long

Branch Saloons, and the hitching rails were full of quarter horses switching their tails and waiting patiently for their owners.

I went into the Long Branch, walked up to the bar, and to be sociable ordered a shot of whiskey. The bartender had a full head of red hair and a mustache, with muscles to match his ancestry. The Irish were known as fighters, and he looked like he could take on an army by himself.

Peering at me he announced, "James McElroy, at your service."

I replied smiling, "I'm Bruce Jacob Ross — they call me B.J. — from Upper McDowell Creek southeast of Junction City, northeast of here, . . . by way of Virginia."

"Aye, me boy, a Scotsman no less, and a kindred soul."

We talked for some time, and a half hour had gone by before I asked about Allen, Dillard, and Slater. He knew the men, but hadn't seen 'em for some time. Slater, he thought, was in Colorado, and the last time he'd seen Allen and Dillard was on the street maybe a couple weeks earlier.

"That don't mean they're not in Dodge," he said, "but they don't frequent my place. I run 'em out of here some time ago. . . . What would ya want with those outlaws?"

I explained about the killing of Reggie.

"I see . . . well, be careful, especially of Slater; he's a back shooter. If Allen and Dillard are in town, they'd be at the Lady Gay — that's where they hang out — but don't ask the bartender any questions, he buddies with 'em."

When I walked outside, my thoughts were on the two outlaws, Allen and Dillard. I didn't know what I'd do if I found 'em, but decided I'd cross that path when I came to it. I figured it was Slater that done the actual killing, and if the two teamsters felt remorse and asked for mercy for what'd happened to Reggie, I'd have to forgive 'em like God commands. But they probably weren't in town anyway.

I looked at my watch; it was half past eight when I walked into the Lady Gay. That place was named right, for the scantily dressed maidens milling with the customers were anything but solemn.

I shouldered my way up to the bar and ordered a beer. The bartender had the head and eyes of a vulture. No wonder he was buddies with the two thieves; they'd be birds of a kind. I turned around, with my back to the bar, and peered at the boisterous room. It rang with piano music and smelled of dust, cigarillos, stale whiskey, and beer. Then my eyes found what I was looking for — they sat across the room, sharing a bottle. I removed the thong holding my six-gun in place and walked over to their table. My shadow loomed over them from the lamplight. At first they couldn't figure out who I was, but when I told 'em I was a friend of Reggie's, a light of recognition widened their eyes. They were startled, and for a moment speechless.

I sat down across from 'em and looked 'em both in the eye. "I need some explainin', about what happened to Reggie."

Dillard, the bolder of the two, spoke up. "We didn't kill 'im; that was Slater. But the old fool got what he deserved."

Dillard hesitated, and with a cold look in his eyes growled in a heavy whisper, "Ya know ya can't get out of here alive; there's two of us!"

He'd said two, but the way Allen was acting, I doubted he'd draw, and if he did, he'd wished he hadn't. The three of us, almost in unison, quickly stood up, and two of our chairs toppled over with an explosive crash. For a moment Dillard and I looked at each other without drawing. When the customers realized a gunfight was about to take place, many dropped to the floor behind tables, then a lady's screams filled the smoky room, as others scrambled for the exits.

In the split seconds of time, I stood there facing the two outlaws. Then Dillard went for his piece. Death winked red in the smoke of my six-gun, and in an instant Dillard slumped to the floor. I'd only used two cartridges; the rest were for Allen, but he didn't draw.

We stood facing each other as he pleaded, "Don't shoot! I had nothin' to do with the killin'. I even tried to get 'em to stop beatin' 'im, but they wouldn't listen."

After two men had carried the dead body outside and cleaned up the blood, I motioned for Allen to sit. He asked for mercy, and from what I'd heard, he was probably the better of the two outlaws and possibly telling me the truth. I didn't know for sure, but his remorse sounded sincere. He surely was the weaker of the two, and probably did whatever Dillard had told him. I kept remembering that Pa always said God tells us to forgive, and so I did. We left it that Allen would start life over again, back where he came from in Missouri.

After most everyone had left the saloon, Allen and I walked outside, followed by the evil eyes of the bartender. I wished Allen well and he took off down the street, happy to be alive. The next day the hostler told me he'd left town.

The following morning I went to see Sheriff Charlie Bassett, to give him the details of the fight at the Lady Gay. I didn't want my name bandied around without my side of the story being told. After my report, Bassett replied, "Dillard had it comin'; it was just a matter of time. If it hadn't been you, it would've been someone else." Then with a wave of his hand he said, "You're free to go, but I'd appreciate no more gunfights in Dodge City."

"Sure," I replied. "I'm leavin' town in the morning; but if Slater shows up before that, I can't make any promises."

Bassett nodded his head. He had been named Sheriff of Ford County law enforcement, which included Dodge City, in 1873, but until '75 the town was for all practical purposes lawless, and it would remain so for another year, when the City Council hired Wyatt Earp to be Marshal.

As I walked out the Sheriff's door, he told me to ride wary, for Slater had no scruples. And then he added, "He's a bad one, and he'll not give ya a break. Best shoot first and ask questions later."

Eleven

WHEN I LEFT the Dodge House, the world was velvet black, the darkest time near dawn. But when I reached the stable, a hint of gray daylight was showing in the east. My gelding was anxious to travel, and I rode out the doors into a fresh lemon light gleaming across Front Street.

Prince wanted to move apace, and when I reined him into the short-grass plains I let him go from a trot, into a gallup, and then to an all-out run. After maybe a mile he settled down into a ground-eating walk.

Overhead, in an unbelievable blue sky, a golden sun rose and rested her warming hands upon my back. Out of the peacefulness of the plains a single hawk circled low in the sky looking for breakfast.

I stayed north of the Arkansas River; I knew that when I'd reached the Big Sandy River in Colorado, I'd have to blaze my own path north-west to Denver. I rode a lonely trail of golden days and purple nights, resting in fireless camps, as I traveled along the Arkansas. I figured cold meals were better than having a horde of Indians come down on me, for the Indians knew where to look for loot and weary travelers. Those of us on our way West all traveled the creeks and rivers, never straying far from water.

Two days out of Dodge City, I saw a herd of at least fifty antelope. Something had spooked 'em and they were bounding and leaping in the air as graceful as anything I'd ever seen. At lightning speed they raced across the prairie grass and disappeared into the southern bush. Then behind the antelope, from out of the north, came the unmistakable rumbling sound of a stampede. A horizon lined with buffalo came into view and I spurred Prince, reining the gelding southeast to a lone pinnacle of rock. Behind the upthrust I watched as the massive wooly animals rumbled by for at least ten minutes. I'd heard tales, from some of the old-timers, of herds years back as far as the eyes could see, and although the one I watched from the safety of my perch was not that large, still there had to be well over a thousand buffalo that passed by.

The next afternoon I was near the Colorado border with the Big Sandy River not over forty miles in the distance. I was riding the flat country along the Arkansas River bottoms with low rolling hills several miles away. I was making good time — too good. I'd covered a lot of miles that morning, and when I rounded a bend in the trail, from out of the trees along the river there swarmed upon me a war party of a dozen Comanche Indians. Too late to put a goodly distance between myself and the warriors, I caught an arrow in my shoulder.

I spurred Prince, reined him north, and he took off toward the low hills. He was one fast horse, and under normal conditions I'd have no trouble getting away; but he was already worn to a frazzle from the miles we had laid on, whereas the warriors were on fresh mounts. For a time Prince left 'em in the dust, but I could see he was laboring hard, and I didn't want to ride him to death. I had to find somewhere to stop and fight it out.

Ahead of me was a buffalo wallow. I rode into the depression and when I fell off Prince, I pulled him down and lashed his legs with a pigging string to keep him low and in the pit. I quickly grabbed handfuls of grass from along the edge and curried him as best I could to distract him and let him know I cared. The Indians were soon within firing range. With my hands in the soft soil, I pushed up earth around the wallow for better protection.

As the mounted assassins rushed up to overrun my position, I sent two to their final hunt. The other warriors then threw themselves off their horses onto the ground, and flattening out, they disappeared in the tall grass. Not a stem of it moved, but I knew they were inching closer. I listened but heard nothing, only the buzzing of a bee as it flirted with a wildflower somewhere close by. I knew I was in trouble, for they'd soon be close enough to rush me. Arrows were now dropping into the wallow from a short distance. I took on two and Prince took three, but their penetration wasn't deep and I quickly pulled 'em out, I was losing blood from the wounds, and it all looked hopeless; but I knew one thing . . . I'd go down fighting.

When they rushed my position, it was fast and furious. I managed to get one of the attackers with my pistol before it was knocked flying from my hand. I had no time to grab my dirk; I was too busy warding off the lances coming from all directions. I'd lost a lot of blood and was nearly helpless, but I made what I thought would be a final defiant stand, on my feet. As their Chief loomed close by, poised to make the final thrust with his lance, I shouted, as if for all the world to hear . . . "*By the Blood of the Lamb, no harm can touch me!*"

The warriors stopped in their tracks. I stood as steady as I could, with a dozen wounds besides the arrow in my shoulder. The Chief, who only moments before had been ready to finish me off, stood silent. It was then that I recognized him as the warrior I'd saved from death in '71 when on my way to Texas. As he moved closer, I could feel myself losing consciousness. The sky turned black, and that was the last I remembered.

When I awoke, I was surrounded by darkness; I could tell I was covered with a buffalo robe. I had no idea where I was, but I could smell smoke and dried animal skin.

Then a stream of daylight poured in as an Indian maiden pushed back the flap of what I realized was a tepee. She entered carrying a bowl of food, came close, lifted my head, and fed me the watery mixture. What it was or what was in it I had no notion, but it tasted good.

A week later, after much-needed rest, I felt better, though the blood I'd lost had left me weak and I could hardly walk. A warrior brought my horse to me, and motioned for me to mount. After I'd crawled up on Prince, the Chief appeared and pointed northwest, telling me, "*Go! We efen!*"

My face mirrored my confusion, and he repeated, "*Go! We efen!*" Then it came to me that he was saying we were "even."

He attempted to ask, as near as I could tell by his words and sign language, who the "Lamb" was that could stop him and his warriors from committing further bloodshed?

My heart was pounding as I tried to explain to him. "Jesus the Christ," I replied. Then I added, "The God of the sun," as I formed my arms in a circle.

He nodded, as though he understood.

The magnificent-looking Chief stood expressionless; I thought the conversation must be finished. I thanked him for his hospitality, and he simply grunted. I realized it was time for me to leave, and rode out of camp with all my weapons replaced and food in my saddlebags. No doubt, if we were to meet again in their hunting grounds, there'd be no mercy, for now, as he had said, we were most surely *efen.*

After I'd gone a good distance from the Comanche camp, I looked back. The warrior hadn't moved. He watched me until I disappeared from sight. Whether he was wary of my circling back, or admiring my tenacity to live, I'll never know, but I'd like to think it was the latter. I certainly had respect for him, and I think he did for me. I'd heard that a body was safe in a Comanche village, but that after leaving, all bets were off. . . . However, they didn't follow.

As I rode out, I was awed by the beauty of the country thereabouts, and I could see why the Indians didn't want the white man taking it away from them.

I learned later that the twenty-five-year-old Comanche Chief was the renowned Quanah. His father was Nocona, Chief of the Nocona Comanches, and his mother was Cynthia Ann Parker, the white girl taken captive in 1836 when the Kiowas and Nocona Comanches had attacked "Parker's Fort," in northwest Texas. They not only killed many defenders, but took five women captive. At the time, Cynthia was close to ten years old. Four of the captured women were later ransomed and returned, and their accounts of the cruelty and barbarous treatment by the Comanches had enraged the Texans. Some years later, Cynthia became the wife of Nocona and bore him three children. But she and a daughter had died in 1864, when Quanah was going on fifteen. Then, after Nocona's death, Quanah rose to Chief, in 1874. Word had it that Quanah remained on the warpath after refusing to acknowledge the 1867 Treaty of Medicine Lodge, the attempt to encircle the southern Plains Indians on a reservation. He'd raided throughout Texas and Mexico, it was said.

Two days after I'd left the Comanche camp, I could see the Rocky Mountains in the distance. They saw-toothed above the plains against a sky of ashen clouds. That evening, the backdrop of escarpments and canyons lured me with the same mysterious charm I'd felt in Virginia when the Blue Ridge Mountains had beckoned; but the Rockies were more magnificently massive and I was filled with a restless eagerness to step foot on their high gravel trails.

The next day I rode into Denver and thought no more of my wounds. Seventeen years earlier, in '58, Denver had been nothing but a trading post, and in August of that year, on Cherry Creek near the confluence of the South Platte River, gold had been discovered. Overnight, Denver grew into a thriving city. But it didn't take the miners long to figure that the gold flowed down from the higher elevations, and in 1859 it was found in Central City and Black Hawk, northwest of Denver. News traveled fast that a rich strike had been found, and the boom was on, as miners came from everywhere. Gold was soon found all along the eastern slope of the Rockies.

As I rode through Denver, I could see to my right the Kansas Pacific Railroad that had reached the city five years earlier. I rode easy among buildings spreading in all directions before the impressive backdrop of mountains. Then I dismounted from Prince, and led him into the stable near the center of the city's marketplace. After settling my gelding in for the night, it was nearly five o'clock. I talked to the hostler for several minutes, before I walked a block west to the hotel.

I noticed some permanent buildings going up, made of native stone quarried from the nearby mountains, but the rest of the village was like most boom towns, quickly constructed of wood frame and false fronts. The main street was of hard-packed earth, and it'd be a typical quagmire after a rain.

With saddlebags over my shoulder, I checked in at the Statler. Later that evening I ate at a cafe down the street. It was packed, but I found a seat at a long table, and ordered their special of deer meat and potatoes.

After supper, I visited at least six saloons within two blocks, inquiring at each about Slater, but I gleaned no particular information, though they all knew him. One of the bartenders thought the outlaw hung out in one of the cantinas on the south side of town. He warned me, "They're tough places and ya'd best tread wary if ya go lookin' for him or anyone else."

My soul was at war when I walked back to the hotel. Part of me said to drop the search, for there'd been enough killing; the other part of me was sure that letting Slater get away clean wouldn't be fair to Reggie.

I knew I'd have to let God lead me in this. I determined I'd try to talk to Slater; maybe he'd want forgiveness. And if he did, I'd have to grant him that, revolting as it seemed.

The next evening I went to the south-side saloons — but only after I'd made sure my six-gun was cleaned and its chambers full. Pa always told me to be ready for any circumstance, and if it then turned out your preparation was not necessary, no harm had befallen; either way, you were still among the living.

Slater was nowhere to be found, but I left word with the bartenders that a B.J. Ross was looking for him. He could leave a message at the Statler Hotel, and I'd meet him anywhere in public he chose.

A week went by, and I heard nothing. Then one evening while eating supper at the cafe I noticed a suspicious-looking hombre at another table. I caught him glancing my way several times with more than a casual interest. When I'd finished, I peered over to check on the man, but he was gone. I paid my bill and walked outside, pausing by the doorway as my eyes canvassed the street. I saw nothing. Then, near the alleyway ahead, I was sure a shadow had moved deeper into the darkness along the frame building.

I looked at my watch, it was half past eight. The alleyway before me was between the leather shop and the hotel — a dark place, where those who wanted to rob could lay in wait for victims without being seen. They could commit murder, and dash away down the alley to the next street.

Commit murder! The words rang through my mind as I was about to step into that ten-foot space between the buildings. I stopped. A loose two-by-four, some six feet long, was laying on the boardwalk. I picked it up and put my jacket over one end. When I shoved the coat into the alleyway, at shoulder height, all hell broke loose. Gunfire racketed the night. I dropped the two-by-four and could hear feet racing off down the alleyway. I could see two men at the far end of the narrow passage, and fired three shots as they disappeared around the corner. But they didn't slow down, so I figured no one had been hit. I looked at my jacket and could see it was nothing but a rag, nearly cut to pieces with bullet holes.

John McCallin, the Denver chief of law enforcement, showed up and asked what was going on. I told him what'd happened, and he peered at me with disbelieving eyes.

"You must have had your guardian angel watching over ya."

"Yeah," I told him, "I guess maybe I did."

When I later entered my hotel room, I wedged a chair under the doorknob. I was tired and didn't want any uninvited guests calling in the night. But I wasn't sleepy, and lay in bed thinking, with my hands behind my head. It seemed Slater sure didn't want to talk. The gunman wanted action, the kind that could get a man killed. I had to give him a chance — handle it the way I thought God would want me to — but I'd cut Slater no more slack. I'd give him an even break, if it were possible; however, there were just some things a man had to do to maintain his honor.

I went to south town several times during the next month, but Slater was nowhere to be found. He apparently had left Denver for the gold fields, to fleece some unsuspecting hard-working miner of his gold.

In August, at the cafe, I met an old-timer the miners called Dry Gulch Joe. Joseph Woodman had struck it big back in 1860 near Central City, and had sold out for what he thought was a fair sum of $10,000. It was a hard-rock mining claim and Joe was a placer man, preferring to pan for his gold. Selling the mine was the thing for him to do, but he'd sold too cheap, and since then the owners had removed millions in gold ore from the claim. But that never seemed to bother Joe too much.

Old Joe took a liking to me and told me about all the places he'd searched for gold. He'd gone to the fields of California in 1854 when he was thirty, and he'd been hunting for treasure ever since. In 1859, he came to Colorado.

Joe was a lonely sort of fellow, and we buddied around together for about a month before he suggested we might do some panning up in the high country west of Georgetown, at a place he'd passed through back in '70. He told me the formations in the batholiths — what they called the deep intrusions of former molten rock that had inched into the rock strata — and the surrounding escarpments looked promising.

"I've never prospected there, but I know there's gold's in the gravel of the streambeds. And what you don't know about prospecting, B.J., I'll teach you."

I hadn't made the trip just for the gold; my main interest in going to Colorado had been to see the mountains, take in the sights, and soothe my soul. But after listening to Joe tell his tales of his mining experiences, it became exciting.

"*Why not prospect for gold*?" I thought. I could see the country at the same time. It seemed a good way to put together a little extra stake for my future. I still had nearly $600 in my Wells Fargo account, but I didn't want to get into it unless necessary. You never knew when an emergency might come along and take all of your savings.

And so I told Joe, "I'd like to go with ya."

The next day I went to the leather shop and bought some well-needed boots. I'd never seen so many boots, bridles, and saddles in one place. Joe picked up what other supplies and equipment we'd need at the General Store.

I had found a pretty fair pack horse for $20, and two days later, with Joe and me each leading a packer, we trailed west out of Denver. That evening, we rode into Central City, and after several days in the area, we talked it over and decided to stay put. We planned to hit the high-country streams above Georgetown in early spring.

Twelve

IT WAS LATE November 1875 and my eyes peered up into an overcast sky. From out of the gray misty clouds came the snow, silently and softly, through an atmosphere of breathless air. In no time the large flakes had covered the dark beaten-earth streets of Central City. I paused along the boardwalk to canvas the scene of hazy escarpments and talus slopes in the surrounding area. Almost invisible through the veil of falling flakes were the numerous prospect holes and shacks above the town in the narrow canyon.

I stomped snow from my boots on the gunny sack just inside the door of the cafe, and walked over to join Joe sitting at a table along the far wall.

We'd been in the Central City-Black Hawk area for three months, panning the streams above the two towns. We'd made good wages. I'd found a nice deposit of nuggets in a gravel bar, where I'd dug down to bedrock. When we cashed in our gold, we'd split $360. I'd not need touch my bank account, as the $180 would nicely run me through the next few months.

That winter I stayed at the Teller House Hotel on Eureka Street. It was a long season, and had a person wanted, he could get himself into all kinds of trouble. The street saloons were full of miners, and the loud clamor of talk, laughter, and music was almost deafening. Inadequately dressed women continually roamed among the miners, doing their best to relieve them of their money.

Each saloon had its games of chance, and I watched some of the poker games a few times, to acquaint myself of its workings. The gamblers at first tried to get me to join in, but I'd have none of it. From what I could see, the slick gamblers always won, and the poor chap who'd worked hard for his money was soon broke. I couldn't tell if the gamblers won from skill or by cheating, but probably it was the first, unless they needed to cheat to win. I noticed once in a while, though, that they'd come up with cards that should've been in the discards. At times, when the gamblers would be called for cheating, the game ended up in gunplay and inevitable death. And once again, usually the miner was the one carted off to the morgue. I wanted no part of that kind of life, and stayed away from the saloons unless I was looking for information.

The year 1876 was memorable in many ways: Bat Masterson had his first gunfight, in Sweetwater, Texas, killing Sergeant Melvin King in a dust-up over Molly Brennan; the well-known and always confident General George Armstrong Custer was killed by the Sioux and Cheyenne — a shock to everyone — at the battle of Little Bighorn in Montana; and, most important to my life, my Grandfather John Ross died in Loudoun County, Virginia.

Following upon the long winter of '76, suddenly and without warning, spring came sallying forth like an invading army. Only two days earlier we'd been under six inches of snow. Then, on the first day of April, the snows almost disappeared and the miners worked in shirtsleeves. What had seemed like an empty countryside was now full of men with their picks and shovels ringing against the rocky slopes.

That day I went to the General Store to select a few items of clothing I'd be needing for the season ahead. While the clerk was packing up my purchases, I wandered over to the wooden case holding the handguns. I was admiring the new Smith & Wesson .45 when the clerk walked up and told me I could try it out if I wanted. Back of the store, thirty yards away against the rock bank, was a target. I soon realized at that distance the new handgun was more accurate than the Remington I carried. When I left the store, I had a new Winchester rifle in hand, my Remington in my saddle-bag, and the Smith & Wesson tight in my holster.

On April 10th, Joe and I picked up our horses from the livery and were on the move southwest. The next day we rode into Georgetown. The booming town lay in breathless high country, the surrounding area covered with pine, spruce, fir, and aspen. At the edge of town ran Clear Creek, a crystal stream of melted snow that came down from the peaks in roaring cascades. We saw vistas of far-away canyons, escarpments, and slopes of aspen working their way into wildflower meadows. To be there in the remote community was a pleasure hard to describe.

After checking our horses at the livery, we walked to a nearby boarding house and rented a room. That evening we cleaned up and went to the Hotel de Paris, owned by Louis Dupuy, Joe's friend. The hotel was to become known as one of the finest in the West, along with the quality of its meals. Dupuy had been a miner for a time, but was injured and opened a Georgetown bakery in 1873 that he soon turned into a hotel. Back in '69, Joe and Dupuy became acquainted when they'd partnered together in the mines.

We'd no sooner sat down at a far table when Dupuy spotted Joe and came over. After I was introduced, Dupuy took our order, and the waitress soon was bringing our supper. I'd thought when I saw her earlier that she looked familiar; it was Susannah Longstreet, the young woman I'd met in Abilene who had headed for Denver to find her betrothed.

Joe and I had a grand supper of duck meat and potatoes, with all the trimmings. The next day we moved to the hotel at Dupuy's insistence. That night I talked to Susannah after she had finished work, as she'd asked me to stay on to visit after I finished my meal.

Susannah'd had no luck in finding Devon Hamilton, and asked if I would help by questioning other miners in my travels. She had inquired of those around the area of Georgetown with no success. I promised I'd see what Joe and I could find out in the mining camps, and she gave me a picture of Devon to take along.

After two days of being spoiled to the core at the hotel, Joe thought we'd better head for high country. I acknowledged that I thought we already *were* in high country, but he laughed and added, "Not as high as we're going!"

Most of the first day of travel we passed many a miner, working placers along the streams and prospect holes on the slopes. We saw a few shacks of stone and logs, but mostly they were of canvas.

On our second day out of Georgetown we saw no one. We rode a trail that no man had traveled before, at least there appeared no signs of it. But that was the way I liked the wilderness — places where man hadn't disturbed the countryside. It made a body feel like you'd passed through God's country.

We rode careful, without disturbing the land. I felt a peacefulness that man sometimes feels on occasion, and usually when alone. Joe and I talked little; I just followed his lead, and figured he knew exactly where he was going.

At midday we rode the eyebrow of a sheer cliff that must have dropped three hundred feet to a sliver of a stream rushing white water below. The trail was around eight feet wide, but there were places my left foot and stirrup hung out over the vast open.

The view was breathtaking, but I was too busy looking straight ahead to enjoy it. I was nervous, and all I wanted to do was get off that ledge. The way my gelding's muscles tightened up when I coaxed him out onto it, I knew he was wanting no part of that trail either, but he trusted me, as he stepped out on tender feet. Almost before I could start up a good sweat, we were past the cliff and in a wildflower meadow with patches of aspen and pine scattered along its slopes.

When I looked back down the narrow way, I shuddered. I doubt it was over five hundred feet in length, but it'd felt like a mile.

I questioned Joe. "Ain't there a safer way into this place?"

"There is, but it's too steep for horses," he replied.

An hour later we came to a stream that poured down out of the mountains. We made camp in a widened area of the narrow canyon of uplifted rock. I removed Prince's saddle and curried him down with a comb. He dipped his unbridled nose into the stream for a drink, then wandered his way into knee-deep grass.

After I'd cared for my pack horse, I noticed Joe was busy fixing supper, and decided I'd take a walk. The stream twisted slowly across the meadow to the rim of rock, then pitched off the edge. Earlier my curiosity had gotten the best of me, and I'd wanted to view the falls I could hear roaring from our camp. But when I reached the fluted rim, I wasn't prepared for the sight that spread out before me. I could see at least five falls, and the bottom cascade must have descended another hundred feet into a large pool of deep blue water. The twilight view along the peaks and escarpments of the mountains was a scene I'd never forget.

The sun sets early when mountains rise high above you in the West, and the last of day's sun glows like yellow flame on the rock and underbrush. I watched as the golden-lit grassy thicket paused, blazed up for a moment, then slowly turned from brilliant gold to purple. When I got back to camp, after wading through the low shadows of coming night, Joe had supper ready.

After a meal of salted deer meat and wild greens, we sat quiet around the campfire, mostly listening to Nature. Joe pulled a pad from his shirt pocket and spent at least an hour writing something; I figured it was probably a diary.

"Joe," I asked, "where're ya from?"

"Boston," he answered.

"I'd never have guessed it," I replied, then told him I was originally from Virginia.

"Yes," he answered. "Almost everyone in the West is from back East somewhere if they're over the age of twenty."

I don't know why, but I never thought of Joe as someone from the East. He just fit the mold of what I thought was Western — steady, strong, self-contained. But he was right; almost no adult at that time had been born in the West. After my prodding, he told me a little of his life in Massachusetts. He had been raised in a family of means. His Pa had owned an iron mill, and when Joe had graduated with a business degree from the prestigious Harvard University, he went to work at the mill.

In 1849, Joe's Pa began to come onto bad times. He'd carried his help on the payroll too long, and the next year ended up losing the mill. His Pa died the year after, and his Ma, with just a small stipend on which to live, died in '53. Joe, on his own, bounced from one job to another, then in the spring of '54 he packed his belongings in one suitcase and took off for California where he hoped to make his fortune in the gold fields.

"Ever been back to Boston?" I asked.

"No," he replied. "There's nothing for me there; after all these years, I have no reason to go back. I love the West and consider it my home."

But I thought it strange that Joe never talked about his life back East, for he'd lived in Boston some thirty years. The only thing I could figure was that something'd happened he wanted to forget.

Joe and I stayed in the high country 'til fall, a six months filled with new experiences. We found little gold, but I'd gained a quantity of knowledge, for each day Joe would carefully show me what soils and what rock formations to look for to find the hidden wealth.

"Look for quartz," he'd told me. "Find it, and gold should be close by."

And when Joe wasn't talking gold, he was showing me what plants were edible and those medicinal.

Joe was as happy as a rabbit in a summer garden the entire trip. I think he knew all along we'd not strike it big, for he had a familiarity with the area like the back of his hand. I don't think he cared whether he found gold or not. He just loved the place so much he wanted to share it with someone, and, in truth, I praised God that Joe had picked me.

The evening before we were to head back to Georgetown, and after we'd eaten our supper, the mountainside turned quiet. I lay on my groundsheet listening to the serenade of a nearby brook humming joyful tunes and looking at the stars. There was something heavenly about those lonely times in the wilderness that made the heart sing.

Joe was sitting by the campfire writing. A bit later he slipped the book into his saddlebag and stared off into the western distance to far deserts below. Then, like a poet of old, he began in a melancholy voice.

How heavy do I journey on the way,
When what I seek my weary travel's end
Doth teach that ease and that repose to say,
"Thus far the miles are measured from thy friend!"

He said no more, and I felt I dare not break the silence. Then he spoke again.

"Many a time I've quoted that verse from Shakespeare, when traveling alone. Although I'm with you, I still have that special solitary feeling as we prepare to leave our sanctuary."

"Aye," I replied. "I understand your thinkin'. Ma liked poetry, and I've read many a verse myself. I like it too, but I remember little of what I've read."

Joe smiled. "Well, I guess I can recite many of Shakespeare's lines, especially those that have touched my heart, but I met a man prospecting in California who could repeat all of the sonnets!"

I was surprised at finding out one more bit of information about Joe. I'd heard of men who could retain what they read and then recite it later, but none I'd known personally. There was more to Joe than I'd first thought, and if anyone had told me that he'd turn out to be my closest friend, I wouldn't have believed 'em.

It came to me then that we — all people — travel in but the same short-measured world. It would seem not so, with all the separate miles and directions we move, yet the company we keep maintains a small, close place. We associate with but few people and travel our lives within that orbit of friends, even though outside that boundary we are among unknown millions.

In early September that year we were back in Georgetown. We cashed in our four pounds of gold nuggets, and out of my share I deposited $400 into my account at Wells Fargo. Earlier, when at home, Pa had wanted to deposit all of Dandy's stud fees into my account, but I'd refused and we'd settled on half. Since that time, he'd put in deposit for me another $300. For someone who's never had much money, the $1,200 in my account seemed like a near fortune.

I spent the winter in Georgetown, staying at the Hotel de Paris and spending a big share of my spare time talking to Susannah. It wasn't long, and I was smitten. But then who wasn't? It seemed like every cowboy who came into the hotel dining room was soon gazing her way.

Thirteen

I'D COME TO KNOW the manager at Wells Fargo, Bill Elliot, who was also staying at the Hotel de Paris. One night after supper as we were visiting I queried, "Have ya ever had a holdup by an hombre called Slater?"

"No," he mulled. "I've heard of him, and others have told me he outlaws for a livin', but he hasn't bothered us here at Georgetown, though that don't mean he won't. We freight a lot of gold from the mines, and that makes us a target."

"Well, if you're haulin' a lot of gold, he'll be around, probably waitin' until the time's right." I told Elliot about my run-in with the fugitive in Denver, and that I'd sure like to catch up with him. Then I added, "I'm sure he'll show, with all the gold hereabouts, and when he does, let me know."

It was then that Elliot told me he had an opening for an express messenger on the Denver stage. I could have the job, he said.

I asked what I would have to do — my charge — and if I'd be qualified.

"Oh, you're qualified all right," Elliot told me. "I know a bit about your past. The job requires helpin' to look after the passengers, along with handlin' the mail and strongbox that goes under the driver's seat in the front boot; but your main duty will be ridin' shotgun on the Concord stage from Georgetown to Denver."

His explanation gave me a few reservations, but I accepted the job with the condition I'd be quitting in the spring. A sprig of trepidation later hit my wary bones, but I'd given my word, and I'd just have to tough it out until April. The pay was $100 a month, more than three times the wages of a wrangler. That should have told me then and there that the job could be dangerous.

My usual day started at six o'clock. I'd dress, breakfast at the hotel, and be at Wells Fargo, the home station, by half past seven. We'd leave at eight o'clock sharp for the fifty-mile trip to Denver. The weather especially, but other conditions too, could dictate our arrival time. Then that night we'd bunk at the home station, and make the return trip to Georgetown the following day. Between the home stations of Denver and Georgetown were four swing stations where the stock-tenders — usually two of 'em — would quickly hook up our coach to a new team of harnessed and ready-to-go mustangs. Many a time we'd veer over to Central City and Black Hawk for a stop with cargo and passengers.

After my two-day run, I'd have a day off to loaf. Earlier I'd told Elliot I'd not work Sundays, and that was the way he arranged my runs. Each trip I carried my own handgun, along with my Winchester rifle and a hundred rounds of ammunition. Besides my own firepower at hand, I held a company-furnished double-barreled, twelve-gauge, sawed-off shotgun across my lap. Just the look of that scatter gun would scare most people away from wanting to cause trouble, especially if they ever looked at the results of what a twelve-gauge can do to a man at twenty feet.

I'd started work on September 8th, and was at the Wells Fargo office by twenty past seven. I had a few minutes to spare, and peered inside the Concord stage, which was almost new and a magnificent-looking coach. It could seat nine passengers on three leather-upholstered benches. Wood paneling decorated throughout the interior, with polished metal fittings. On each side of the coach near the doors hung an ornate kerosene lamp. Twelve more passengers could ride on the roof, but at such full capacity, everyone would be cramped, crowded, and uncomfortable.

That morning the sun was glowing a warmth into the cold air, especially when out of the wind along the break of the frame building where I stood. I couldn't help but notice along the slopes the aspen leaves were in the process of changing into their proud, golden autumn color.

Just before eight o'clock, the driver, Clint Thorson, who I'd just met that morning, shouted his call to the passengers inside the station, "All *aboard!*"

Nine men and three women stepped out onto the wooden walk; one of the women carried a crying baby. As I helped the womenfolk step up into the coach, three men also ducked inside; the other six, who were miners, climbed up and settled on the roof.

Earlier I'd loaded the mail and strongbox below the seat in the front boot, so after tending to the passengers, I sat a minute to ready myself for the trip. I felt like a bird on a lofty perch, and suddenly realized I was duck soup for anyone wanting to shoot me from cover. But the driver climbed into the box at that moment and settled down into the seat to my right. He gave me a smile, then asked, "Ready?"

When I nodded, he took hold of the reins, released the brake, cracked his whip above the six mustangs, and shouted "*Haaaaaa!*" The animals leaned into their harnesses and left Georgetown in a rush of pounding hooves. We hadn't gone a quarter mile before the coach had rocked the fussy baby to sleep.

We made the trip to Denver in record time and without a hitch, arriving at six that evening. I made two trips to Denver that first week, with no major problems; even the weather was calm. But my intuition told me it wouldn't stay that way much longer, that surely something would happen to make life unpleasant.

When I'd started with Wells Fargo Susannah became angry — well, not angry, but upset; she'd started to cry, insisting the job was too dangerous.

"What if you're killed? Then I'd have no one."

In my travels among the miners I hadn't found anybody who'd known or seen her fiancé, Devon Hamilton, and as time went on I knew Susannah was becoming more despondent. I think she had finally given way to the thought he might be dead.

But before I could respond to her fears about my new Wells Fargo job, she rushed off, back to the kitchen.

September 25, 1876, was still dark when I rolled out of bed. Besides our regular mail, freight, and passengers that day the stage would be carrying $50,000 in gold. After I'd finished breakfast, I walked briskly to the Wells Fargo station, the only sound the hollow steps of my boots on the boardwalk. By that time, the aspen along the slopes and streams had all turned color, but down around Denver, at the lower elevations, the leaves were still green. In the glow of morning light I paused and peered up at a country of emerald slopes, purple escarpments, and golden aspen spilling like fountains of water into lonely dark canyons.

As was usual, I arrived at the station ten minutes early, twenty past seven. James King was to handle the reins of the six mustangs, and there was none better riding a box. Two guards carried out the gold and put it in the front boot. They'd also be making the trip, one on the roof, the other in the coach.

Six passengers stepped up into the stage, two ladies and four men. One young lady, I recognized, worked at the saloon two blocks south of the hotel. She seemed a bit upset, and I figured she probably had a fight with her young man. I recognized the men, local miners, except one was an hombre carrying two tied-down guns and looked like a gunfighter. He seemed a confident sort, but when he glanced my way he had a nervous smile. What concerned me most was his black smoldering eyes that reminded me of a striking snake. Ma'd always told me ya can tell a man's character by his eyes.

"Look in his eyes," she said. "He may be a charlatan, but if he's evil, it's transparent and the one thing he can't hide."

King had told me the man was John Terrill, a gunfighter out of Louisiana. He'd been in Georgetown about a week, hanging around the dives, gambling in the south end of town. I couldn't believe it was circumstance that he'd be taking the one stage carrying $50,000 in gold, and I could see both guards were keeping a wary eye on the gunslinger.

About the time King snapped the whip and shouted at the mustangs, I thought of Slater. If he knew about the shipment, he'd try to take it if he could figure out a way to do it safely; he was a sure-thing outlaw, but he'd not chance getting himself killed. I'd told King about Slater and my suspicions, and he agreed we should be wary. He had heard of him, but it was rumored that Slater and his gang operated farther south along the eastern slopes.

"That don't mean they're not in this area now," King added and continued. "I know of many an outlaw notorious for robbin' stagecoaches, and believe me they know we're carryin' gold today, but they're also figurin' the odds of pullin' it off. I'd say with me drivin' and you ridin' shotgun they won't take the chance. Too risky."

"D'ya really think so?" I asked, almost doubtfully.

"I do. You have a reputation with a gun. You'd be surprised how many men have heard of your gunfights in Abilene and Dodge City. That kind of news travels like a prairie wildfire."

"I didn't know," I said. "Anyway, I'd not have survived those fights without God."

"*Hmmph*," King muttered.

The day before, on the 24th, in an area called Robbers Roost, northwest of our swing station at Lawson, in an abandoned cabin, Slater and four of his henchmen were drinking whiskey and plotting on how and where to rob the stage, which they thought to be carrying over $100,000 in gold. The informant Slater had hanging around Wells Fargo had over-estimated the amount of the shipment he'd heard bruited around town. Slater should have realized that such an amount of gold would probably be transported in an express wagon with at least four guards. But, nevertheless, the $50,000 we actually had with us was still a lot of money.

Slater and his men had decided on a narrow stretch of road halfway between Lawson and Idaho Springs, estimating the stage to be at the location around eleven that morning. They'd be in place by ten, in case the stage had left early. The place of ambush was at the top of a long uphill grade. They'd checked several stages and, rightly so, the horses were tuckered out at the crest where the coach would stop to rest its mustangs. What they didn't know was that I'd been studying the Denver run for likely places of a holdup. The spot the outlaws had chosen I also had figured to be the most likely.

After everything had been decided, Slater's informant, as an afterthought, hastened to add, "Oh, by the way, I also heard James King would be handlin' the reins. The talk was with him at the reins and Ross ridin' shotgun, it'd be no easy chore for anyone to rob the stage and live through it."

Slater removed the cigarette hanging from his mouth and almost screamed at his informant. "What did ya say? Who's ridin' shotgun? Did ya say B.J. Ross?"

"Yeah . . . well . . . Ross was all I heard, and from the rumors bandied around, no one wants to tangle with him or King."

Slater sneered. "It *has* to be him; I been wantin' to see Ross dead, and now's my chance. This calls for a drink!" he roared, lifting the bottle to his lips.

We were making good time, and after a short stop at Lawson, where we changed to fresh mustangs, King cracked the whip and the team of six rushed out of the station in a cloud of dust. The passengers had closed down the leather curtains to keep out the billowing dirt, though the effort didn't help a lot, for it still managed to get inside the stage. At the swing station, I told King about my suspicions, and he agreed that the road divide was a likely place to be hit, and in fact had been several times, so we made plans. If there would be no ambush, we still weren't out anything, but if there was, it could mean the difference between life and death.

The long grade was forested with green pine and golden aspen. From the crest you couldn't see over a hundred yards downhill due to the road curving out of sight. Below the curve was where we would stop and rest the horses. Any noise we made would be covered by the roar of the stream close by.

It was a quarter past ten that morning when we stopped in the grove of pine trees and aspen to rest the horses. We decided to stay for thirty minutes, then move uphill. At the crest, the horses would still be in fine shape and raring to run. We kept an eye on Terrill while stopped, for we didn't want him leaving, to sound the alarm of our ruse, if he was part of a robbery attempt. But he never acted suspicious. I doubted he was part of a gang, but he could be an opportunist. To me he seemed more a loner who was fast on the draw.

King moved the horses slow up the slope, and at the divide, maybe fifty yards away, five armed outlaws rushed into the road with guns at the ready. Spread out, they waited for us, and when we were within thirty feet of them, Slater shouted, "*Stop!* . . . Throw the box and gold on the ground and no one will get hurt!"

King looked at me and at the top of his lungs called out "*Now!*" while snapping the reins and cracking his whip. When he lunged forward in his seat, I lifted my handgun, crouched over, and fired at the nearest outlaw, just as the team of mustangs in unison surged forward. As the gunman went down, I grabbed my shotgun and fired at another hombre only a few feet from the stage. The upper part of his body fell and then his legs crumpled. The remaining thieves, surprised at our furious action, were now firing their rifles. We flashed by so fast I had no chance to shoot at Slater who'd stationed himself along the right shoulder of the road.

A few miles ahead, we stopped to assess the damage. We'd need not worry about the thieves; they'd be off somewhere licking their wounds. But the guard on the roof was dead, and one of the male passengers had been hit in the right shoulder, though it wasn't death threatening.

The rest of the trip was without incident. Terrill had not been a problem during the shootout. The guard said that Terrill had his pistol in hand — he assumed to shoot at the outlaws — but the man never fired his weapon. I wondered later about Terrill's drawn gun. What if the holdup had gone in the outlaws' favor? Who would he have shot?

In late November of that year we had four to five inches of snow on the ground. Following a break in the weather, Elliot had me make a run to Denver. We traveled in snow until we hit Idaho Springs, and then we made good time the rest of the way. The next morning we left Denver with four men and two women passengers. One of the ladies had been on my first trip to Denver.

"Looks like we're riding together again," she noted.

"Yeah, welcome back," I told her.

"I've been visiting my sister in Colorado City, who was not well. She's better now, and I'll be glad to get back to work."

When we reached the foothills of the mountains on our return trip, the sky had turned a gray overcast. At Lawson, snow started to fall. The box of a stagecoach is no place to be in any kind of bad weather, and I burrowed down into my sheepskin coat to gain a little warmth. Visibility lowered, as we rode into a maelstrom of blinding snowflakes. We were still ten miles from Georgetown, and at the rate it was coming down, we'd be snowbound before we could reach town. Nevertheless, we determined to push on, and the snowfall seemed to ease a bit.

There was no wind, but the air was cold; the temperature was dropping. We'd gotten stuck twice in deep drifts that'd crossed the road, costing us at least an hour in time. The men on the stage had gone to work shoveling until the coach could get clear of the drifts. Then, suddenly, the snow quit, and the western skies gleamed a familiar sunset of pink along the peaks.

At six o'clock we slowly and carefully rounded a sharp bend in a foot of snow. Nestled away and below us glowed the welcome lights of Georgetown. What a relief it was to realize we'd made it back to civilization. I peered around at the gray escarpments fast losing the light of day, and along the roadway at snow-covered brakes. Juniper branches hung heavy to the ground alongside hillside houses buried in snow hanging over rooftop eves. Below, the varied character of the town flats had disappeared beneath a white blanket.

Six black horses exhaling steam in the crisp air stamped cautiously down off the mountain into the silent town . . . as silent and breathless as the backdrop of the frozen escarpment looming farther west. The mustangs slowly came to a stop in the glowing light from out of the window at Wells Fargo. The frosty stagecoach gleamed in the golden lamplight welcoming us from out of the bitter cold.

Time moved snowbound into December, and all the countryside around Georgetown was buried in drifts up to ten feet.

Fourteen

ON A SNOWY December day, when all outside was white, Joe and I walked a deep narrow path between drifts accumulated along the boardwalk to the Golden Nugget Saloon. Inside, we stopped near a man at the rail — his name was George Jensen — who'd been prospecting for gold in the Rockies since the late '50s. I showed him Devon Hamilton's picture.

"No," he said, as he handed me back the photo, "I've not seen him." Then . . . "*Wait* a minute!" he exclaimed. "Let me look at that again; there's somethin' about the gentleman that looks familiar." Jensen examined the photo carefully. "Yeah, that's him all right. It's his eyes. The reason I'd not recognized him before was that the miner I'd seen had a full beard coverin' his face; the man in the photo has no whiskers. He's got a claim down on the Animas River, near a minin' town called Silverton. He was there last fall when I came north. He has a decent claim, so I'm sure he'd still be there." Jensen then explained the location of Hamilton's placer above Silverton, gesturing south.

"I stayed with him a few days. He's a decent sort who seems lost; doesn't seem to care about much. What d'ya want with him?" Jensen queried. "I hope he hasn't committed a crime. . . . You're not the law are ya?"

I reassured him. "No, his fiancée's been tryin' to locate him for nearly two years, and she'll be pleased to know he's alive."

"Well, if you go down there, best be careful; it's not safe in that part of the country. There're claim jumpers everywhere. A lot of gold is being found along the streams, and it's easier to find the gold than to hang onto it! Hamilton told me he'd been hit three times by outlaws, but had managed to keep 'em at bay. He had a partner with him, but he looked like no one I'd want to trust."

On the way back to the hotel, Joe told me he knew right where Hamilton's claim was on the Animas. He'd been through there back in '65, and he'd also found gold in the area. He'd come across several large jewelry-type nuggets, and then all at once there were no more.

Joe explained, "The source of the gold was a mystery . . . surely there's an answer. I searched for a week before moving on, and always figured I'd return sometime, but I've never been back."

I asked why not. He sighed. "I don't know; I should have. There's a mother lode close to where the nuggets ran out, I'd bet my life on it."

"Why are ya so sure?" I asked.

"Because the last nuggets I found had sharp edges; they weren't smooth and worn, so the source would be close by. Nuggets carried in fast waters are bounced around in the gravel and lose their rough edges if carried any distance. The smoother the nugget, the farther it is from its source."

Joe looked over at me again. "So when do you want to leave for Silverton? After we locate Hamilton, we can check out my area, and maybe between the two of us we can find that mother lode."

Excited, I eagerly agreed, "Sounds good to me; I'd say we pull up stakes sometime in early April. We might still get snowed in along the way, but that late in the year it wouldn't be for long. The sooner the better, especially if Hamilton was bein' harassed by claim jumpers — he might need our help."

That night I told Susannah the news at the hotel. It was her turn to be excited as I added, "Joe and I've decided to leave in April, locate Devon, and tell him where he can find ya."

I was happy for Susannah; she had just about given up, for it'd been over three years since Hamilton had left Atlanta. Yet, much like that day I had left Virginia for Kansas, I felt as if I was losing something — like there'd been a death in the family. It was then I knew I was in love — a love I couldn't profess, a love I had to keep to myself.

That winter of 1877 Susannah, Joe, and I attended the Presbyterian church together most every Sunday. At a service in January, Susannah was born again, according to the Scriptures, and two months later Joe likewise received the Holy Ghost. Later he told me his conversion came about because of the peace he'd noticed I had with life. He figured my surety must have come from God, along with my steadfast reading of the Bible and my daily prayers.

I acknowledged it had become a habit with me, morning and night. "Ma'd got me started on prayer and readin' the Holy Word when I was six or seven, back in Virginia. On a summer Sunday, she'd explained to me that the food you eat, you need for your physical well bein'; and not only that, without continual nourishin', your body would waste away and die. Likewise, Ma'd said, you need spiritual food, and God's word is spirit and life to your body. If a man doesn't continually feed his spirit, he's soon dead within. Ma told me I needed to read the Bible, meditate, and pray at least three times a day, like eatin', to maintain that spirit, and that I had to especially pray before goin' to sleep at night and when I got up. Ma was pretty certain about all that."

"Tell me," Joe asked, "why pray particularly before sleep?"

"Well . . . ," I told him, "Ma always said it was so I could be with Jesus in my dreams. It let me visit with Him without being hindered by outside worldly influences. . . . And I found it worked, for I'm then continually with Him, night 'n day.

"And that next Sunday, after Ma's talk, I'd received the Holy Ghost."

It was a deep winter in Colorado that year, and Wells Fargo was practically shut down, so I had a lot of leisure time, from most of December until the following March. In early April I was assigned to ride shotgun on an express wagon carrying $300,000 in gold. The gold was to be picked up at the Polar Star mine and hauled to Denver. James King was the driver for the shipment, and I was relieved to know he was at the reins of the team. Four Wells Fargo guards would ride the wagon with us, and we had a lot of firepower; but we were also sitting ducks riding out in the open and bunched up together.

King and I came up with a plan for traveling the areas of likely ambush. As before, I don't doubt every outlaw in that part of the country knew of the shipment, and we were at the mercy of their whims. At one point of possible ambush, the most likely, where several holdups had taken place and where a nest of large boulders crowded the road, a dozen outlaws could easily hide within a few feet of the inclining road. The other side of the way was a hundred feet of fluted cliff to a stream below.

Thirty-some yards before the boulders, all six of us stepped off to walk along the wagon, keeping it between us and the boulders. In other words, the wagon was our barricade. We passed the boulders without incident, but I caught the glimpse of reflecting light — surely from a rifle barrel — and we figured the outlaws in ambush decided it'd be suicide to attempt a robbery. We made the rest of the trip without a hitch, and I breathed a sigh of relief when we reached Denver.

Then on April 15th, I quit my job at Wells Fargo. Elliot wanted me to stay on, but I had places to go.

The sun rose red, and while climbing its ladder in the sky it turned gold amidst the bright blue. It was nearing May, and a rainbow of flowers had come up and blossomed almost overnight. Spring had come late to the Rockies, and there was still a lot of snow in the gullies, north slopes, and shady places.

Joe and I were packing our belongings and buying supplies for our trip to Silverton. The next day we'd be leaving for the town of Ora City. Gold had been discovered there in California Gulch back in 1860, and miners had been prospecting the area ever since. Neither of us had been there, and we were curious; we'd heard so much about the discovery we wanted to see the place. Besides, it wasn't that much out of our way to the south.

That evening I had supper at the hotel. My heart skipped a beat when Susannah appeared from the kitchen and walked over to my table. She had that special way of crossing a room that I'd remember for the rest of my life. In my eyes she was the most beautiful woman in the world. I didn't know for sure, but I think she'd come to care for me too. Several times that past winter I noticed her looking at me a bit longer than normal, like maybe she also had feelings for me; but if she did, she kept them to herself.

After ordering my meal I explained, "Joe and I'll be leavin' in the morning. When I've located Devon, I'll tell him you're here workin'. I'm sure he'll come a-runnin'."

Susannah thanked me, then added, "But, B.J., I've done some thinking and decided I'd like to ride along with you. I've quit my job and bought a pretty little sorrel mare for the trip."

I blurted out, "Ya can't, Susannah; it's too dangerous among hundreds of unscrupulous miners. And not only that, it's rough terrain we'll be travelin', and the ride without niceties at hand would be a hardship on ya."

But she was feisty, telling me, "Don't you think for a minute, B.J. Ross, that I can't rough it! I talked to Joe earlier, and he said it was all right with him."

What could I do? I knew the trip could be dangerous, and I also knew I didn't trust myself to be that close to the woman I loved . . . but I caved in to her pleas.

Fifteen

WE LEFT GEORGETOWN behind us in the darkness, and when the sun came up we were trailing our way through a long-grass meadow. An eagle screamed as he soared against a backdrop of snowy peaks, with his golden sunlit wings spread wide. Then he screamed again, looking down long and hard on our lonely little caravan, like he didn't appreciate our crossing beneath his country in the sky.

Joe led the way, followed by Susannah, and then I brought up the rear leading two supply-loaded pack horses. Earlier I'd asked Joe why in the world he'd told Susannah she could ride along, and he just smiled that curious grin he had at times and replied, "Probably the same reason you did. How are you going to tell her no?"

Around noon the next day we rode through Ora City. It was a desolate place near the Continental Divide, and resembled a wasteland with piles of debris next to prospect holes everywhere. We wound our way through the maze of canvas huts, and those miners not working their claims stopped to watch us pass, with a greeting and "Godspeed."

The following year, approximately two miles northwest of Ora City, would be a rich silver discovery, and the city of Leadville would spring to life.

At the time we were traveling, it was cold and freezing at around ten thousand feet; we decided to head for lower elevations. The foothills of the Rockies would make for easier going. Ora City was near the headwaters of the South Platte River, so we'd follow the Platte east by southeast until it turned north, and then head south.

The afternoon turned cloudy, and the wind switched to the north. We plodded on into a light drizzle of cold rain that made for a miserable ride. We stopped early and found a small cabin beneath a large ponderosa pine — a shelter that had been abandoned for several years by the looks of it. The cabin was leaking water, but I covered the roof with a canvas. Joe started a blazing fire in an old stone fireplace, then disappeared into the forest of pine and aspen with his rifle. It wasn't long until a shot rang out racketing sharply along a nearby escarpment. Some ten minutes later Joe carried a small doe into camp. After I'd cared for and staked out our horses, we had a quick and hearty meal of venison.

Inside the shelter felt like heaven on earth as we listened to the angry howling wind outside, tearing at the canvas. On the earthen floor, over cut willow, we laid our groundsheets and turned in beneath blankets for the night.

By morning the winds had calmed, but a bitter cold sparkled breathless in the air. Our tethered horses from the wet night before had churned up the ground and were standing in a frozen wallow of rough ridges, deep with hoofprints. Our shelter had ice hanging from the eaves, some pieces over a foot long. When Joe and I went outside to care for the livestock, I pointed to the icicles. He looked at them for a moment and softly spoke:

When icicles hang by the wall,
And Dick the shepherd blows his nail,
And Tom bears logs into the hall,
And milk comes frozen home in pail,
When blood is nipped, and ways be foul,
Then nightly sings the staring owl,
To-who;
To-wit, to-who, a merry note,
While greasy Joan doth keel the pot.

I looked at Joe as if to ask "Who's work was that?" and with a smile he said, "Shakespeare."

I shook my head. "I should've known." Then before I could say anything else, Susannah leaned out the cabin doorway and invitingly called, "Breakfast's ready!"

Joe and I looked at each other and broke into laughter. Susannah seemed a bit perturbed until Joe recited the rhyme again; then she also laughed, and playfully said, "I don't know what I'm going to do with you two, but it's made my day; now get in here to breakfast."

After a meal of deer steak and scalding coffee, we packed up our supplies, and with the extra deer meat, our pack animals were heavily loaded.

We mounted our horses and moved out from our campsite to a narrow trail, riding single file. We rode deep in our coats beneath a heavy sky of overcast. Within the hour, our visibility had dropped to almost nothing. Then from out of the gray and empty sky a large snowflake struck my face and quickly melted. Behind the big fluffy flake came thousands of others that soon had covered the dark gravely earth of our trail. In an hour we were encountering twelve-inch depths of new snow. At the rate it was coming down, by nightfall we'd be stranded somewhere.

We'd about decided to leave the trail to find cover when the snowfall stopped. Desperate for lower elevations, we urged our horses down grade. It wasn't long until we saw a break in the cloud cover, and we rode out of the storm. By the time we'd made camp that evening, the eastern sky was clear and we were out of the snow.

The next day we were riding in sunshine. With the change in the weather and temperature, we now traveled a peaceful land that welcomed our caravan along its fine-gravel slopes with the glowing warmth of hospitality.

We plodded slowly through a beautiful passage of magnificent views — a forested land of pine, fir, juniper, cactus, and aspen; beige gravely trails, sheer cliffs, escarpments, and fluted canyons; long-grass meadows and wildflowers; clear cold streams, white-water rapids, and waterfalls; soaring eagles, owls, hawks, buzzards, Jays, hummingbirds, and songbirds; and chipmunks, squirrels, rabbits, deer, bear, and wolves.

That night we camped along the South Platte. While Susannah was cooking supper, I made our beds close to the campfire, again laying a groundsheet over cut willow that I'd selected along the river.

The next morning we left the river and took a trail southeast that would take us north of Pikes Peak. Two days later, we stopped at Soda Springs, which would one day be known as Manitou Springs, and a couple miles west of Colorado City.

I'd tried to keep my distance from Susannah, but at Soda Springs Joe said he wanted to see an old friend in Colorado City and wouldn't return until the next day. Twilight came early into the foothills and shadows of Pikes Peak. The canyons were first to disappear into the purple darkness that slowly spread to grassy meadows. Susannah and I had finished supper and were sitting at the campfire, listening to the Fountain River singing songs of happiness and watching a full silver moon come up in the east. It always seemed that the chorus of rushing water sang louder at night, and the rippling music was flowing beautiful when we decided to take a look at the stream.

It happened natural, my taking Susannah's hand as we walked the moonlit pathway to the river. There's nothing prettier than a stream of water beneath a bright moon, as it was that night. At the river we sat on a boulder, with our feet at the water's edge. When the moon rose above a patch of aspen, the reflecting moonlight crossed the water with a silver pathway that traveled back into the heavens.

Susannah moved over and laid her head on my shoulder. It must have been the moment, for before I knew what was happening I was holding her in my arms. I wanted desperately to kiss the lassie I loved . . . but I didn't, and we sat there together for a few minutes. I knew she belonged to someone else.

Susannah spoke softly. "I think we better go back to camp."

I stood and took her hand to help her up from where we were sitting. We remained for a moment hand in hand, peering at the water . . . but I saw no water. We never spoke, then walked the pathway back.

I felt terrible, and had a hard time sleeping, as did Susannah, for I could hear her rolling and tossing all night. The next morning I got up before daylight. Susannah lay asleep, with her back to the campfire that had burned out, except for a long red winking ember buried in the ashes, fingering a light trail of smoke skyward. I added a few pieces of wood and immediately leaping tongues of fire flashed into sticks of golden flames.

Susannah was soon up and fixing our morning meal. She mentioned nothing about our walk to the river, nor did I. I didn't know what to say, and figured I'd let her take the lead if she had something to note about the night before. Then, as we were eating, a somber Susannah apologized.

"B.J., I'm sorry about last night; and thank you."

"Thanks for what?" I asked. "Anyway, I'm the one who should be askin' your forgiveness."

"No, B.J., you must have sensed my feelings, and I want to thank you for being thoughtful. I feel despondent and ashamed, for when I awoke this morning I caught myself wishing I wasn't betrothed; and it's not fair to Devon."

"Susannah you mustn't feel that way; I think Devon is the luckiest man in the world."

"I don't know; but thank you, B.J., for being a gentleman."

We ceased the conversation at that and went about our chores. I think Susannah's airing the situation was her salvation. An hour later I could hear her singing an old Southern tune, coming from the river where she'd gone to wash some clothes. I'd kept to myself how much I really cared for her. What good would it do? She was a lady that honored her commitments, and it would only have complicated things and made her feel bad. Now she was her old self again.

Around eight o'clock, Joe returned. We packed up, and were on the trail by nine. Later that morning we left the Fountain River and took a trail southwest. Early the next morning we hit the Arkansas River east of Cañon City. We rode careful, but saw few people as we worked our way west traveling through Cañon City, Salida, and Gunnison. At times I'd catch Joe looking at Susannah and me. I think he knew something had passed between us, but he never said a word.

Six days after leaving Colorado City we rode into Gunnison. It was the last of May when we reached Silverton by way of the mining towns of Ouray, Guston, and Red Mountain. Silverton was a main street of stores and saloons. We didn't know how long we'd be in high country, so we stocked up on supplies.

From Silverton we took a mountain trail northeast. Joe led the way, since he knew the area and was familiar with the location of Hamilton's claim. A million thoughts raced through my mind as we moved through the wilderness. None of us knew what we'd find when we reached the site. Hamilton might be dead for all we knew. Many had died in the West, and family and friends had never heard from them again. In the wilds, a man could break a leg or a horse fall on him, or he could die from some disease, and no one would ever know. Besides that were the elements to contend with — snow, sleet, wind, rain, tornadoes on the plains, and famine, drought, heat, and bitter cold. And if you got through those things, you might be surprised by outlaws or Indians. The frontier was just not a safe place, and it took a brave man and woman to settle in the West.

We were passing through a rugged country of cliff-fringed canyons and had slow going all that day. The next day we were riding a narrow trail when Joe, riding point, stopped; he held up his hand and whispered. "The claim's up ahead. I think maybe we'd better play it safe and injun up on the camp."

Susannah stayed put while Joe and I disappeared into the woods. From a high ridge behind the campsite we counted four men, but from the description I'd had of Hamilton, he didn't seem to be one of 'em. Joe suggested we open up on 'em, as surprise would be on our side.

"Wait a minute!" I told him. "What if one of 'em *is* Hamilton, and we kill him? I couldn't live with it on my conscience."

Joe peered at me for a moment, then nodded his head as though he understood. "You're right. Go back and get Susannah; bring her here. She'll know if he's there or not."

An hour later Susannah looked down on the camp and studied the men as they moved about working the claim. "No!" she whispered. "Devon's not one of those men."

I, too, studied the four men closely, then I realized, "I know one of 'em. That's Slater, the murderin' outlaw I've been hankerin' to catch up with!"

I stepped out of the trees and shouted. "*Slater!* This is Ross! . . . I'm comin' in shootin'!"

The outlaws grabbed their guns, and about then Joe and I started firing. We killed two, but Slater and another hombre got away. They jumped on their horses, crossed the river, and rode into a maze of trees. I'd put a bullet into Slater, and he rode off shouldered over.

Joe and I chased 'em for a spell, but we could see we'd not catch up with 'em without traveling many more miles. Concerned about Susannah's safety, we gave up and returned to the camp.

The sky was in its blaze of afternoon when we dismounted and cared for our horses. Susannah had already started rummaging around the outlaws' camp, but she found nothing that she felt was Devon's, at least nothing she could recognize. I told her not finding anything didn't mean much, especially since he'd been gone so long from Atlanta that whatever he'd brought from Georgia he'd have worn out by then.

That evening we buried the two claim jumpers, and I read over 'em. Two days later we were still at Devon's campsite. We'd found a little gold on the two dead men and in the tents — maybe a pound of metal altogether. Joe figured Slater'd be back once he healed up from his wound, and I agreed. We'd need to be leaving there in a few days, and that was what we were talking about as we sat around the fire that night.

Devon was nowhere to be found in the area, and we needed to get Susannah back to Silverton. That was where she wanted to go, thinking she could find someone who knew Devon's whereabouts.

Joe and I were sitting before the fire in rambling conversation, and Susannah had seemed unusually quiet all the while. When I looked across the flames, she was staring at me. A tear slowly worked its way down her cheek, and I thought I'd heard a muffled sob as she got up to go to her tent. Joe said nothing, and acted as though he saw nothing.

I wanted desperately to go to Susannah and hold her in my arms, but I didn't. I thought about our night at Soda Springs. When I had taken her in my arms there it'd given my heart a feeling I'd never experienced before; it was a happening in my life I'd not forget — a half hour of joy that I'd remember forever. I wondered if those were the same feelings Romeo and Juliet had felt in the garden . . . then my thoughts were interrupted with a start.

"Hello, the camp!" shouted a voice out of the darkness across the stream. Joe and I shot to our feet and faded out of sight away from the fire. Susannah rushed out of the tent.

"It's Devon! . . . *Devon! . . . It's Susannah!* Come on in!" A rough-looking bearded man came splashing across the stream with his rifle held high. Then Susannah and Devon were in each others' arms.

After several hours, Devon and Susannah had pieced together the cause of their losing track of each other. Circumstance had created a vacuum. During Devon's months of prospecting, he was unable to mail letters. Susannah, not hearing from him, grew concerned and she'd decided to go to Colorado to find him. At about the time Susannah was heading there, he was writing to her from Ouray. But when all his letters had been returned, he was at a loss as to what he should do. He was broke at that time, and still looking for his first good strike, barely making enough to keep searching. A year later, he'd about lost hope, and then he made his find north of Silverton. His plans were to lay up enough gold to buy a ranch somewhere and then return to Atlanta to find Susannah.

In the meantime, another miner, Clyde Taylor, had moved in next to Devon. Devon's claim had almost played out, so when Taylor began working the claim, Devon didn't object. He then searched afar, and several miles upstream, on a side branch, he found a richer claim. He cached most of the gold at the new site, but Taylor happened to see some of it and asked to partner with him. Devon refused, as he didn't trust the man, and made certain to leave for his diggings early each morning before daylight. Though Clyde tried to follow a time or two, Devon always was able to lead him off in the wrong direction.

Devon's nuggets were locked in the seams of a rock ledge at the bottom of a three-foot gravel bed. Growing more and more suspicious of Taylor, Devon began to cache all the gold he found near the site before returning to camp.

When Slater and the claim jumpers showed up one evening, Clyde Taylor welcomed them, foolishly showing them the four pounds of gold he'd panned at the claim. Devon knew they were both in for trouble.

The outlaws quickly confiscated Clyde's gold, and immediately rummaged through Devon's tent, where they found maybe a half pound. Clyde had told Slater he knew that Devon had more gold stashed, and Devon heard him whisper to the outlaw, "I've seen some of it; it's a lot! A lot more than I've found!"

It was then that Slater had pulled his gun and shot Clyde, killing him, Devon said.

By that time night was coming on, which probably had saved Devon from the same fate as Clyde. They tortured Devon for a time, to find out where his gold was hidden, without success. Devon said he lay in a heap, for the outlaws' beatings had left him in near unbearable pain, with broken ribs, and cuts and bruises.

Meanwhile, hunger had overcome the outlaws, and they decided to eat before they continued working on Devon. Slater growled to him, "Think about it. What's comin' to ya will be worse, so ya'd better tell us where you've hidden that gold. . . . Tell us and we'll let ya ride out of here with your life."

Devon knew better. His only way to live another day was to escape. The outlaws tied him hand and foot, but luckily they left him lying back away from the campfire while they rustled through the tents for food. Finding what they wanted, they gorged themselves, then uncovered three bottles of whiskey stashed away in Clyde's tent.

Old Clyde, it seems, turned out to be Devon's lifesaver, for it wasn't long after swilling down the liquor that the thieves fell asleep around the warm fire — except one, who'd drank little.

It was after midnight before Devon was able to free himself and slink quietly into the darkness. Soon he heard a shout at the discovery of his escape, but he stealthily made his way to his other workings where he had stashed an extra rifle and ammunition. He hid out from one place to another, and the outlaws searched but never found him. Almost every day he'd move to another location.

After a week of searching, the thieves gave up and returned to the campsite. It was a month before Devon felt healed enough to injun back to his claim. He didn't care about the campsite itself; what he wanted was the rest of the gold he had cached nearby.

The dark of night had settled in when he came up to the camp, and after watching for several hours he realized the claim jumpers were gone. He saw a woman enter the tent, and figured anyone who'd have a woman along would be friendly. That was when he'd shouted, "*Hello . . . !*"

A week later, we were in Silverton, checked in at the hotel. Knowing well how gold draws outlaws, we stashed ours in the hotel where one of us stayed on guard at all times. We would need to take the gold to Animas City for deposit.

A new church had been built on the high ground overlooking Silverton, and we found the preacher on the dust-blown street on the search for sinners. Something told me he could stop about anyone that came along!

The preacher was overjoyed to have a wedding, and that Friday evening at eight o'clock Susannah and Devon were married — she in a white dress and he, clean-shaven, in a black suit. They made a handsome couple. I was best man and gave the bride away.

Two days later we were in Animas City, where Devon and Susannah deposited sixty-three pounds of gold at Wells Fargo. Those days, $16,000 was a goodly amount of money, and surely sufficient for the two to start life together.

We watched as the overland stage came rushing into town to a quick stop at the stage office, carrying along a cloud of dust that settled over man and horse. Devon and Susannah had their tickets. They planned to stay a week in Denver before heading east. Devon had wanted to buy a ranch, and so I told him about my homestead on Upper McDowell Creek, in Kansas. He acknowledged that they just might decide to settle in that part of the country.

"It sounds like good ranching territory," he added, "so we'll look it over when we travel through; but first Susannah wants to see Atlanta again before we settle down."

Susannah gave me a hug and whispered, "I'll always love you, B.J." When she quickly mounted the steps into the stage, I thought I saw a little sadness behind her smile.

Devon and I shook hands. "Thanks," he said. "I owe you."

I'd known Devon only a few weeks, but I knew in my heart that Susannah was getting a good man. I felt no remorse for what could have been, as I wished the pair well.

The driver shouted, snapped the reins, and the six mustangs took off in a rush down the dirt street. The coach tooled a fast turn to the east on the trail leading to Alamosa. By the time the dust of Animas City had settled and the thunder of hooves had faded, it was as if the stage, Susannah, and Devon had never been there.

Sixteen

WE'D LEFT ANIMAS on a beautiful mountain-country day, and the sun on my back felt warm as Joe interrupted my thoughts.

"It looks like a good day for traveling; how about getting lost in high country, up where the eagles fly?"

"I'm ready," I eagerly replied. "Let's go!" I paused a moment and wistfully looked around at the dusty street, then mounted my gelding. At the edge of town a large black dog came out of cover to bark at our heels. He followed us for a short distance, as if he wanted to go along, and then retreated to his hovel.

Our camp lay among tall pine, and below the needled branches the area was scattered with delicate cones nestled about in lonely patches of grass and on worn gravel trails traversed by the many chipmunks in the area. Across the stream to the west stood battalions of aspen, waiting for some kind soul to travel their vistas of shimmering leaves.

June nights can get cold at nearly ten thousand feet, and the warmth beneath my blanket made for good sleeping. I hated to get out from under it, knowing that bathing in the cold mountain stream would be like washing in ice. I lay watching the stars turn out their lights one by one while Joe was busy at the campfire. He was cooking bacon, and the aroma drifting my way turned out to be all the incentive I needed to hop up.

For several weeks Joe acquainted me with what he knew of the area, a landscape filled with escarpments, high pinnacles, canyons, and beautiful meadows. When we weren't panning for gold together, at times I'd venture out to spend time alone with Nature, to get a sense of the land. Words could not describe the bond deep within that I soon had for that beautiful country.

On one of my wanderings I rode down vistas of forest, on narrow game trails, swerving in and around trees like in a twisty creek bottom. I stopped to let Prince drink in a fast-flowing bubbling stream coming down out of the mountains. He dipped his muzzle into a pool of cold water, disturbing the mirrored reflected shadows of landscape and morning sky. I'd traveled to higher elevations that day and was returning to camp when I dropped down into a trail of switchbacks. Slowly plodding the narrow way, I looked over at a white fall of water plunging into a gorge that must have dropped two hundred feet. I marveled at the scene and figured the water surely came from the stream I'd stopped at earlier. Along the escarpment face, and at least a hundred feet above ground, a large pine tree graced the sky. How that pine gained foothold on the solid rock face was hard to understand; I could see one main root, almost as big as the bole of the tree, that traveled horizontal at least thirty feet, then turned into a crack of the rock. Down near the bottom of the waterfall, the chasm was choked with manzanita evergreen. I doubt a rabbit could have found his way through the maze, but thankfully the trail veered off away from the green entanglement.

Sometime later, in August, I took another day off from panning gold. In the shadows of morning I mounted my gelding and reined him northwest. I hadn't been that direction, and was curious to see the area. Around noon, and some ten miles later, riding through aisles of forest and switchback trails, I came to a stream rushing in cascades down the mountain. An old trail followed along the stream. I could tell it wasn't a game trail, but a manmade path from years past. The trail encroached with foliage, and where not overgrown, it was some six feet wide.

Up the graveled way, I could see a plateau that covered an area of at least a hundred grass-covered acres. A dark object caught my attention, and I almost passed it by — an old wooden beam, just east of the trail. Riding closer, I found the remains of a ghost town, aged, forlorn, and abandoned. The surrounding silence would have been almost deafening if not for a happy songbird, unseen in the brush, and my gelding cropping grass. Occasionally I could hear the nearby buzzing of a honeybee running his busy fingers into the heart of an Indian Paintbrush blossom.

As my eyes scanned the deserted landscape, I found a few bones — traces of human life, now gone. I was shaken by the ancient catastrophe that had occurred there. At that moment there came a slight breeze that rustled a moan through the grass, like the far-away cry of the dead. A forlorn feeling came over me when I realized that the indifferent mountain had no remorse or concern for the long dead lying on its shoulder, or for what they'd built, now in permanent decay.

It appeared that a garrison of men had been wiped out, probably by Indians, centuries earlier, for as I walked over the area during those several hours, I found an old piece of Spanish breastplate and a rusted *arrastra* used for breaking up rock to separate gold. I realized then that the dead were the Spanish who had mined the area. A half mile west of the ghost town, along the base of a gorge through which the stream passed, their mine was visible.

I grieved for those who had died along the mountain, with no family close by to care for their bodies; and then I thought it was probably as good as any place to meet one's God. It had been a bustling place of vitality years ago, on the ever-turning wheel of time. But they now rested in silence.

For three months I'd been hunting for the mother lode along the Animas River, but Joe seemed unconcerned as to the source of any gold we'd found. It was into September and the mountain was turning color. The far slopes were blanketed with seams of gold aspen leaves spilling into dark canyons of flowing water, sparkling like nuggets and waiting for some lucky prospector.

We'd dug out around three pounds of nuggets, worth some $720, from cracks in the bedrock beneath the gravel bars. It was a nice amount of quality, jewelry-type gold for three months of work. But the pieces had noticeable sharp edges, and less than a half mile upstream the gold ran out. What few nuggets we did find up there apparently had traveled far enough that they were smooth, though we noticed that the gravel bars on the west side of the stream had contained the sharp nuggets. Back away from the stream, the canyon wall was all fluted rock. My eyes scanned along its rugged face for quartz, and found nothing.

On a day when we were relaxing after our morning meal, drinking Joe's scalding coffee, he concluded that within no more than a month we'd better pull stakes.

"Better play it safe and get into low country. October can turn cold, and we could get caught in a snowstorm up here, and maybe not get out 'til spring."

That same morning, upstream from camp several miles, the tall rustling aspens were calling to me from across the way. I mounted Prince, splashed across the water, and rode into the maze of golden leaves. I didn't go far in the dry wash, for it was a box canyon. The sun was high above the trees when I dismounted and fixed a lunch. As I settled down to eat, Prince trailed his reins over to a small meadow and dropped his muzzle into the grass.

I sat peering at the canyon; something about it seemed strange. It was what I'd heard called ancient, incoherent, unstratified rock, but everywhere else in the area were precise later formations. And when I studied the terrain, it looked as though I was in an ancient streambed. The old dry wash appeared to have carried a lot of water at one time. It was clear that some time in the past there'd been a catastrophic upheaval within the mountain and it had caused a massive avalanche, filling the gorge. Where I sat must have been the river, now relocated to its present channel. I realized that such being the case, the mother lode we'd been searching for was probably buried beneath tons of rock behind the box canyon.

From the canyon's dead end it was less than a mile to the Animas River. The canyon's dry-wash entrance was covered with aspen, and I didn't have to look to know there would be gold beneath the old streambed.

That evening, after a hearty supper, I looked across the campfire to Joe and announced, "I found the mother lode, but we can't get to her; she's buried in the mountain."

Joe shook his head and smiled. "Ah, you found the old streambed and the canyon. I knew you would; you're a smart lad."

"You mean you knew all the time where it was?"

"Sure. But I wanted you to find it. Now it's yours."

I couldn't help but smile. "You mean 'ours,' you old rascal. I ought to dump ya in the creek."

I don't think Joe really cared about the gold, otherwise he'd have been in there digging it up. I realized at the time I'd grown to love that old man . . . a loyal man of integrity and most surely unselfish.

A month later we pulled stakes, with nearly a hundred pounds of nuggets on our pack horses. We could have stayed and taken more, but it didn't seem right. Someone else might come along and figure out what'd happened those thousands of years ago and receive their reward too.

It was late afternoon when we rode into Silverton. The sun was barely above the peaks, causing long purple shadows to cover most of the dust-blown streets. The hotel looked inviting, but we never stopped. With the gold we were carrying we thought we better keep away from those who liked to steal for a living. We'd thought that hopefully, by riding on for five or ten miles, we could be back in Animas City by the next afternoon.

As we passed the saloon, a local tough with a cigarette hanging from his lips was standing out front, watching us ride by with more than casual interest. He was still watching when we'd reached a block farther down the street, but a moment later, when I looked back, he was gone. I wondered why he had such an interest in us, with all the other miners crowding about the streets. A mile out of town I turned around, to check our backtrail, but no one had followed, and I felt easier; yet we'd have to ride wary with all the gold we carried.

On the trail, Joe and I were contemplating what he called the "elusive treasure." Joe concluded, "Searching for nuggets is kind of like hunting morel mushrooms; you never can find them all!"

An eagle made a wide swing high overhead in the sky. Looking down, he could see us riding horseback, leading our two pack horses. We hadn't thought about it at first, but the eagle had a better view than we did of movements below, for he continued to watch with interest something besides our little caravan. I peered at him as he hesitated, wings wide, unmoving in the sky, and screeching indignation off into the distance, back up the trail. Whatever it was had alerted the bird of prey, and though it probably was just an eagle's complaint, instinct told me he saw an intruder in his domain. Had I wings to soar, I'd have known it was Slater and his gang.

Slater spoke to the hombre riding behind. "It's Ross alright; I'd know his horse's prints anywhere. They must be carryin' a lot of gold; their pack horses are trackin' deep. I'd say they're about a mile ahead."

Slater had planned to hit us at midnight, when we were camped and asleep. He warned his men, "Leave that bastard Ross to me. I've a score to settle with 'im. I've put up with a lot of misery from that homesteader, and I've got a bullet in my left shoulder to remind me. To now, he's had all the luck — but it just ran out. He's gonna pay for the misery he's caused."

Slater reminded his men of the other gunfighters I'd faced, like Kennedy in Abilene. "But Ross's never faced a *real* gunfighter, like me," he told them. "I heard say that Kennedy outdrew the kid, but Ross had him flustered and he missed his target. Well," Slater boasted, "I'm faster than Kennedy, and shoot a hell of a lot straighter!"

Joe was building a campfire when I went to look at the water rushing down out of the mountain. I could see a nice fishing hole upstream, below a cataract of falls. Later, when it was turning dark, and distance disappearing, I cut me a long willow, tied on a light cord, and took out a small hook from the tin box in my pocket. After turning over several rocks, I caught five crickets and put 'em in a tobacco can for fish bait. In less than thirty minutes I had a half-dozen rainbow trout. We had a fresh-caught meal that night.

After supper, we were sitting talking when I told Joe of the gold on Fourmile Creek, south of Council Grove. When I'd finished he asked, "You haven't tried to find it?"

"No," I replied. "After Reggie was killed I didn't have the interest in lookin' for it."

Nothing more was said, and in the silence of the darkness I thought of the eagle, wondering again if he was trying to tell us something. For some reason, it all made me uneasy. I told Joe I was going for a walk and would be back in an hour. I'd remembered some high ground where I could see for miles, not more than ten minutes from our camp.

At the pinnacle I scanned our backtrail, but saw nothing. Then just as I was about to leave, I caught the smell of smoke. Looking upwind, I searched the black night and finally spotted what I knew was a campfire. I'd had the suspicion earlier, and now I was sure that we were being followed. Slater and his gang were on our tail.

I hurried back to camp. Joe was already asleep, and alongside his hand lay his King James Bible and six-gun.

"*Wake up!*" I insisted. "We got company. If my hunch is right they'll hit us when they think we're sleepin'."

As Joe jumped up, I told him what I'd seen. After a short debate, we decided he would head on to Animas City with the gold and I'd stay behind and hold them off his trail. He didn't want to go, but I finally convinced him it'd be better for me to handle the outlaws. I could injun around better, being younger and with a more agile and faster horse. He still didn't want to leave until I promised him I'd be careful, and work my way south. If I hadn't caught up with him by the time he'd made Animas City, he would go ahead and make our deposit.

In minutes, Joe was leaving camp. I'd let the fire burn down and covered over some cut branches to look like two people asleep. I'd saddled Prince and had him ready to move in a moment's notice. A hundred yards southwest, I found a high spot covered with small trees and brush, and from the copse was a trail, another few hundred yards south, leading to the road to Animas City. I waited in the cover.

An hour later, the moon rose up over the snowy peaks of the mountains to the east and lit a glow of blue light across a mixed forest of pine and aspen. At least another hour passed without a sign of the outlaws. I hoped that maybe I was wrong . . . maybe the campfire I saw was nothing more than travelers passing through.

It was after midnight when I heard the movement of horses and Prince began to expand his belly. I grabbed his nostrils to keep him from whinnying. Then I heard a low hissing whisper.

"*There's their camp!*"

Softly they made their way through the underbrush to our campsite. They stood quietly for a moment, then opened fire on what they thought were two figures beneath the blankets that I'd left lying by the fire. When they realized they'd been duped, I heard their cursing. What they didn't know was I was watching them. Sighting down my rifle, I honed in on the silhouettes of four outlaws, and after they'd shot into the blankets, I opened fire. I saw two of 'em take bullets. The two others slipped away into the cover of darkness.

I grabbed Prince's reins and moved as quietly as I could toward the trail to Animas City. I dared not get cut off from heading south, and decided to travel two or three miles, then pick some easy ground to defend and pin down the remaining hombres for three or four hours before moving on to catch up with Joe. But when I stepped onto the main trail, from the far-off darkness along the east shoulder came a gleeful shout.

"*Ya-hah!*"

A shadowy figure opened fire, and before I could respond I had taken two slugs from Slater's six-gun winking eyes of ruby flame. I fell into the brush, hanging onto Prince's reins. Out of sight, I crawled onto my horse and took off back up the trail. I was slumped over the saddle horn, onto which I'd managed to lash my hands.

I softly whispered to Prince, "You're on your own, boy; let's find someplace we can hole up."

Seventeen

I WAS IN a bad way. I couldn't go on to Animas City, nor back to Silverton, for Slater had the trail blocked. I should have known he would cover the path below the camp. There'd been five outlaws instead of four, and now I had not two, but three, hunting for my hide.

Prince took off northwest. I couldn't see a path, so the gelding must have been making one of his own. I figured I'd passed out now and then during the night as we trailed higher, for there were times I just couldn't recall. I could hear them behind me ever so often, and Prince was doing his best to keep ahead of 'em. I'd been hit in my left lower shoulder and left thigh, and I knew I needed to find someplace where I could dress the wounds and rest. I'd lost a lot of blood, and didn't know how long I could keep on riding. By daylight I was in throbbing pain and felt myself getting weaker. I was in no shape to face three vicious outlaws.

I untied my hands from the saddle horn and took a game trail along the top of an escarpment. I was in the open and not a mile ahead when the three outlaws burst out of the brush onto the trail to the south.

They had me. I had nowhere to go, and I couldn't handle a fast ride.

The cliff beside me must have been five hundred feet above the canyon floor. I could see a sliver of a stream below, gleaming diamonds from the surface of a large pool at the bottom of a waterfall. Had I felt better, it would have been a beautiful sight, but in my state I was in no condition to enjoy it. That was when I wished my horse had wings. If I could get down to the bottom of the canyon I'd be safe — at least for a while — until they could get down there, and that could take 'em up to a day or more. But at that moment I had no chance.

It was about then I pleaded with God. "*If there's a way to escape the infidel, Lord, show me now.*"

I know it's hard to believe, but like a miracle, a way opened up before me. Maybe a hundred feet ahead, the escarpment had a narrow passage to the bottom — an almost straight up-and-down steep talus slope of slide rock and shale. It was so steep I began to sweat when I realized I'd have to go down the slide to escape. But I nudged Prince to the precipice. He stopped at the edge, then when I urged him on again, he stepped off as if into empty space. That horse trusted me, and down he went. His hooves had hardly touched the slope before he started sliding. He settled back on his haunches, making a wave in the talus of shale he carried along with him as he slid by a boulder not over ten feet away. After what seemed an eternity, the steep slope finally gentled out to where Prince could stop his slide. He then walked slowly on down to the base of the canyon.

The gelding came through the drop-off to the bottom without a serious injury. It was a miracle that both horse and I hadn't been killed, and I praised God. Prince shook his head as if to say he might not want to try such a route every day.

I looked up to the top of the escarpment and saw the outlaws at the edge, with rifles in their hands. I rushed Prince to a safe place, then dodged behind a large boulder just as a bullet whizzed by my head. I could see 'em at the top of the slope talking amongst themselves, but I wasn't worried about them coming down into the canyon the way I had. Yet I was hoping they would, for anyone going off that cliff, without God's help, was a fool. After ten minutes or so the outlaws mounted their horses and backtracked off out of sight.

I untied Prince and followed him to the stream, where he dropped his nose into the cold water. I drank long as well, then crawled onto the gelding and reined him downstream, wading in the water, trying to leave as little trail as possible. I knew I had to find a place to hole up and treat my wounds, for I was weak and felt like I had a fever. Two hours later, I stopped. I'd spotted a shallow cave, hidden by brush, and it provided protection from the north. I was close to the timberline, and could see the recent bluish-white snow surrounding that lay several inches deep in the shaded areas. Where the sun could get to it, the snow had melted, easing a path. I needed to prepare for a cold night, so selected some willow for a bed, stitching others together for a cover.

I'd saved some of the willow bark to make a broth, and pulled out a tin cup from my saddlebags to boil it in. I built a small fire, then slowly drank the broth. Joe had told me it was good for fever

I boiled more water and washed my crusted wounds, then found some glacier lily nearby and made a poultice with the crushed leaves. I wrapped the wounds with a clean cloth from my saddlebags. I was worn out, and when I lay down, I went right off to sleep.

It must have been close to daylight when I awoke, shivering with cold. I forced myself to get up and cut more willow for added cover, then went back to sleep. The sun was high when I woke again.

I heated more willow broth, and was hungry — an encouraging sign, I thought, that I was healing. I slowly, painfully rigged a willow pole and was able to catch a few trout. Along the valley floor, as I scanned the area, I could see some watercress, and walked over to pick a hatful of leaves, for I knew watercress was used to treat wounds and bleeding. I crushed the leaves, adding some water, and after washing my wounds again, I put on the new poultice wrapped with a fresh bandage.

I slept off and on throughout most of that day. Earlier, in the morning, I'd seen some stonecrop stems sticking through the snow, maybe a hundred yards upstream, along the talus slope of the canyon. Joe had told me you could find the plant in the wintertime above the timberline; the whole plant was edible, roots and all. When uncovered of snow, the leaves would be as green as if it were a summer growth. Many a man had survived a winter caught in high country by eating stonecrop. That night I ate a hearty meal of stonecrop and trout for supper, and was feeling better by the time I went to bed.

Although I wasn't up to full strength, I decided to leave my shelter in the morning, knowing that if Slater was still looking for me, he and his thugs would surely be about to close in. I'd need to be wary and try to find a trail around 'em to where I could continue south and make my way to Animas City.

The sun was edging upward in a blue sky toward ten o'clock when my sore body slowly crawled onto my gelding, reined him around, and pointed him south. The canyon floor was narrow and dangerous, with fluted escarpment walls that shot up several hundred feet; and through the chasm ran rushing water with intermittent falls. At times, the rock passage would widen, but I found no way I could ride out of the gorge.

I knew that where I traveled would be no place to be in a rainstorm, for I could see scatterings of driftwood as high as fifty feet, left there by flash floods. But not only the elements concerned me. If Slater and his henchmen were to catch up with me, I'd be cornered in a narrow passage, with no way out. I was thinking of those things when a bright flash caught the corner of my eye. I knew what it was . . . sunlight reflecting off a rifle barrel.

Shortly, about a mile downstream, hunting their way north, I saw two gunmen. I quickly moved into the cover of some dense willows, where I'd be hard to see. From my hiding place I saw Slater edging his way south. I was cornered, and it looked like another running fight. It'd been only two and a half days since I'd been shot, and I still was in no shape to run again, anywhere. I knew the outlaws couldn't help but find my gelding's tracks soon, and then it'd be only a matter of time before they latched onto me.

I shouldered low on Prince to hide myself better, knowing it might take them a while to find my tracks on the rock ledge I rode across. I dodged in and around brush, upthrust rock, and boulders, making my way to a forest of aspen below the escarpment. I rode quiet, well hidden. Then suddenly before me appeared an eroded area. It had been well concealed from my searching eyes, a narrow game trail that angled up the slope, along the escarpment, to the west — a way out of the canyon. I rode higher and higher through the brush, scattered pine, and aspen covering the trail. The narrow way then leveled off, but it had me concerned, for I was still a good hundred feet below the escarpment rim. I silently prayed for God to either direct me out of the canyon to safety, or have me stop, and I would hole up behind the brush and shoot it out with the renegades.

As I paused on the unfamiliar trail, I could see 'em below. The three had come together, and were talking and searching about for my tracks. They were slowly working their way toward the path I was on. It wouldn't take long, and they'd be hot on my trail.

I was wanting to stop and just face 'em, but it seemed as if God was prodding me ahead. The trail took me to an escarpment ledge, a hundred feet to the south, without any cover. Not only was there no cover, but the traveled way soon narrowed onto a mere sliver of rock ledge. There was nothing but space below it, a two hundred-foot drop to the valley floor, where the rushing rapids of water roared. The ledge looked like it was five to six feet wide for a stretch of maybe two hundred feet. That was as far as I could see, for the fluted wall then turned west and out of view. It made the eight-foot ledge Joe and I had taken above Georgetown look like a highway. I rode to the ledge and hesitated.

"There he is!" echoed a shout from below. Following fast behind came a bullet that hit the rock face of the escarpment some ten feet away.

I could see animal tracks leading to and from the ledge and figured that if animals used it, surely it went somewhere. If I could find a place for protection around the bend to the west, and if the outlaws followed, I could pick 'em off one at a time — that is if I hadn't already passed out from exhaustion. By then I was thinking I surely had a lot of "*ifs*" to consider.

I dismounted and led Prince onto the ledge. The gelding rolled his eyes and snorted. He didn't like it much, but he followed. He was stepping softly and once again putting all his trust in me. I was scared, but I also wanted to live, and all I could think of was getting away from the danger behind me. Another bullet spattered on the rock face not over three feet away. The outlaws were getting closer and moving fast up the slope.

I spoke to Prince as I cautiously walked on. "It's okay boy, we'll make it. . . . And after we get through this, we're headin' for Kansas."

I don't know if he understood or not, but I heard the metal of his bridle rattle as he shook his head. By that time the palms of my hands were sweating and I quit looking down, as it made me dizzy. With my eyes straight ahead and watching our every step, in what seemed an eternity, I finally made the bend.

Instantly my heart pounded, for I could see at least another four hundred feet of treacherous cliff to cover. But I quickly realized that not more than a hundred feet ahead, the ledge widened out to at least eight feet. The pathway stopped at what looked like a cirque or hanging valley. I could barricade myself there and pick off the outlaws as they came around the bend.

I was just starting to halfway feel good when terror struck. Behind me, at the bend of the ledge, I heard the ominous crack of rock. Prince jumped forward just in time, as part of the cliff gave way behind him. I stood frozen for a moment as I watched the avalanche of boulders cascade and splash into the river below. Relieved that the gelding hadn't gone with the debris, I rushed him ahead and into the hanging valley.

On firm ground, I looked back. It appeared that a massive part of the cliff was gone. No man or beast would be using that trail again. I realized I was safe from the outlaws.

Except for the roar of the river below and Prince munching grass in the meadow, there was silence. Then from behind the broken cliff came laughter, the insane laugh of someone deranged.

Slater shouted. "*Die Ross!* . . . Die the slow death of thirst and starvation! I couldn't have picked a better way for you to suffer!"

Then quiet returned to my sanctuary, with a deafening silence that seemed to invade my weak body. I lay down in a natural bed of grass by a grove of aspen. I felt the wound in my thigh bleeding again, but I was too weary to do anything about it.

Heavy with exhaustion, I peered around at a beautiful refuge of maybe thirty acres of scattered pine and aspen with open areas of grass, wildflowers, and yucca. The amazing valley amidst the mountain peaks had no way to go up or down out of the meadow that I could see. I was a prisoner; but I recalled once again how Pa had always told me that with time, there was no problem a man couldn't think his way out of.

With that in mind, I dropped off to sleep. When I awoke, the sun was high and pouring its bright glaring beams onto me, a light that came flashing through the wind-stirred leaves of the aspen. I lay covered with golden coins of yellow leaves that had fallen overnight. I felt better, not so tired; maybe it was the relief from the pressure of imminent danger and not having to worry about the outlaws.

I peered over at Prince grazing in the meadow. He was still saddled, and I whistled. The gray lifted his muzzle and looked my way, then tossed his head, and trotted over to me. As I removed his bridle and saddle, a pain shot through my shoulder. It'd been three days since I'd been shot. I softly talked to Prince and rubbed him down with handfuls of grass, something I should have done the night before, but I'd been too weak.

When Prince walked back out into the grass, it came to me that I now had another problem. How was I going to get out of the cirque where I was marooned?

But, first, I was thirsty. I'd have to try to find water. I nervously wondered what I'd do if there was none in the hanging meadow, and about the time I started to panic, Prince walked over to the escarpment and nosed into a patch of watercress — a sure sign of fresh water. The pool was spring fed and covered some three hundred square feet, maybe two feet in the deepest part. Most of the area was covered with the watercress.

I drank long from the pool, and felt refreshed, then cleaned and redressed my wounds. I ate the smoked trout I had in my saddlebags, and finally satisfied, I slept most of the day.

The next morning I still felt like I was running a fever, so I drank a tea brewed with aspen bark. The meadow had a wealth of edibles — watercress, plantain, stonecrop, wild raspberries, elderberries, evening primrose, even horsetail. I could live on the plants and berries, though I knew I needed some fat in my system, and so that evening I shot a deer. Though deer had only the barest fat, I knew it would have to do for the time being and I was grateful for what I had.

Eighteen

I'D BEEN A WEEK up in the high meadow. There'd been a two-inch snow the previous night, and thank God it hadn't been a bad storm. The temperature was near freezing and the jacket I carried in my saddlebag was not enough. I'd made a blanket from the deer hide, and though it helped, I wasn't equipped for a long winter. I knew I'd have to find a way out of the cirque.

That day was the first I'd felt good, my strength having returned to maybe half what it should be. I hadn't had the energy to survey the whole basin before, but that morning I walked west toward the far escarpment. It was the first time I'd been any distance from the shallow cave where I'd camped. Halfway to the parapet wall I realized I hadn't seen Prince since waking. That wasn't like him, for he'd usually be around to muzzle me for attention. As I walked across the base of the entire escarpment, I could see no way to get man or horse out of the imprisoned basin.

Where was he? I was baffled. I'd whistled, but he still hadn't shown up. I wondered . . . had he found a way out? Horses don't just disappear. I whistled again, louder. Then not over a hundred yards away, Prince suddenly rose out of nowhere, tossed his head, and trotted over to me. It looked like he'd come from the escarpment.

From the distance, I could see just a crack in the fluted rock that went to the surface. I walked a game trail over to where the gelding had appeared, and after reaching the rock face realized that what I'd seen earlier had been an illusion. My perspective had been wrong. The crack was actually the left edge of a narrow wall that stood out from the front face, leaving a four-foot-wide passageway, which ran parallel to the front face for maybe ten feet and then turned west. Inside the rock cleft, the walls shot straight up to a thin blue ribbon of sky. About six feet into the cleft, there gaped a ten-foot-high cave. Inside the cave a few yards I could see a sliver of daylight in the distance. My heart raced . . . I knew I had my way out.

The escarpment top was a narrow hogback, and the cave turned out to be a thousand feet of walkway to freedom.

Two weeks after I'd been shot, I rode into Animas City, with the sunlight on my right shoulder and my six-gun in my holster. I'd not seen Slater and his gang of thieves since that day on the cliff, but I rode able and ready to meet him or anyone else he sent my way. The previous misery he'd caused me had for a time left me discouraged, and though I was a slow person to anger, I'd had enough of that hoodlum. I'd not go looking for him, but if he came after me again, he'd better have his gun in his hand, for I'd be shooting first.

After getting Prince settled in at the nearest stable, I walked down the street and checked in at the hotel. I asked the clerk if Joe Woodman had a room and learned he'd been there a week. I walked up the steps to the second floor, down the hallway to room 203, and knocked.

"Who is it?" came Joe's voice from within.

"It's me, B.J."

I heard the squeak of bedsprings and a rush of feet across the floor. The door flew open and Joe grabbed hold of me with a big hug.

"I thought you were a goner, B.J.; but I prayed, and my faith stayed strong. I waited here for a day, and when you didn't show, I went back to look; but I never could catch up to you. And besides looking, I was busy keeping out of sight of Slater and his two henchmen. By the signs left, I figured I'd found your camp about a day after Slater."

I nodded. "Yeah. I'd been hit and waited as long as I could before pullin' stakes," I told him.

Joe figured I'd been wounded, and downstream he'd spent another day looking for me after Slater and his thugs had left the mountain. He'd found tracks leading to the ledge pathway, but thought it had only gone the two hundred feet.

"Well," I told him, "the ledge broke away behind me and fell into the canyon."

By that same evening, Joe said, he'd become concerned, for he knew Slater wouldn't leave the mountain if I was still alive. He'd wondered if they'd killed me and maybe buried me in a ditch somewhere, but thought sure he'd have found some sign.

"I was puzzled," he added. "There wasn't sign of a struggle. But I decided you were alive somewhere, so I returned here to Animas. After a week, I was being put to the test, as I was about to be getting discouraged. I was just lying on my bed thinking it over when you knocked."

Joe and I spent the next ten days loafing around and resting up. He had already deposited my half of the split, a $12,500 windfall, at Wells Fargo the day he'd returned to Animas City. The town was a bustling place with miners coming and going at all hours of the day. You wouldn't know it at the time, but in three short years Animas City would be a ghost town, for in 1880, when the railroad from Alamosa stopped at a rail head two miles south, Durango was born. The residents of Animas City just picked up and moved there.

After supper the evening I'd arrived, Joe and I walked down the street to the saloon, hoping we could find out a thing or two about Slater and his gang. I wasn't on the hunt for him, I just wanted to know if he was around. I always figured it paid to know all you could about possible trouble.

The bartender told us he'd heard Slater had moved to the Georgetown area. I felt sorry for the hard-working miners, tending their claims, unwary of Slater nearby. That night I told Joe I'd decided to be heading for the rimrock country south of Manhattan and Junction City.

Back in 1854, when the state was still a territory, Joe had crossed Kansas by wagon train, and he remembered well the Big Blue River area. "I like that part of the country," he confided. "Mind if I ride along? I might even buy me a spread, if I can find a nice place close to yours."

I was pleased. "There's no one I'd rather ride the trails with," I told him. But I wanted to do one other thing before we headed east. I wanted to see Santa Fe, and the Rio Grande River.

Joe was eager for that venture, and four days later we rode into Española, New Mexico Territory. From there we followed the rim of the Rio Grande River basin into Santa Fe. It was in the throes of afternoon when we saw Santa Fe in the distance.

We stopped early to make camp along the rim of the valley's escarpment, mainly to enjoy the mysterious desert. It was coming on to evening when I sat on an upthrust rock and watched the most glorious sunset I'd ever seen.

After we'd eaten, Joe and I sat around the campfire talking, mostly about my family's homestead above the Humboldt rim. Then we lay back in silence watching our gleaming campfire painting orange and red onto the fringes of darkness. After a time, Joe took out his note pad and went to writing. Following upon one torn-out page that he threw in the fire, he finally seemed satisfied with what he'd set down, and he put his pad away.

That night I had asked, "What're ya writin' Joe?"

He seemed reluctant to answer, then sheepishly replied, "Poetry."

"Oh . . . I'd always thought ya was keepin' a diary. . . . I like the way some poets put words together, but many of the bards that Ma used to read to me I couldn't figure out what they were sayin'."

"I know what you mean, B.J. A person has to write about what others can understand, and they need to feel the emotions. Poetry's just a way to tell a story in as few words as possible. And you need to try different approaches — different techniques — in a way the reader can figure out what you want to say, or the poem fails.

"It's important to understand the poet's perspective on what he's writing," Joe added. "I've read all the English poets — they're the greatest and the most prolific. And I like some of the American poets — even some of the homegrown ones . . . like me."

After a bit of persuasion, he read to me the verse he'd just set down.

Rio Grande Sunset

Beyond the painted desert cliffs,
I watched the sunset low,
Leave painted purple shadows,
Beneath the afterglow.

Along the banks of sandy shores
Ancient, twisted, and gray,
The Rio Grande paused gleaming,
Then faded off with day.

Heaven's skies were turning dark,
When to the stars, God told,
"Fill up your lamps with kerosene,
And light their wicks in gold."

I admired Joe's talent and though I'd known he had graduated from Harvard, I was never put off by his learning. He'd seemed more to me as just someone like myself, who'd roamed and loved the beauty of the West all his life. I knew the West was full of men just like Joe, for many professional men from the East had come West to find fortune. And some did, but most met with failure and disappointment. The town drunk may have been a doctor before falling to that demon liquor — the famed Doc Holiday had been a dentist before turning gunfighter, of necessity, in the untamed West.

My education sure couldn't compare to Joe's. I'd gone to a country school for eight grades, and, with some extra courses, was considered to have a tenth-grade education. It was enough to get me in most colleges of the day, if I'd wanted. Ma had encouraged me to further my education, and in 1868, when fifteen, I'd enrolled at Washington College back in Lexington, Virginia.

The Confederate General Robert E. Lee had been appointed president there in August of '65, and I was beside myself to think I'd be attending a school run by such a great and revered man. I'll never forget that year. I've always had a thirst for knowledge, and the school library had an abundance of information that took up all my spare time. On a cool day in

October of ’68, I was walking to my dormitory, unaware of anyone else around, daydreaming while treading on a pathway through falling leaves. My attention was on a gathering of downed leaves that swirled around my feet. Mesmerized by the whirlwind, I bumped into General Lee.

“Pardon me,” I apologized. “I guess my mind was on the leaves!”

“They *are* beautiful,” the General acknowledged, “and I, too, am mysteriously taken by them each autumn.”

He asked my name, and I responded, “Bruce Jacob Ross, sir.”

“And whereabouts is your home?” he queried.

“Loudoun County, Virginia, sir.”

“Ah . . . and would you be related to one Captain James Franklin Ross?”

I was surprised. “Yes, sir! He’s my father.”

I was proud to listen to the General tell me that Pa was a great soldier, as were many in the war. “But that’s behind us now,” he added. “It’s time to move on and do what we can to make a better world.”

I never spoke with General Lee again, but I did see him a few times from a distance. I finished that year and went home in the spring. I had planned on attending college one more year, but that autumn Grandfather fell from his horse and was laid up with a broken leg. He needed help, and I never returned to school.

In October of 1870, General Lee died, and the South grieved, as did I. But I was pleased when in February 1871 the school officially became Washington and Lee College.

Joe and I spent the next day in Santa Fe looking at the sights, then that afternoon headed out of town on the Santa Fe Trail. It was the 25th of October, 1878, my twenty-sixth birthday, when we rode with golden sunlight in our eyes. We each led a pack horse up the trail to the community of Las Vegas in the valley, and knew we’d better enjoy the warm weather, for the winds of winter would find us well before we’d reach the Humboldt rim.

Nineteen

THE WEST in 1878 had many stories to tell besides my own. In March, in Dodge City, Kansas, Ed Masterson, Bat's brother and town Marshal, was killed in a gunfight. His brother Jim, a policeman at the time, replaced Ed.

On the 13th of July that year, in New Mexico, the Lincoln County War began. Lincoln County included almost a fifth of the entire New Mexico Territory, and was then the largest county in the United States. The fighting, which lasted into 1881, was brought about by the greed of two men — James J. Dolan and John H. Riley — who'd wanted to control the county's merchant trade, just as it had been earlier by the powerful Lawrence G. Murphy, following the Civil War. Gunfights, cattle rustling, and murder came to a head in the eventual war, and one of the off-and-on again participants was William H. Bonney, who'd become known as the outlaw "Billy the Kid." He'd dealt himself into the war, killing as many of Dolan, Riley, and Sheriff William Brady's men as he could find. In July 1881, the Kid himself met his death.

Killing and lawlessness had been ingrained in the American West.

But meanwhile, on May 8, 1878, far to the north, in Kinmount, Ontario, Canada, a young girl named Hughena — "Enie" — MacArthur had turned fourteen, the youngest of ten children. Kinmount, a logging town, was located on the Burnt River in the southern part of Ontario, some thirty-five miles northwest of Peterborough. Between the two cities lay the southern edge of the Canadian Shield, a vast upland plateau unfit for cultivation and sparsely populated, but a beautiful glacial land of lakes and dense forests.

Enie's mother, Ellen, had been a widow for nine years, since Enie was five. Enie's father and mother, with eight children, had moved to the Ontario frontier in 1860 from Martintown, after spending a few months in Ottawa City. Two years had passed in Kinmount, when baby Victoria arrived; then another two years later, Enie was born.

Arthur Duncan MacArthur, Enie's father, had worked in the logging industry, at the local sawmill, and when the logging company was short-handed, he also worked as a shantyman, skipping across the river on logs, breaking up jams. For a period of time he had been the Sheriff of Kinmount.

After each year's spring thaw, when the huge logs were readied along the Burnt River banks and branded, the shantymen climbed atop the unhewn pieces of timer and rolled them into the river. On one of those cold spring days in 1869, after the ice had melted, logs were started downstream. With no railroads in the area, it was the only way to transport them to market. The river was full of the timber, and it was the shantyman's job, using his pike pole, to keep them parallel, to prevent log jams. On that freezing day, Enie's father was called from the mill to help out, for the river was running fast and extra men were needed to keep the logs straight.

But Enie's father never returned home; nor was his body ever found. It was not uncommon those days to be killed running logs, for the shantyman's work was dangerous.

Enie was a month short of five years old when her father was lost in the river. It was then that she, her mother, and her sisters — Victoria seven, Genevieve ten, and Margaret twelve — moved in with her brother Alex, who was twenty-five, and sister-in-law Grace. Then eight years after Enie's father died, her sister Victoria had gone to Kansas, traveling with family friends, to live with another older brother, Andrew, who'd homesteaded on Upper McDowell Creek, not far from where my own Ross family had settled in.

Back in 1867, Enie's brother Daniel, twenty-five, had been the first of the family to come to Kansas, along with John and Donald Cameron. Three years later, her brother Andrew, twenty at the time, sister Isabella, nineteen, and brother Tom, eighteen, followed. They'd traveled by boat to Newport Landing in Kansas City and then by wagon westward, the one hundred-fifty-odd miles, to Junction City.

Dan MacArthur and the Camerons had planned to work on the railroad, but homestead land to develop and prove up was available. They liked the Junction City area, with its winding rivers, plush valleys, and rolling hills, and so they stayed. And that was when Dan MacArthur decided to settle on Upper McDowell Creek in the Welcome Community.

Andrew, Isabella, and Tom MacArthur came to Kansas to homestead the same year my family moved to Kansas. Only two miles of prairie grass separated the two home sites, but though eighteen at the time, I'd never met the MacArthur family.

After the spring of '71, I was away from home, spending most of my time west of the Humboldt rim. It'd be another seven years before Andrew and I would meet, in the fall of 1878, when I went to the MacArthur place looking for help to drive a herd of cattle to Junction City.

In 1877, Andrew had wanted his mother and his sisters Victoria and Enie to move to his place on Upper McDowell, but only Victoria made the trip. His mother had thought it might be too much of a hardship on Andrew if they all three came to Kansas. Andrew was disappointed, and wrote again inviting his mother and Enie to come live with him, explaining it'd be no hardship and to quit worrying about being an imposition.

It was summertime in the forests of Ontario when Ellen decided, after all, that she and Enie would make the trip. Enie was excited about their adventure to America. She'd heard much about the endless horizons of blue sky and prairie and its frontier dangers, but she wasn't much worried, as most of the hostile Indians had been pushed farther west, and were not the threat of earlier years. Andrew had written about the outlaws, particularly in the cowtowns, but not even they, except on rare occasions, would treat a women with irreverence. Prairie fires, they knew, could be a threat, but surely no worse than the forest fires that were an ever-present danger around Kinmount.

Ellen and Enie had to be in Parry Sound, on the eastern Georgian Bay, by the 25th of August to board ship for the journey to Chicago. The entire trip to Kansas would take some thirty days and cover nearly twelve hundred miles by boat and four hundred by land.

The small house where Enie had lived for the past nine years, two miles northwest of Kinmount, was located in a remote area covered with spruce and pine. The one-story country home, barn, and out-sheds sat lonely in an area of few houses, with their closest neighbor a half mile away.

Ellen and Enie were leaving for Kansas the next day, and Enie was anxious and excited about the trip, though her feelings were mixed. She wondered if others leaving the only life they'd ever known felt as melancholy as she did.

Afternoon would soon slant down through the trees, and Enie later said she'd decided to take one last look at the places that had been special in her life. She strolled down the lane from the house in the dappled shade of pine needles to the wagon road that led to Kinmount. Ahead was the bridge over the Burnt River she'd passed over so many times going to and from school. After crossing the bridge, she wondered if it would miss her sweep of step so familiar to its wooden deck. She continued on down the road toward Kinmount.

At the edge of town was the nondescript one-room schoolhouse. School wasn't in session, as it was summer, but Enie had just wanted to look and revisit its familiar atmosphere. It was in that room that she'd felt love for the first time, she'd said. Not the love she'd had for family, but the first love she'd felt for a boy. She was in the sixth grade when a new student, John Sinclair, her age, had recently moved to Kinmount.

"He was so handsome," she'd whispered, as she described him later and blushed at the thought. But he never knew about her love, nor did anyone. Yet her steadfast ardor remained strong, even though he seemed unaware of her feelings. Two years later, he moved away, but even so her dreams remained loyal.

That final day, as Enie reminisced, the schoolhouse door was unlocked and she went inside. She sauntered slowly to the front of the room, paused for a moment, peered around, and took a deep breath. Later, when she walked toward the door, she stopped at John's old desk and swept her hand across the varnished top with delicate fingers. Across from his desk was her own. She sat down and gazed at the mottled brown surface that had several initials embedded in the varnished wood. A few minutes later she walked out the door and never looked back.

Between the schoolhouse and the bridge was a shanty. It was from the shanties along the river banks that the shantymen got their name — the long narrow buildings with bunks on both sides, and a long table down the center where the men ate. As Enie passed by, she remembered back four or five years, when she and Victoria were on their way home from school. They could smell the delicious aroma of bread and cakes baked in large black kettles coming from the shanty. The chef had invited them in and offered them one of the cakes; she remembered the pastry as the most delicious she'd ever eaten.

And Enie remembered that carved in the old wooden bridge over the Burnt River that she'd crossed each day was a poem. She stopped on that last visit to read it again . . . words she'd surely read a hundred times.

Here's to the wind that blows
and blows,
Here's to the boys that wear
rough clothes,
Here's to the girl who leaps
with joy,
To . . . grasp the hand of a shanty boy.

Enie stood on the bridge, unmoving, as her pretty blue eyes stared downstream, remembering the day her father had made his last trip down the river. The water looked peaceful enough, and she wondered, after all her heartaches, if the river was sorry it had claimed him for its own, depriving her of a father she had loved so dearly.

She remembered him as a kind and generous man, and felt a pang in her heart as she recalled the lonely sleepless nights her mother had endured. *"How could life be so cruel?"* she thought to herself. *"Did I fail You?"* she asked of God, as she listened to the rushing water. Then from out of the forest of whispering aspen leaves she heard a voice . . . or was it the wind . . . that sounded like the Scriptures?

"You must honor your father and mother for a long life."

Enie thought to herself that she had tried to do those things that pleased the Heavenly Father, and recalled the past Sunday.

Most Sundays Ellen and her children would travel to Kinmount to attend the Presbyterian Kirk. Enie loved Sundays, for they were a day of worship and rest. And she liked attending Reverend Ferguson's church; he was a nice man, of integrity, and Enie'd learned her lessons well, worshiping God with supplication and prayer. Reading the Bible daily was an encouraged habit Enie'd picked up from her mother.

That last Sunday, two days earlier, unable to attend church in Kinmount, Enie's mother held church at home. Her text was from Isaiah, Chapter 55. Afterward, in meditation, Enie realized how true the text had been in her life. God's thoughts and ways were higher and different, His Word always accomplishing its mission. Enie realized that all her prayers had been answered, except maybe two, but given patience they would be also, as long as she stood fast in faith. What seemed strange was that almost all her prayers had come to her in ways she hadn't expected, proving Isaiah's anointed prophecy, as she remembered a verse of that chapter.

> *For ye shall go out with joy, and be led forth with peace: the mountains and the hills shall break forth before you into singing and all the trees of the field shall clap their hands.*

The woods had taken on the purple hue of afternoon by the time Enie had returned home. Before stepping inside the house, she decided to spend an hour at her favorite place in the forest. It was maybe a half mile north, through battalions of spruce and pine, with areas of scattered maple, beech, and walnut. She walked a pathway almost invisible to the eye, a path she'd taken many times, edged with occasional berried shrubs and wildflowers, to a place for dreamers and the romantic of heart.

Her sanctuary was a crescent-moon-shaped ridge of glacial deposit, a drumlin, like a small hummock. In front of the drumlin was a small pond along the crescent. There atop the Canadian Shield, glacial action from thousands of years earlier had left behind a flat plain without mountains or hills. It was a slight undulating spot, with few hillocks, but Enie's favorite place, with its drumlin, was one of those isolated beautiful areas.

Enie was ten when she'd stumbled upon the lonely refuge while in the woods looking for wildflowers. The small concealed meadow was sparsely populated with pine, spruce, and aspen. Her mother loved the glacial flowers there, and Enie had been in the habit of picking a few when her mother felt melancholy.

Enie was the first in her family to find the oasis, but someone else had been there years earlier and built a bench of rough-sawn walnut, in the shade of a tall pine. As she sat on the bench and peered around the site, long shadows began to invade the pool of pristine crystal water and the grassy areas. A stand of blossoming mayflower grew along the edge of the forest, as did the yellow lady-slipper orchid. Along the earth-covered rock of the crescent grew golden foxglove with stems of fern-like leaves. Higher among the exposed glacial rock grew vines of blue blossoming morning glory. In front of the pond, in the short grass, waved patches of red cardinal flower, her mother's favorite.

The refuge was where she'd go when lonely and sad . . . where she'd go when all was right with the world. It was her place to escape from reality and dream the dreams of a princess.

But in those final hours at Kinmount, realizing time was running short and that it was the last she'd see the place, Enie turned despondent. Teary-eyed she picked a bouquet of red cardinal flowers and walked slowly through the woods to the house.

It was dark beneath the stars when Enie was awakened for the trip. Her brother Alex, standing by the wagon, waited patiently. After all the luggage had been loaded, daylight was beginning to brighten the sky above the dark green forest. Two large shire horses stood by, shaking their harness bells. Then her brother slapped the reins of the team and the wagon lumbered down the lane. Enie took one last look at the silent house.

It was over; a part of her life was behind her now. Feelings of new beginnings raced through her mind and her heart as the wagon moved past the landmarks of her childhood. The sun hung high when Alex reined the horses northwest onto the wagon road to Parry Sound.

Four days later Ellen and Enie were boarding the boat for their transit to Chicago, and by nightfall Ontario was out of sight. It was another four days before they docked in Chicago and made arrangements to travel overland the one hundred-fifty miles west to Moline, Illinois, on the Mississippi River. After three hundred miles down the twisting Mississippi, they changed boats in St. Louis. The steamboat then traveled slowly up the mighty Missouri River. The sights were vast and exciting to Enie, especially the high bluffs along the Missouri River valley.

Two weeks after leaving Chicago, the steamboat docked at Newport Landing in Kansas City. Andrew was waiting for them when they walked down the gangplank.

A week later, Andrew tooled his horses down the dusty earth lane to his house on Upper McDowell. Enie had arrived at her new home, and when she stepped down from the wagon, Victoria rushed from the house. It was a reunion of tears and happiness as Ellen, Enie, and Victoria walked with their arms wrapped around each other. Enie paused at the door and canvassed her eyes across the far-flung horizons. After a week of traveling in Kansas, she was still amazed at the spacious skies and the endless prairie.

She shouted to Andrew, "The land, it's so beautiful . . . so vast! I can hardly wait to have my own horse. I want to ride across the prairie with the wind in my face!"

Andrew listened as he stood by his team and quickly turned away, leading the horses to the corral. He never answered for fear of discovery; it wouldn't do for the womenfolk to see tears in a man's eyes, or witness the shudder that went through his body. But these were tears of happiness, for his mother and two youngest sisters were with him at last.

Enie looked around and saw Andrew at the barn, removing the harness from the horses and putting away the gear.

"I guess he never heard me," she whispered, and went into the house.

Twenty

IT WAS A HOT summer day in 1879 when I once again rode Dandy along the divide, with the Humboldt bluffs over my left shoulder and Upper McDowell on my right. The stallion had missed me, and we rode the hills together. For weeks on end, whenever I'd head for the barn, he'd be waiting for me along the corral fence. It was as though he was worried I'd go off somewhere without him. But I dared not neglect Prince too much, for he'd never shirked from whatever I'd asked him to do in our often perilous journeys out West. I divided my time between both horses.

I'd caught up on my work and was riding over to see Joe. He'd bought a section of grass, six hundred-forty acres, a half mile northwest of my place that straddled the divide between Upper Humboldt and Upper McDowell. The site had a decent house with two apparently good springs, and in April he'd bought eighty head of steers to summer pasture.

It was around eight when I rode up to the barn where Joe was working on a corral gate. It'd probably been a month since I'd seen him, and he was happy to see me. He dropped what he was doing, and we went to the house. I was surprised at how clean it now looked — I'd seen it when he first bought it! After a cup of coffee, Joe suggested we go for a ride. "You haven't seen all my spread."

We spent the day riding the range and talking about past times. It was late afternoon and hot when we rode into a patch of oak trees. Nature had spaced them to a canopy of shade, and in the middle of the sanctuary was a spring flowing out of the hillside into a clear pool of water.

The horses watered downstream, and then they trailed their reins to a nearby meadow to crop grass. Joe and I drank from the pool, and I was surprised at how cold the water felt to my parched throat. We sat next to the water until the afternoon began to paint a purple hue on the trees. Nearby a songbird began its melody in the brush, and it gave me a feeling of contentment. I listened to Joe once again recite from one of his favorite poets.

Thou wast not born for death, immortal bird!
No hungry generations tread thee down;
The voice I hear this passing night was heard
In ancient days by emperor and clown:
Perhaps the self-same song that found a path
Through the sad heart of Ruth, when, sick for home,
She stood in tears amid the alien corn. . . .

I peered at Joe in the dimming light and asked, "Shakespeare?"

"No," he replied, laughing. "John Keats."

"I should've known you'd pull someone else on me," I told him.

By the time we rode into Joe's ranch yard, dark had settled in. After a supper of steak and canned peaches we went outside and sat on a bench to check out the stars. They reminded me of my home in Virginia, I told Joe. "And wherever I've been, the stars remain unchanged. They're like God . . . the same forever."

"Yes, I know what you mean," he replied.

I was reluctant to ask, but I wanted the best for Joe, and I just came out with it. "Joe you've a nice place here, but it must be lonely. Have ya ever thought about gettin' married?"

He wasn't shocked or disturbed by my question, but a melancholy look crossed his face as he replied, "I'm already married."

"Oh! . . . I didn't know."

He said no more, nor did I. I figured if he wanted me to hear about his situation he'd tell me. After other small talk, mostly about the ranch, Joe invited me to stay for the night, and I accepted.

It was late October, and I'd been home almost a year when Joe wanted to ship his eighty head of steers to Kansas City from the rail head in Junction City. I rounded up the needed wranglers for the drive to Junction from the Welcome-Upper McDowell Creek area. I picked up Andrew and Tom MacArthur, who lived two miles north of my place, and two of the Horne boys, from their homestead east of the MacArthurs. Joe and I figured that was all the help we'd need for the drive. We would start at sun-up, for it would take a long day to reach the stockyards in Junction City.

Joe and I often got together those days, sometimes just to exercise our horses and look at the countryside. Usually we were checking and fixing fence. Joe liked working cattle, but he wanted no part of breeding and raising his own.

"Too much trouble," he told me.

I wasn't much for wanting to work cattle, but I loved raising horses. Pa and I had forty quarter horses, not counting four magnificent stallions, including Dandy, and a gray Pa rode. Of the forty horses, we had ten mares, nine geldings, seven colts, and fourteen fillies. Pa figured we'd sell eight geldings and two mares at the next livestock sale in Junction City.

I had told Pa earlier, in the winter of '73, the story of the buried bullion near Council Grove. I'd explained to him about the remaining ten wagons of gold the Union had taken on to Topeka, then shipped by rail to Virginia. Pa thought it was probably the same gold he'd captured, when a Confederate, from the warehouses along the Orange and Alexandria Railroad at Culpeper, Virginia, back in '64.

The next day Joe came by the house, and I told him a bit more than I had before, in Colorado, about the hidden gold on Fourmile Creek.

He shrugged. "If you want to go get it, B.J., I'll help you and expect nothing for it."

"No," I insisted, "if I decide to dig it up, we'll share. We're partners when it comes to huntin' gold aren't we?"

"Sure, B. J., we're partners. But you know, I'm not greedy. If I was, I'd head back to Colorado."

"I know, Joe . . . but I'm not sure if I want to get the gold or not. I'll mull it over, and pray about it."

Joe nodded.

In December of that year a Friday night box supper was held at the Humboldt School. Nobody those days missed a box supper — especially the single men. It was one way to meet the pretty local girls. By four that day I'd cleaned up and was ready to go. Ma, Pa, and James had already left for the schoolhouse. The program was to start at six, and the boxes were to be auctioned off around seven. Over the past two years, my three sisters had married — Susan wed Walter Pepper; Harriet wed William Clark; and Virginia wed Thomas McKinley, a distant relative of William McKinley, who was at the time in the U.S. House of Representatives, and later became president, in 1896.

I was waiting for Joe to come by the house, as we'd planned to ride the three miles together to the school. I had on a western black suit, black boots, white shirt, and black bow tie with short ribbon strings. After looking in the mirror, I had second thoughts, wondering if maybe I should dress down a bit. But it was too late to change. There was a knock at the door; it was Joe. An inch of dry snow had fallen during the day, and when I opened the door a skiff of flakes flew in. Joe wiped his feet on the gunny sack and stepped inside. I threw my cartridge belt around my hips, and slipped on my sheepskin coat and black flat-crowned hat.

"You look mighty handsome all duded up," Joe exclaimed.

"Well, you do too, Joe," and without thinking I added, "we'll have to find ya a woman; it's about time ya settled down."

Joe glanced at me out of the corner of his eye, then he smiled. "What about you? You're getting on yourself."

He was right. I was twenty-seven years old and didn't even have a lady friend to be courting.

I was riding Prince that evening, and he kind of blended in with the snowy countryside. Old habits die hard; I figured it never hurt to be cautious. Two miles later, lonely on the prairie, we could see the schoolhouse. It was lit up like a glittering Christmas tree, with golden shafts of lamplight falling out of each window, and glowing a comfortable welcome into the icy darkness.

We tied our horses to the manger of a long shed on the grounds, pitched 'em some hay, and walked a snow-trodden path to the building. We stepped inside to a blast of warm air. It was a little after five, and the local people had already filled the room.

Five minutes later, Andrew MacArthur came through the door with his brother Tom and four pretty women; one of 'em was absolutely beautiful. Andrew introduced me to his mother, Ellen, and his sisters Isabella, Victoria, and Hughena. When Andrew got to Hughena, she boldly spoke. "They call me Enie."

She was the one that'd captured my heart, and later that evening I asked Andrew if Enie was dating young men. He looked at me with a slight frown. "No, not yet; she's just fifteen."

I was shocked. I knew she was young, but I thought she looked to be at least eighteen. I told him I'd thought she was older, and changed the subject.

When the program started, I went to the far side of the room where all the bachelors were scrambling to get to, away from any "hussy" who might want to speak to 'em. I ended up in front of most of the men, for I wasn't about to fight my way through that pack of flesh. I did manage to see Joe, who'd retreated to the back, leaning against the wall. The program was directed by the lady teacher and put on by the school kids, mostly reciting rhyme and putting on little skits. I paid a dollar for a neatly wrapped box, which belonged to Andrew's mother. She came to where I stood and took me to a desk where we would eat. We'd no sooner sat down when Enie came flying over with Joe.

"Mother," she pleaded, "may I change partners with you; it's okay with Mr. Woodman."

Mrs. MacArthur was somewhat startled by the suggestion, and looked at Enie questioningly, then smiled. "Sure, why not."

And that was how I ended up eating my box supper with Enie MacArthur. She was bright and interesting, and she completely stole my heart. She told me about her life in Canada, and when she stopped talking, she straightened her back and searched my eyes with hers.

"Now tell me about yourself," she ordered. "I already know two things; I know you're not married, and you're from Virginia."

"How'd ya know that?" I asked.

"Andrew told me when I asked him."

"Ah, I see."

Enie gazed up at me and smiled. "You remind me of a boy I knew in Kinmount, B.J."

It piqued my interest, but she said no more, and then asked me again to tell her about myself. After that, Enie hardly talked as she listened intently about my tales of the West.

It was late when I left the schoolhouse and said goodbye to the MacArthurs. Joe had decided to travel home a different way, a shorter ride.

The cold was not bitter, and I was enjoying the night beneath the bright stars of Orion. I was thinking about the evening and realized Enie was someone I could love, if she were only at least marrying age. Being twelve years older was a hindrance. Surely someone would come along for me. But I wasn't going to push myself into a bad marriage.

Riding relaxed my thoughts, which rambled off in all directions. When I'd passed a clump of shadowy wild plum, I'd thought the leafless branches looked strange, but my observation was too late. I heard the blast of gunfire. I was hit, but as I fell from the gelding I pulled my six-shooter and started firing at the shadows behind the thicket. I heard running, and the hooves of horses rushing off into the distance.

Then silence settled in. I'd been hit in the side, and it began to hurt; but it didn't feel like I'd been hit bad. I crawled onto Prince, standing next to where I'd fallen. I was only two miles from home, and in ten minutes I was walking into the house. Ma and Pa heard me in the kitchen and came downstairs as I was looking at my wound. The bullet showed up as a lump just under the wound entrance, and Pa took his knife and removed it.

I wondered why the bullet hadn't penetrated deeper, then Pa looked in my coat pocket and discovered that the bullet had gone through a book I'd been reading and left there. I was fortunate; the wound was shallow and hardly more than a scratch.

Early the next morning, I mounted Dandy and rode to the place of ambush. I found the tracks of two bushwhackers, and with all the cigarette butts scattered around, they must have been waiting a while. It must have been Slater. I knew there'd been a stranger at the schoolhouse, though it wasn't Slater.

I trailed the hombres into Junction City, but there was no use trying to track farther, as any evidence was lost among thousands of other hoofprints on the street. There was something to remember though; one of the horses had a broken shoe.

It was close to noon, and I hit the saloons inquiring, but nobody had seen 'em. One cowboy on the street said he'd seen two men leaving town around seven that morning, and one of 'em matched the description of Slater.

They were gone, but I had a hunch they'd be back. I'd once again have to ride wary with my six-gun ready.

The winter of '79 passed, and on April 10th the day finally felt like spring. The redbud and plum thickets were in full bloom in the creek bottoms, and on the shallow banks of the washes there was a misting of chartreuse along the branches of the softwood trees.

Joe had bought seventy-six steers, and I was heading for his place riding Dandy. The black was in his element and loved the countryside as much as I did. Joe was out by the corral and ready to go when I came down the lane. He mounted his roan gelding and met me halfway. We were soon on the Humboldt Road heading for Junction City, where we'd meet the MacArthurs and the Hornes at the salebarn stockyards around daylight the next morning.

We dropped off our horses with Spencer at the stable, just as the sunlight was dropping below the trees. We'd put them up, then went on to the cafe. We'd invited Spencer, but his wife was fixing roast for supper, he thought, and he figured he'd better head for home.

"But why not come home with me?" he asked. "Katy would like to see ya, and Joe you're invited too."

We offered our thanks, adding we'd go to the cafe that night as there might be a new waitress to meet!

"Well, there is," Spencer noted, "and she's a pretty one. Julie's her name. But you'll have to get in line, for everybody not nailed down wants to court her."

"Sounds like my kind of girl," I replied.

Spencer laughed. "Yeah, most of 'em are."

That night Joe and I slept in the hayloft at the stable. After a breakfast of flapjacks and eggs at the cafe, we were pushing cattle by daylight. Late that afternoon we crossed the Clarks Creek riffles, and before dark we were watching the steers spread out into Joe's prairie-grass pasture.

After Joe had paid the wranglers, he and I went to the ranch house where Joe fixed a supper of beefsteak and Irish potatoes. When we'd finished our meal, Joe spoke.

"I been thinking about the gold south of Council Grove," he said. "It's not as if Nature put it there. So why leave it where it does no one any good?"

"Yeah, that's been botherin' me too," I added. "But I don't feel right in takin' it for myself." I told Joe how it originally had belonged to the Confederates States, then the bulk of it was captured by the North. "From what Pa's told me, and I think so too, he believes he'd recaptured that same gold for the Confederacy at Culpeper back in '64 as that same amount corresponds to what the Union had when they left Council Grove, and the dates coincide.

"You could make a case that it belongs to both sides. Yet, by all rights, I think Reggie would want Katy to have a part of the bullion. I've been prayin' about it, and God will tell me what should be done. I just don't feel qualified to decide on my own."

It was the middle of May 1880 when Pa'd received a letter from his brother John in Virginia. It contained the usual family information, and all seemed to be as well as could be expected. The part that interested me was at the end of the missive:

> *. . . I received a letter from Washington and Lee University asking for donations. Since the war, there's no money in the South. The reconstruction has decimated everyone. The greedy carpetbaggers from the North have stolen what little we had left, and there's not much we can do about it.*
>
> *The university is in need of money, and many of our Southern boys would like to further their education, but*

cannot afford it. I did manage to scrape together a hundred dollars for the school, and wished it could have been more.

Sincerely, your brother, John

I knew when I read the letter it was God's way of telling me what I should do with most of the gold. The poor boys in the South would get an education!

The next time I was in town I took Spencer aside and told him about the bullion. He was astounded. Surprisingly, he murmured, "I always knew there was more to Reggie than met the eye." Then he added, "If Katy is to benefit, I'd like to help."

"Sure," I replied, "as soon as Joe and I talk it over and decide what to do I'll let ya know."

After several days and more prayer I came up with the plan for Washington and Lee to receive eighty percent of the gold, some $100,000. I'd not planned to take any of it for myself, but I was overwhelmed with objection from Joe and Spencer. I'd prayed about it again, and felt I would measure my share in a proper way later. After talking it over, Spencer, Joe, and I decided we'd make the trip for the gold sometime in the fall.

Twenty-One

ON A WARM day in late May of '80 I read of a mare for sale in the Junction City paper. It interested me, for I'd been looking for one to mate with Dandy. The owner lived in Abilene, and on the spur of the moment I decided to make the trip.

Joe was busy, so I decided to travel alone. There were times I liked riding on my own. I had more time to fellowship with God, and He with me. When someone else was along, they naturally took up most of my thoughts.

I stayed the night in Junction City, had business to take care of, and wasn't on the trail until the sun was high over the eastern bluffs along the Smoky Hill River. I rode the Smoky Trail, meeting few travelers. I could make Abilene before dark, if I didn't dally — but I did.

I'd reined Prince off the traveled way, wading into the prairie grass. I wanted to look at the river, and decided to take my time. The water was running shallow and clear. At a low-water crossing I reined Prince into the stream up to his hocks, the fast current splashing around his legs. While he drank his fill, I peered around at the peaceful scene. The riffle ran into a deep hole along the south bank where willow branches hung out over the water.

I wasted away almost two hours beneath the shade of some walnut trees on the north bank, and Prince waded into the grass to eat. I fixed a bite myself after catching a channel cat below the riffle on a wee toad I'd caught. Well contented with the day, I mounted up and made my trail north away from the twisting river. It was long into afternoon, and I knew I'd not make Abilene that night.

I rode in a lonely prairie, as the sun painted gold on the wind-shifting silver-green bluestem. Prince plodded into a slight headwind pushing through the waving grass that moved across the meadow like a creeping beast, as far as the timber along the river. In the west, cumulus gathered, forming massive, towering cathedral clouds that misted into vistas of pinks and blues. But a half hour later, the sky had turned an ominous purple, and was moving fast in my direction. In moments the storm front hit with gusts of wind and scattered pellets of raindrops. I stopped and put on my slicker from out of my bedroll. With a stroke of God's hand, the land lay dark as far as eyes could see and then thunder rumbled in anger along the hills. I rode with my hat tied down as the wind tore at my raincoat, with only its buttons keeping the slicker from being torn away. Behind the wind came the rain, and visibility dropped and far horizons disappeared, as did the hills south over my left shoulder. Along the dense river bottom, the trees next to the water grew faint and ghostly behind the veil of downpouring rain. I pushed my gelding onward through the darkening grass brushing against my legs. Deeper into the emerald prairie I rode, a wet, lonely, insignificant figure of a man bobbing in the vastness of a swelling sea. Suddenly in the dark swirling clouds, a sly window opened and splayed a brilliant arm of golden light upon the purple countryside, like a bright bracelet inlaid with pearls of gleaming raindrops, each precious gem clinging to its long-stemmed blade of grass.

When the sky cleared into the evening twilight, I stopped and made camp in a looping bend along the Smoky. I cut some willow to make a cushion for my bed, and one extra piece for a pole. The fish I'd eaten at noon had tasted good, and I decided to catch a few for supper. What little daylight that had filtered into the woods had now disappeared. The only light was that coming from my campfire.

I almost always caught fish that time of day, especially after a rain. Below the bank on a gravel bar of the river I tossed my line, hooked with an earthworm, into a pool of water below a roaring riffle. In less than five minutes I had two nice catfish. It was tempting to keep on having fun, but a familiar voice said, "*That's enough.*"

The fish were delicious, as they always were when cooked over an open fire. Later, as I was lying on my makeshift bed, looking up through the leaves at the stars, I heard the swoop of an owl soaring on invisible wings down through the corridors of dense trees. Owls had a way of waiting for complete darkness to hunt for unsuspecting prey, and from the scuffling noise I heard in the distant leaves, I think he found a victim. I lay listening to the riffle singing its familiar tunes I'd heard so often, yet I never grew tired of its music . . . a melody that always made me sleepy, like a rhythmic lullaby.

A rippling of crashing, on gravel stones splashing,
In swift waters roaring, its tinkling tunes soaring,
With mandolins stringing, and soft chorus singing . . .

I slept like a log under cover, with my handgun along my leg. The riffle had put me into a dreamland I hadn't experienced in a week.

What woke me was a slight breeze stirring the branches of a cottonwood, causing sunlight to flash down through its leaves into my waking eyes. I fixed a quick breakfast and was mounting Prince by seven o'clock. Around mid-morning I rode into Abilene. I dismounted at the Twin Livery stable. I'd met Jeff Olson, the hostler, back in '72, when Reggie worked there. Jeff was standing by the large, open swinging doors when I tied Prince to the hitching rail. We greeted each other, and he asked, "What ya doin' in these parts, B.J.? I haven't seen ya for years.

"I was sorry to hear about Reggie; I believe he was on his way into straightenin' up his life."

I acknowledged it was a shame, noting it was Slater and his bunch that'd done Reggie in. "Ya haven't seen Slater lately, have ya?"

Jeff hadn't, and said he didn't want to see him either. "That's one bad hombre; I keep my twelve-gauge handy for the likes of him."

I visited with Jeff about the ad he had in the Junction City paper. "The mare ya described could be what I've been lookin' for."

"Well, she's a beauty," Jeff admitted. "Come take a look."

We walked through the stable and out into the corral. I whistled, and turned to Jeff. "I've never seen a prettier mare in all my days!"

She was a blue roan, and from her teeth I could see she was a four-year-old filly.

"She's broke to ride," Jeff explained, "and gentle as a lamb around womenfolk."

I'd never seen better lines for breeding; she was just what I'd wanted to mate with Dandy. Jeff was asking $150 for her — a high price — but I'd have paid double if he'd have asked. I named her Princess.

In June of 1880 I was kept busy taking Dandy around to those who wanted him for stud. On Deep Creek it was the Barrys and the Gehrts. On Upper McDowell it was the Pooles, Hornes, Camerons, MacArthurs, Fechners, Germanns, and Simontons. On McDowell it was the Brannicks, Tullys, Shanes, Lichtenhans, Hannigans, and Estes.

Pa had deeded to me one hundred-sixty acres of grass along the Humboldt rim, half of what he'd purchased in '71. With the eighty I had, it gave me two hundred-forty acres — plenty of land for raising horses.

I'd put up a one-room cabin in '71 on my homestead, but that July, with Pa and Joe's help, I built a four-room house and outbuildings. We finished the house and barns in September. Pa had built his house close to the road, but I made mine a thousand feet back in a grove of oak trees that gave a welcome feeling when coming home on a hot day.

Before moving in, I cleared out the brush and scrub trees, and those too close together for good growth. I wanted no tree closer than fifty feet to another, enough space to where someone couldn't sneak up on me without my having a line of fire. It wasn't perfect, but you have to give up a little safety if ya want some shade.

I had a piece of high-ground prairie grass northwest of the house a hundred yards that remained a concern to me, a place that had a view of my front and back doors where an enemy, with a rifle, could lay in wait for the right moment. Because of that drawback, I built a secret way out, on the east side of the house, to a shallow ravine. The dry wash went north and paralleled the east side of the barn.

I was riding Dandy, Joe his favorite roan, and Pa his gray — three men with rifles in their saddle boots, and armed with handguns on the Humboldt trail. I couldn't help but notice the men at my side. Joe and Pa rode straight in their saddles, tough men, confident men, that had faced many a rough situation. I peered at them beneath my hat brim, the two people I most admired in the world. It was a privilege to ride beside them and know there was no situation they couldn't handle. Neither man asked for a thing; it was their will to help with what I wanted to accomplish, and my heart was full. By mid-morning we were splashing across the Clarks Creek riffle.

It was an unusually cold day for early October. The temperature was above freezing, but it was windy, overcast, and damp, the kind of weather that chills a man to the bone. Yet in the past nine years, I'd learned one thing about Kansas: the weather'd probably change the next day.

I hadn't wanted for Pa to go along to Council Grove, but he wouldn't have it any other way.

"After all," he'd said, "I'd captured most of that same lot of gold in the War Between the States, and it's only right I be in on the last of what's left."

I wasn't going to argue with him; he was my father. Ma just smiled when he told me he was going, and she peered over at me as if to say, "I told you so."

I told Pa, "I'd like nothin' better than for ya to ride along." By that time I'd decided we might need him. He was more experienced with fighting than the rest of us, and I think after being tied down on the farm since the war, he wanted the adventure.

We rode into Junction City, turned our horses down the main street, and pulled up at Spencer's stable before noon. He was waiting for us, and excited about the trip.

By twenty before eight the next morning, the four of us — Pa, Joe, Spencer, and myself — had finished a leisure breakfast at the cafe. We were mounting our horses when I heard the hollow moan of a train whistle in the distance — the eight o'clock Missouri, Kansas, Texas Line they called "The Katy." It was the railroad from Junction City to Council Grove, and had been in operation since '69.

We rode up to the depot just as the train pulled into the station. The iron wheels squeaked to a stop and the train rested alongside a rusty water tank. Railroaders dropped the hose into the thirsty boiler as the engine puffed and steam hissed along the drivers.

We pulled a ramp up to the stockcar and loaded our six horses — our own mounts, along with two pack horses belonging to Spencer. At ten minutes after eight I stepped up into the passenger car behind my three companions.

We'd no sooner sat down in our seats when came the "All *aboard!*" The train jerked as the iron wheels began pulling against the rails, then gathered speed and finally came to a smooth roll.

The countryside flashed by as my eyes took in the autumn colors of a beautiful endless painting. We stopped at Skiddy, White City, and an unscheduled whistle stop, for passengers waiting to ride that day, before pulling into Council Grove at noon. By half past twelve we'd unloaded our horses. We were hungry, and ate dinner at the Saddlerock Cafe across the street, south of the depot.

After a dinner of fried chicken, mashed potatoes, and gravy, the four of us mounted up and reined our horses west. We rode by the Blue Duck on our left, a dance hall and saloon that sat along the Missouri Pacific track. Farther west, on our right, was the large oak tree where the U.S. Commissioners and the Osage Indians, back in 1825, had signed a treaty giving Americans and Mexicans free passage along the Santa Fe Trail through Osage Territory. Moments later our horses' hooves were stamping a rumbling echo on the wooden deck of the wagon bridge across the Neosho River.

West of the river, along the south side of the Santa Fe Trail, sat a trading post owned and operated by Malcolm Conn. Spencer was a friend of Conn's, and after crossing the river, we stopped at the store. Conn told Spencer we could stable our horses in his barn. We accepted, realizing our numbers might not create as much attention there as they would at the town stable.

While caring for our horses we decided on a plan of operation. Pa and I would ride out of town the next morning an hour before daylight. We'd take the two packers and go for the gold on Fourmile Creek. Joe would follow behind and stop, posting sentry, at the top of the hill leading down into Fourmile. Spencer would post at the south edge of Council Grove. If anyone left town heading our direction, he'd follow. We wondered if maybe we were being too cautious, for the area we were going to was not populated and the grounds probably hardly ever stepped on by humans.

Nevertheless, we determined that Joe would stay at the Saddlerock Hotel, Spencer would stay at the Hays House, and Pa and I'd stay in

Conn's barn. I decided to keep away from the hotels, being the more well-known in the area, especially if Slater was around. He'd be suspicious if he was to see me in town.

At six that evening, and coming onto dark, Pa went to the Hays House for dinner. He saw Spencer eating, but they played the part of strangers. Two other men, along with three couples, were also having their supper. After his meal, Pa motioned to the waitress.

"That was a mighty fine supper," he expressed to the lass, and added, "Fix another to take with, will ya; I've not had a lot to eat lately."

While I waited, I was getting hungry. We had food in our packs, but I figured we might need it on our way home, though I was about ready to get into the supply when Pa finally came back with my supper.

It was five the next morning when Joe and Spencer showed up at Conn's. The pack horses were ready and stowed light, for they'd soon have an additional two hundred-fifty pounds apiece to carry. Spencer had seen no one suspicious at the Hays House, but, much as we'd feared, Joe had seen Slater at the Blue Duck Saloon. He was with two other men.

"Rough-looking characters," Joe had described 'em. "Slater didn't recognize me; as far as that goes, he's never seen me up close. After an hour the men left the saloon and rode out of town, heading west. Out of sight, I tracked them for several miles, and figured they must have a hideout somewhere in that direction. But when they left the saloon, they were stumbling around as though they'd had too much to drink. I don't think they'll be up and around yet this morning."

That relieved my mind a bit. "If everythin' goes well, we should be back this way by twelve o'clock." I wondered to myself what Slater was doing back here, for surely Colorado would be better pickins', unless he'd caught wind of a big shipment on the Santa Fe Trail. I thought that might be it. They were probably robbing unsuspecting souls traveling on the trail, or it could even be things got too hot for 'em in Colorado.

We'd earlier decided that the quickest and safest way home with the bullion would be on the wagon road east of the Neosho River, and it'd also be the shortest route through Council Grove. When Pa and I were ready to leave the site of the buried gold, I was to signal Joe so he would know we were loaded and moving out. Joe would then backtrack to town, pick up

Spencer, and wait for us north of Council Grove. From there we hoped it'd be a safe ride home.

That was our plan; but plans at times can go awry.

At half past five, with almost an hour's head start, Pa and I were riding out through the barn doors and leading two pack horses. An hour later, in the dawning sunlight, I spotted the large gray sycamore tree from the hill looking down on Fourmile Creek. That was one of the landmarks I needed. The tree was some two miles southeast and stood guard at least ten feet above the other trees along the creek. In minutes we were sitting our horses across the creek from the sycamore.

Along the east side of a deep draw running into the creek, and hidden from view, lay a half-buried limestone boulder. How it got there was a mystery, but I'd reckoned the force of Nature deposited it maybe a thousand years earlier.

Lining up with the sycamore, I stepped off ten paces south of the boulder. The bullion wasn't much more than a foot deep, and in less than an hour, with shovels from the pack horses, we'd removed it. We put the gold in two large canvas bags and then strapped 'em on our packers. We replaced the dirt, then sifted dust and old leaves over the disturbed area. With no way to hide the shovels in our load, we broke the handles and pitched the remains out of sight, into the ravine.

Satisfied, I rode out into the open where I could see Joe in the distance along the hilltop sitting on his horse. It was a sunny day and with a mirror from my saddlebags I flashed a reflection of sunlight to let him know we were ready to leave. I watched as he took off north to get Spencer.

We'd been lucky no one had ridden down the trail where Joe had waited. Ten minutes later, Pa and I splashed our horses across the Neosho at a low-water riffle.

When we rode past the Saddlerock, I looked at my pocketwatch. It was eleven o'clock. A slim-looking cowboy was leaning on the canopy post in front of the cafe. He acted surprised, and I could tell by the way his eyes followed us up the trail he had more than a casual interest in our caravan. He looked familiar, but I couldn't put a handle on just where I might have laid eyes on him.

Before we were out of sight of the cafe, the man had mounted his horse and was hightailing it west. It was then I recalled he was the same man I'd seen at the Humboldt School box supper; no doubt he rode with Slater. But by the time that hombre could get to Slater's hideout, we'd be far ahead of 'em. I didn't much care if Slater caught up; we could settle things for good. Slater'd be a fool to attack us with the firepower we had in our possession, though knowing him, he'd rather wait and bushwhack his quarry.

Joe and Spencer were waiting on us just north of town, and we moved north like four small specks, lost in the vast emptiness of the universe. Around dusk, we passed a promontory bench of land on my right shoulder, in the upland of rolling hills. The plateau, near the headwaters of Mill Creek, in seven years would be the site of a new town, Alta Vista, fed by the railroad.

Later that evening we rode up to Joe's ranch house. He would keep eight bars of bullion at his place, until I was able to take 'em to Wells Fargo. Spencer took the other two with him, to Junction City. I thought it better that I didn't stash the bullion at my place. That way, if Slater did come nosing around he'd be out of luck. Maybe my imagination was working overtime, but I had a disturbing premonition he'd be calling in the near future, and I hoped so, as I was getting tired of watching my back trail all the time.

But I'd have to be cautious, and not become careless; one misstep could mean death.

Twenty-Two

SLIM DILLON jumped off his gelding, ran to the cabin, and threw open the door shouting. "*Slater! . . . Slater!*"

"Damn you Slim. Shut up, ya idiot!" growled Slater, who'd been trying to sleep off the splitting headache of a hangover. He rose from his cot, staggered over to the kitchen table, and fell into a chair, then reached for the whiskey bottle and took a swig.

"It helps to have a little hair of the dog, after a night on the town."

Slim slipped over to the other side of the table and sat down. He was twenty-two, and had gotten himself in with the wrong crowd when he was eighteen. It was easy to do if you hung around the saloons. Slim was not a bad sort, and had he ridden with a different — law-abiding — crowd, he'd have fit in on the straight and narrow. Slim's problem was he was a follower, and wanted someone else to do the thinking. He'd been with Slater for a year, after a night of drinking in Colorado.

It wasn't long until Jake Snodgrass stumbled over to the table. He sat down and reached for the bottle. Slater grabbed it away.

"There ain't enough for both of us. You can do without!"

Jake, middle-aged, had a scar that sliced across his crooked nose and right cheek. He glowered at Slater for an instant, then leaned back in his chair without saying a word.

Slater was a hard man on partners, and if they tried to leave his outfit for some reason or another, he'd shoot 'em. Jake had been with Slater four years, and that was some kind of a record; most of 'em didn't last that long.

After thirty minutes of intermittent silence and a few angry words, Slater peered over at Slim. "Now what the hell did ya want, comin' in here howlin' like a pack of wolves?"

"I wanted ya t'know I saw Ross ridin' by the Saddlerock, with an older man. They were leadin' two pack horses that looked to be carryin' a lot of weight."

Slater's eyes widened. "Which way were they headin'?"

"North."

"Why didn't ya tell me when ya come through the door?"

"I tried to boss, but ya shut me up!"

Slater was furious again, and he scowled, staring through black scorching eyes embedded deep in his whiskered face. He jumped up from the table and knocked his chair backward, spinning across the room. His face had turned ugly, and he angrily demanded, "How long ago was it?"

"I'd say a good three hours."

"*Damn!*" he called out, and kicked the chair Jake was sitting on, tumbling the outlaw to the floor.

Jake jumped up, shouting at Slater. "For Christ's sakes, Johnny, settle down!"

"You *bastard!* You don't tell *me* to settle down!"

Then before Slim or Jake knew what was happening, Slater pulled his six-gun and shot Jake between the eyes. With a glassy vacant stare, Jake appeared to look at Slater, tried to speak, and then slumped to the floor.

Slim said nothing as Slater paced with gun in hand. Slater rambled on, mostly to himself. "It's too late to catch 'em now. I know that Ross was carryin' the missin' gold. He won't get away with it! I'll dog him 'til he begs me to take the gold off his hands . . . then I'll kill 'im!

". . . I still can't figure how he got off that mountain in Colorado . . . or how he lived through that ambush last winter. I know I hit him good, but that fool comes up shootin'! He's got more lives than a cat. . . . But I'll kill 'im yet, if it's the last thing I do. I'll shoot 'im in the belly and watch him beg me to kill 'im. I want 'im to suffer before he dies!"

Slater rampaged on for at least five minutes before he finally settled himself down. He pointed to Jake. "Take 'im out and bury 'im — and not too close to the cabin! I don't want him stinkin' up the place."

Slim did as he was told. He laid the outlaw across his horse, then mounted his own, and rode into the hills. Slim was doing some serious thinking, and knew if he wanted to live out his life he had to get away from Slater. He figured it was only a matter of time before he too was killed.

"*God!*" Slim thought to himself, *"Slater killed Jake without blinkin' an eye."*

To murder a man he'd rode the trails with for four years meant nothing to Slater. Killing, as far as Slater was concerned, was no different than stepping on a bug.

On his way back to the cabin, Slim decided that Slater must never know he planned to leave him. He'd pick a time that'd be safe . . ."*Or I'm a dead man*," he voiced aloud.

Back in the cabin, Slater was sifting ideas through his brain. He decided he'd let things settle down for a while before going after the gold. "Ross'd still have it buried somewhere on his ranch," he figured. "And in time, he'll think everythin's safe, and I'll catch him with his guard down."

Slater was netting all kinds of morbid ideas in his dark mind, then he quietly gloated and chuckled. "I'll get the bullion and kill Ross at the same time. Five hundred pounds! . . . That's a lot of gold."

At daybreak, two days after our return with the gold, Pa and I rode down the lane to Joe's ranch with a peeking sun watching our every move. As we were dismounting at the house, the light glanced golden off our horses' flanks, and along the barn it brushed a pale lemon glow into the purple shadows.

Joe'd made plans to meet a cattle buyer that morning in Junction City and was unable to make the ride with us into Manhattan. By seven o'clock, Pa and I had loaded up the eight, fifty-pound gold bars on two pack horses. I'd not been in Manhattan more than a dozen times since coming to Kansas, but we wanted to make our deposit at the Wells Fargo there where we weren't as known. Andrew MacArthur had told Pa that the clerk and manager there was from Georgia, and a decent man.

We arrived and found the Wells Fargo office; the clerk was middle-aged, of average height, with a receding hairline, and wore dark-rimmed glasses. He'd been sitting down, but stood up when we entered. He peered askance at us when we each carried in a gold bar and laid them on the counter. After three more trips outside for more bullion, he had an unbelieving look on his face. He walked over to the door and looked out, but all he saw were our two riding horses and the pack horses.

He shook his head back and forth and whistled. "Man, that's a lot of gold! What do ya'all want me to do with it?" He had a distinctive Southern drawl.

"Put it in deposit," Pa told him.

The clerk stretched out his hand to Pa. "My name's Dal Peterson."

Pa introduced himself, then nodded my way. "This is my son B.J. Ross."

"Glad to meet ya, Mr. Peterson," I responded.

Peterson examined the bars. "That's a strange brand on the bars. Most bullion I've seen had an identification number on 'em." He walked over to his desk and pulled out some papers. Then, as though it was an afterthought, he walked over to his holster and handgun hanging on the chair, picked up the cartridge belt, and threw the belt around his hips.

He looked at Pa, then me, and smiled.

"That's a powerful lot of gold. I better be prepared if some undesirable would happen to get wind of that kind of wealth."

He went back to going through the papers on his desk. After maybe ten minutes, he said with an almost sheepish smile, "You're in luck. This gold isn't on the stolen list."

I spoke up. "I could have told ya that."

"I'm sure ya could, son, but I had to check it out. I'm full of questions, but if it's not stolen, it's none of my business."

Peterson walked to the front door and shouted. "Bill . . . come in here a minute."

Bill was loafing up the street and came running. "Yeah, Mr. Peterson, what can I do for ya?"

"Go over to the market and bring me back Larry's large scales. After that, I want ya to arm yourself, then get hold of Mike. I want the two of ya here for guard duty."

Bill took off across the street like he'd been shot.

Peterson peered over at Pa. "My scales only go to ten pounds and won't weigh those bars. I usually deal with no more than a couple pounds of metal."

Five minutes later, Bill brought in the scales. Peterson weighed each bar. "Fifty pounds exactly for each," he observed. "That's four hundred pounds.

"You have any idea how much money we're talkin' about?"

"Yeah," I replied. "I'd say around a hundred thousand dollars."

"That's right," he responded. "With that amount of gold in town, I'll have to hire at least two guards while it's here, and day after tomorrow I'll need an extra guard on the train when I ship it to Kansas City. I wish I could ship it today, but I'll have to make arrangements. I can't get shut of this gold too soon to suit me.

"What name should I use for the deposit?" he asked.

"Washington and Lee College, in Lexington, Virginia," I replied.

Surprised, Peterson peered over at me, then looked at Pa as though to ask if it was all right. Pa nodded.

I added, "I'd like the receipt for the deposit sent to the college with a letter tellin' that the money's from an anonymous source; the donation's to be used only in helping boys from the South that want an education but can't afford it."

The clerk's earlier uncertain attitude changed. I could see a look of respect in his eyes as he responded, "I'll personally take care of it. Just give me a few minutes.

". . . But could I ask ya . . . I've a nephew in Atlanta that's been wantin' to go to college for several years, but my brother just doesn't have the money. Would ya mind my writin' to my brother about your endowment?"

"No, sir, I wouldn't mind," I told him. "As a matter of fact, put the boy's name in the letter as someone I'd like the college to help."

Peterson was genuinely appreciative and thanked me, then turned away to attend to matters of business. Maybe fifteen minutes later he handed me a copy of the deposit and the letter. He looked over at Pa and asked, "Are you the Captain James Ross who was with General Jackson in the valley, and later with General Ewell?"

Pa acknowledged he was. "But mostly with the Stonewall Brigade."

Peterson nodded. "I thought so. I was from Georgia and fought with Longstreet — in late '64. There were rumors bandied about that you'd captured a large amount of Union gold from the warehouses at Culpeper. It passed through my mind that maybe this was part of that seizure, but you'd been wounded and captured, and all that bullion had been turned over to the Confederacy.

"People are nosey — and I'm no exception. As you carried in the bars I wondered how a homesteader in Kansas come by that amount of gold. But you know, it's really not my concern; and may God look kindly on generous souls."

I'd given the two remaining gold bars to Spencer to melt down. He had experience in blacksmithing, and would turn the bullion into one-ounce plain round coins — gold that we could turn to cash whenever we wanted.

It was mid-November when Joe caught me riding fence line. He'd seen Spencer the day before, and Spencer wanted Pa, Joe, and I to ride in as soon as possible. The next day, the three of us pulled up at Spencer's livery at around noon. The day was warm for late November. Spencer was sitting on an old wooden chair leaning back against the building and catching the warm reflecting sunlight. We dismounted and tied up at the hitching rail.

"Howdy men," Spencer beamed. "About time you hombres showed up. I was beginnin' to wonder what happened to ya!"

He got up from his chair. "You're just in time to eat. . . . It's on me."

The four of us walked side by side to the cafe, our boot steps echoing off the boardwalk.

Ham and beans with cornbread was the special of the day, and it was what we ordered. After a leisure meal we walked back to the stable, making small conversation, but Spencer spoke nothing of the gold. We walked into the barn, following him to the stock room. From underneath a pile of iron he pulled out four heavy leather sacks with drawstrings tight and set 'em on the counter.

"Help yourself boys."

Twenty-Three

THE FIRST FEW days of December had been pleasant, including the morning of the 5th, which brought with it a bright sunshiny day and the temperature hovering at forty degrees. But sometime that afternoon, the blue sky turned gray and the temperature started dropping. By six o'clock there were a few flakes of snow in the air, and a half hour later the snow thickened and the winds picked up. Visibility dropped, along with the temperature, to almost zero. I could barely make out the barn not over a hundred yards from the house.

I started a fire in the stove and was thankful I was inside. The storm raged, and sudden panic took hold. The nearby horses would be fine — they'd come to the barn for protection — but fifteen, including two colts and four fillies, were in the west pasture with no way home. I'd planned to bring 'em in to near the barn before the weather got bad. But it had been so nice the past week I'd just left them there in the plush grass. I knew I'd have to go get 'em.

I put on my heavy clothes, boots, sheepskin coat, scarf, and hat. When I opened the door, it flew from my hands, caught by the wind, bringing a gust of snow that settled across the floor.

Prince and Dandy were nearby in the barn, and even the clapboard siding couldn't keep the wind from swirling inside. I saddled Prince for the ride, and for once Dandy didn't seem to care. I covered him with a blanket for warmth and rode Prince out the barn doors, leaving 'em open for the horses when I'd return.

Snow had covered the dark earth of the ranch yard by this time, and although it was night, the atmosphere had a glow to it. The problem was you couldn't see anything over fifty feet away.

I angled into the north wind, keeping the ravine of trees over my right shoulder. I knew that'd get me close to the pasture gate. The pasture had no trees except for a few plum thickets, so landmarks would be hard to come by. It was a bitter cold wind that blew; my toes and fingers were starting to freeze.

When I reached the pasture fence, I opened the barbed-wire gate and laid it out of the way. To find the horses could be a problem, and with no windbreak for protection, they might be anywhere. With nothing to stop the winds in the high pasture, it roared unabated.

Angling into the blow made for hard going, but I figured the horses would be bunched in the small patch of plum trees for protection along the north fence. Prince kept wanting to turn downwind, but I wouldn't let him. It seemed like it took forever before I finally came to the fence. I reined Prince left and found the leafless plum thicket — but the horses weren't there.

By that time I was nearly frozen stiff, and didn't know where to look. Prince was still wanting to head in the opposite direction, so I let him go, thinking he probably had good reason. A half hour later, he found the horses with their backs to the wind along the south fence. I started pushing 'em to the west, and if the truth be known, I'd have been lost without the north wind, for all landmarks by then had been obliterated with a foot of blowing snow. The horses let Prince easily push 'em along the fence line. I think they figured wherever they were going things couldn't get worse.

An hour later, they were safe in the barn. With them out of the storm and cared for, I rushed to the house. On the way I grabbed a bucket of snow, taking it with me. Inside, I poured water over the snow and quickly put my fingers and feet into the cold water. It was what Ma always had me do for frostbite. The cold water felt warm to my icy hands and feet, and they soon were prickling like they were being stuck with a thousand needles.

But in another hour I felt fine, especially in the warm house, which seemed even warmer than it was because of the howling wind tearing at the eaves.

Morning came with a stillness that had an air of desolation to it. Even under a half-dozen quilts I could tell the air was below freezing in the bedroom. The only heat was a wood-burning cook stove in the kitchen. I figured there should be a few embers left to start a fire, but I also knew the stove would need more wood to heat the room. Though I hated the thought of stepping out onto the icy cold floors, I jumped out of bed, grabbed my clothes, and ran barefoot to the kitchen where very little heat radiated from the stove. I quickly dressed, put several pieces of split timber in the stove, and soon had a blazing fire going.

I scraped the frost off the kitchen window to look outside. Not a thing stirred. It was like nothing was left alive. A blanket of deep snow had covered the land, turning it into a neatly undulating plain that rounded over ditch, fence, and underbrush. Along the barn, huge drifts swirled upward, almost to the eaves. The outside was in a deep freeze, well below zero, and I'd not be going anywhere for a while; but I'd have to make a pathway to the barn to care for the horses. Except for my chores, I never stirred from the warm kitchen that day.

I thought of Joe, alone, not more than a mile away, but I knew he'd be safe. That old-timer had been dragged through the wringer, and he'd be prepared for any situation. Joe was no fool; he had no animals to care for except his riding stock. He'd thought it out carefully and wanted no cattle to care for in these winters.

Two days later, the country still lay frozen. Around ten that morning I looked out the window and saw Joe riding up the lane. He put his horse in the barn and walked to the house. When he stepped up on the porch, I opened the door.

I was never so glad to see anyone in all my life, and then I felt guilty. I should have been the one to go check on him. He reached out his hand. I took it and pulled him into a hug. We walked to the kitchen, and with a quick glance, I'm sure I saw tears fill his eyes.

We spent the day talking, and Joe helped with the chores as I fixed supper. We had rabbit, Irish potatoes, and Ma's canned peaches. I'd shot a couple rabbits before the snow, and they were delicious. I'd talked Joe into staying over for the night, and after cleaning up the table, we reminisced in the glowing halo of a kerosene lamp.

After a time, we sat idly without saying a word. Friends can do that and still enjoy one another's company. But I could tell Joe had something on his mind, and he finally asked, "Remember the time I told you I was married?"

I nodded.

"Well, it was a lady named Jane Thompson, from Boston."

"I see. I was curious, but figured if it was somethin' you wanted me to know you'd tell me."

"You're right; I don't like to talk about my marriage, B.J., it's been a thorn in my side for twenty-seven years.

"I was married for nine years before I walked away from the solemn commitment. Jane was from a wealthy family that'd lost everything. My family was well off when we met, and after a short courtship we married. Jane received a trust of ten dollars a month from her grandparents, but that was a mere pittance compared to the life she'd been accustomed to living before her family's financial troubles.

"I was not wealthy, but my father's mill, where I worked, paid me a hundred dollars a month. I apparently was the best catch Jane could find, something I never learned until later. It wasn't long, and I was soon under pressure from her to ask my father for a salary increase; but even so, our first year was fairly happy.

"Then in 1850, my father lost the mill, and I was unemployed. I worked at several different jobs and made enough for us to get by, but not enough for Jane, and things turned ugly. I could no longer support her as she liked, but I felt obligated to stay in the marriage to provide for her, as she had no skills of her own.

"My father had lost everything, but managed to salvage a trust that paid him fifty dollars a month. My parents lived adequately on the allotment and finished their lives happy together. When Father died in '52, and Mother in early '54, the trust was left to me. But after arranging for Jane to receive the monthly stipend, for as long as she lived, I left home.

". . . Last month, my attorney in Boston told me I had six hundred dollars he needed to send me from the trust, for Jane had died in October of '79."

Joe went into no specifics about Jane, but I knew his principles, and the marriage would've had to have been unreconcilable, something he felt he simply couldn't live with, for him to have left. It was a kindness for him to give Jane his trust so that she wouldn't have to live in poverty. Knowing Joe as well as I did, I could tell that whatever'd happened between him and his wife had left him deeply hurt.

I fixed Joe a pallet on the floor in the kitchen, by the heat of the cook stove. The next day warmed up to above freezing, and though there was very little melting of snow, the windless day felt like spring.

Twenty-Four

MY NEW FILLY Princess dropped her first foal in April of 1881, the prettiest blue-roan colt I'd ever seen, with a white blaze on his forehead. He'd hardly been born a minute when he popped right up on wobbly legs. It was two days before I came up with a name for him, then decided rightly to call him Blaze.

By August he was racing around the holding pasture like a thoroughbred. He'd tag alongside his mother wherever she went, then suddenly hop up in the air on all fours, and when he hit the ground he'd take off running, his tiny hooves thundering across the grass.

When I'd come out of the house in the mornings to do chores, he'd be watching for me and then race over to the pole corral by the barn, raise his right leg, and paw at the fence. Thoroughly excited, he'd crow-hop around, race off a short distance, and then return. He'd anxiously fidget, waiting for me to open the gate. Inside the corral, I'd pet him and whisper in his ear, then I'd curry him down. He loved the attention, and I was spoiling him, but I couldn't help it. When he was older would be time enough for discipline.

In early June, at daylight I was riding Prince and leading Dandy north down the road. Our little caravan was heading for the Brannick place on McDowell Creek. On my way I stopped by Joe's. He was ready when I rode up to the house, and quickly mounted his gelding for our trip. At breeding time, Dandy could be hard to handle, and Brannick had told me he'd have his son help, but I figured I'd need an extra hand.

Michael Brannick lived in a two-story stone house in the bottomlands of a plush valley watched over by the bluffs of bluestem hills. East of the house meandered McDowell Creek, maybe a half mile away.

Brannick had contacted me earlier about a mare he wanted bred. He'd thought the $50 stud fee high, but heard such good things from others who had used Dandy that he decided to pay the price.

I rode into the Brannick yard when the hour of the sun's sphere shone at ten o'clock. Brannick looked up from his work along the corral fence, and watched Joe and I approach to where he was working.

I greeted him, and introduced Joe as my friend and neighbor. We shook hands. Brannick's hands were strong and callused and you could tell they'd seen a lot of hard work. I'd heard he'd been a stone mason in Ireland, and in Kansas, along with his farming. Lately he'd worked for the Army at Fort Riley, building stables for the cavalry.

"So that's Dandy," Brannick observed, as he walked around the stallion. "He's surely a mighty fine-lookin' horse."

By that time Dandy had caught scent of the mare in the corral and was becoming restless and hard to hold. As we stood there talking, I could hear the hoofbeats of a horse galloping down the road. It turned into the lane and raced to a stop near where I stood, with an accompanying dust that quickly settled to the ground.

"Pa . . . I hope I'm not too late?"

Brannick acknowledged that the youth had arrived in time, and pointing my way said, "Son, this is B.J. Ross and Joe Woodman." Nodding to us, he added, "This is my son James; we call him Jim."

Brannick looked toward the stallion, advising young Jim that Dandy would be the stud for their mare. Jim was a tall, gangling boy that I figured to be around sixteen; I later learned he was a couple years younger. We shook hands with him as well, and whereas I'd thought his father had strong hands — and he did — Jim's were like holding onto a piece of steel. He was one strong lad.

Jim had rushed back from riding fence for the breeding. His Pa had told him that if he finished his work and got there in time, he could help. The boy was riding a handsome grulla, a mouse-colored horse with black mane and tail. I'd seen only a few, but they were all beautiful horses.

I peered at Brannick, asking where he'd come by the grulla.

"I bought him several years back, from a roamin' cowhand ridin' through the country from the Southwest."

I acknowledged he would have made a good stud.

Brannick agreed, though added, "But he was already a gelding when I bought him."

I heard a screen door slam at the house and saw another young man step off the porch. He was buttoning his shirt as he walked toward our group.

"My son, Josh," Brannick indicated with a swing of his arm.

Josh was older than his brother Jim, but I could tell from his handshake he was not as strong. He seemed irritated that Jim was there, and I saw a look in his eye that made me think of Satan.

The four-year-old mare in the corral was a fine horse. Brannick took his rope, threw a loop over the chestnut's head, then led her into the barn and into a stall. But I could see it was too narrow; I'd heard of men crushed to death in manger stalls.

I peered around at the well-built barn's interior, into a dim hue with a dust-like haze throughout. Blades of sunlight sliced through the darkness from cracks in the outer clapboard siding, giving the mangers and stalls a ghostly appearance.

I looked back at Brannick. "The stalls are too dangerous. We may have to bring the mare out into the open area of the barn."

Brannick mulled. "I have an old breeding stall outside along the west side of the building that's never been used. Tully, my neighbor helped me build the barn, and it was his thought at the time I should have a stall, so he built one for me. It's in an enclosed area where I do my shoeing."

I walked outside and saw that the stall would work perfectly. It was made of poles and laid at an angle from the ground to an approximate height of a horse's flank. It was narrow at the bottom and wide at the top, almost identical to what Pa and I used in our breeding.

We moved the mare outside near the stall. I'd left Joe with Dandy, but the closeness of the mare was overwhelming the stallion's passions as he stomped, fretted, and whinnied. The mare could hear the excited stud and was also becoming aroused. Brannick and Jim were holding her tight by her halter, as they moved her into the stall.

I had Jim put a leather mantle over the mare's shoulders and neck to protect her from any bites from the stallion, then I had Brannick put a pole through the stall behind the mare's rear legs to keep her from kicking. All Josh did was stand back and watch. I could see he'd be no help in handling the mare. I shouted for Joe to bring Dandy inside the fence. I grabbed the stallion's halter, but by then he was almost impossible to hold as he pulled me with him toward the mare. It was all I could do to keep his head down as he pulled and jerked it around, rolling his eyes, snorting, and flexing his neck muscles. The mare began to roll her head and twitch her furled-up tail, and both animals were now fully aroused.

As Joe and I brought the eager stallion forward, he whinnied and trumpeted, his body trembling with waves of lust. He rose up like a conductor over an orchestra, on his two hind legs, held a moment, and then crashed down on the mare's back.

A half hour later we mounted our horses and rode down the lane. Joe and I turned our geldings south as Dandy followed, stumbling along with his head down, completely spent. He looked nothing like the King of Beasts he thought he'd been an hour earlier.

August comes hot in Kansas, and the day was a scorcher. That year we were having a drought, and Joe's two springs had almost dried up. For thirty years, according to those in the area, the farmers and ranchers had never seen it so dry. Joe's cattle were without sufficient water and I was busy helping him haul it in barrels from Humboldt Creek. But even the creek was running low. We needed a rain, and soon. Pa's spring had dried up, but his well was still holding plenty of water, as was mine.

On one of our trips to fetch from the creek we met old man Poole riding his black gelding. We stopped to talk about the drought, of course. After some polite conversation, venting our concerns, Poole peered at us a moment and declared, "Don't fret, boys. It'll rain. It always does."

Then with a cluck to his horse, we watched him ride off, heading for home.

Joe looked at me, shrugging his shoulders. "Well, he ought to know, if anyone does in this country. But I'm gonna play it safe and keep praying."

It'd been almost a year since our trip to Council Grove, and I'd seen no sign of Slater. I was sure it was one of his henchman that'd watched us ride by the Saddlerock. I'd figured Slater would wait for a while before attempting anything, but not eight months. I was sure he'd come after me sooner or later; his hatred was too deep. Forgiveness was not in his make-up, and I'd need to remain wary. He'd not rest until I was six-foot under . . . but I knew it'd be harder to kill me than he thought.

It had always seemed strange to me how outlaws think. They have a different way of looking at things than most law-abiding folks. Even with the murder of an innocent victim, they'll find some excuse to rationalize the killing. I was sure Reggie's murder, in Slater's eyes, had been justified.

I knew Slater'd show up; it was simply a matter of time. It had even crossed my mind to put my work aside and hunt down the bushwhacker. I was at a disadvantage by being the hunted. At least if I took up the hunt, it would end the anxiety of waiting.

Poole was right. It rained in September, and that week we must have had six inches — a rain of blessing, with all the creeks and springs running water.

It was a Saturday, at around noon, when two people in a buckboard, pulled by two black mustangs, pulled into my lane. They looked like strangers to me, and I reached for my handgun. It wasn't there. I was out by the barn, and there was no way I could make it to the house before they did. I began to sweat until I could see one of 'em in the buggy was a woman. I realized it had been stupid not putting on my gunbelt. God was surely watching over me. Had it been Slater and one of his partners, I'd have been a goner.

The folks in the buckboard saw me standing by the pole corral and pulled the mustangs to a stop next to the house. Then I saw it was Susannah who'd jumped off the carriage. She ran over to where I stood and gave me a hug. Devon followed a few steps behind, with a smile on his face and outstretched hand. The Hamiltons had been in Atlanta for three years, and they said they had missed the West. Susannah whirled around with her arms spread wide.

"Devon, I love the prairie and the rolling hills! We have to get us a place just like this! Look at how good B.J. looks from living the country life."

"Suits me," Devon agreed, and turned to me. "You wouldn't know of a good ranch for sale?"

I acknowledged I didn't offhand. "But I'm sure we can find a place somewhere in the area. I'll ask around."

The Hamiltons were with me two weeks before they moved onto a spread of their own. But it was around ten in the morning, on their second day at my place, when Enie MacArthur rode up to the house on a strawberry roan mare. By that time I'd managed to have twenty quarter horses to care for, not including Dandy and Prince, and I was back of the barn in the holding corral shoeing horses.

Enie walked up to the house and knocked; when Susannah opened the door, Enie became flustered, not expecting a pretty young woman to answer. She asked, "Is B.J. home?"

Susannah knew at once that the beautiful young lady who had come a calling had a crush on me. "My name's Susannah," she offered.

"Nice to meet you. I'm a neighbor, Enie MacArthur. It was nothing important, and I'll be going on home. I was out on a ride and thought I'd stop by."

Enie was embarrassed, and she wondered about Susannah. But just as she was thinking that maybe I'd married without her knowing, Susannah added, "He's out back of the barn shoeing horses; come on, I'll go with you."

"Oh, no . . . maybe some other time. I'll just go on home."

Susannah insisted. "Come on, young lady, we'll go see B.J.," and she took Enie by the hand.

When I looked up from my work, two angels were walking around the corner of the barn. Surprised at their presence, I dropped the gelding's leg, straightened my back, and stood up to greet them.

Susannah called out, "B.J., you have a visitor . . . a pretty visitor."

I surely wasn't expecting to see Enie, and I know I must have blushed at her presence, but I regained my composure and welcomed her. "Enie!

. . . I'm so glad ya stopped. I been meanin' to come by your place to see ya; but it seems like there's always somethin' needin' done, and I'd put it off."

Before Enie could answer, Susannah interrupted. "Devon's out on a ride; he told me to tell you he'd be back before noon."

Enie looked at both of us. "Who is Devon?"

Susannah replied, "My husband. We became friends of B.J.'s several years ago."

I couldn't say if Susannah noticed the relieved look on Enie's face, but when Susannah invited her to eat with us, she accepted.

I smiled at Enie. "You can be thankful Susannah's doin' the cookin'."

Enie seemed delighted with the situation and asked Susannah, "May I help? I want to help."

"Sure, come on, we'll surprise the menfolk with somethin' good."

Holding hands and chattering like two schoolgirls, they walked to the house. A few minutes later I heard a commotion out by the chicken house, along with some squawking. I knew what we were having for dinner.

After our meal, Devon and I sat at the kitchen table drinking coffee as the girls cleaned up. When they'd finished with the dishes, Enie looked over and politely explained, "I'm going to have to leave. I've been gone from home longer than I should have, and I don't want mother and Andrew worrying about me."

After saying goodbye to the Hamiltons she walked to the door, and I followed. Outside I told her, "Hold up a minute, and I'll ride along."

Princess, my blue roan happened to be in the corral. She was with foal, and I liked to keep her close by.

"What a beautiful animal," Enie exclaimed. "I don't think I've ever seen a prettier mare."

I acknowledged, "She's beauty all right. She'll be droppin' foal in April."

I mounted up on Prince and we rode down the lane, reined our horses east over to the main road, then turned north.

We could see the MacArthurs' farmhouse and outbuildings when Enie stopped her horse and turned to me.

"I'd better ride on in by myself. No one knew I was going to your place.

It'd be all right with Ma, but Andrew is pretty protective; he might not approve."

"Well, sure, whatever you say." Then I hesitated for a moment, gathering my thoughts on how to ask to see her again, and I bluntly stammered, "Enie would you step out with me? I know you're seventeen, and I'm almost twenty-nine, but I'd like to take you to church Sunday if you'd go with me."

"I've been waiting for you to ask, B.J. I thought maybe you weren't interested. I'll be eighteen in April, and the age difference doesn't matter to me. Ma always said character was more important than age. But you'll have to get Ma's permission. Andrew might balk a little at first, but Ma and I can handle him. By the way, don't scare me anymore. When I saw Susannah I thought maybe you'd gotten married. I want you to know, you're not marrying anyone but me; that's my faith! It was my prayer two years ago, when I first saw you at the box supper."

Enie leaned over, gave me a kiss on the cheek, then rode off in a gallop to the house. Surprised at what had just happened, I sat unmoving on my gelding and watched. "*Well! . . .*" I thought to myself. *"Things are lookin' up."*

I rode home humming an old Scottish ballad that Ma would sing when she was happy.

Flow gently, sweet Afton, among thy green braes,
Flow gently, I'll sing thee a song in thy praise,
My Mary's asleep by thy murmuring stream,
Flow gently, disturb not her dream. . . .

Devon and I had found them a six-hundred-forty-acre ranch for sale north of Council Grove. When Susannah saw the place, she fell in love with it. From the bluffs you could see a panorama of prairie grass for miles. Below the cliffs the valley sloped gently for a half mile to the Neosho River, twisting its way through the rolling acreage, its waters gleaming blue through the fringing willow and cottonwood. It was a beautiful homesite.

The next day I rode to the MacArthurs. Andrew was out by the granary when I came up to the house. I tied Prince to the hitching rail and walked over to where Andrew was filling a gunny sack with corn. After shaking hands, I asked him for permission to date Enie.

To my surprise, he smiled. “Sure, if it will make Enie happy. That’s all that matters.” I thanked Andrew, and as I walked toward the house, Enie ran out the front door, grabbed my hand, and took me inside. I had a few tense moments when I asked Enie’s mother for permission to court her, but she seemed delighted and quickly gave her approval.

Sunday, I picked up Enie and we attended the Welcome Presbyterian Church. I remember little of the service, but I’ll never forget all the curious eyes following our footsteps when we walked in.

Twenty-Five

IT WAS LATE in September 1881 when the Hamiltons left for their new ranch. My place was going to be awfully quiet. I hated to see 'em go, and I'd especially miss Susannah's cooking. I still cared for the lass, but I knew in my heart that Enie would be the love for me; and surely it wasn't a crime to have loved two women in a lifetime.

An early October sun had finished brushing a golden light upon the dark shadows east of the barn when Joe came riding up to the corral on his favorite mahogany bay gelding. While waiting, my eyes canvassed a rainbow of autumn colors as far as the Humboldt rim.

Joe'd sold his cattle and had time on his hands. We visited a while, then I said, "Come on, let's go for a ride. I want to check my fence along the north line. I'm goin' to have to do a little work over there soon. Let's just take a look to see what I'll need; then we'll ride in to Junction City to see Spencer."

Joe acknowledged he was wanting to get away, to do something different.

We found the fence needed some tightening and a few posts, but it could wait. After riding my north line, we reined our horses west for the Humbodt Road. We passed beneath an autumn sun in prairie grass and wildflower that had blossomed into shades of pink, gold, amber, and rust. Patches of sumac had turned a dark red, alongside the golden dainty leaves of the locust that lay like lace on the arms of beautiful dark branches. In the distance, following along the creek and canyons with the remaining green, were the gold and reds of the cottonwood, walnut, and oak.

I looked around. "It's a beautiful sight. Nothin' much prettier than an autumn in Kansas."

Joe added, "Nor a prettier day than this one. But tomorrow could be different. We'd better enjoy the scenery while we can."

We spent the day in Junction City, visiting with Spencer. Later, it was already dark as I was ready to leave Joe at his ranch, and he handed me a sealed envelope.

"I want you to open this if anything ever happens to me."

I thought he sounded a bit melancholy, but I told him, "Sure, Joe, I'll keep it in a safe place."

I figured it was his will, but I didn't ask, nor did he tell me.

Enie and I were now going to church together every Sunday, weather permitting. On the nice days, we had family meals together. A few Saturdays, we'd go on a picnic. Enie would always fix the basket with the food I liked, and the recollection of those days has remained precious.

But, then, another cold winter was upon us, with snow as deep as fence posts for most of January. I loved Kansas, but the winters were not for the faint of heart.

March of '82 came in on the tail of a lion slipping on snow, with a north wind that was bitter and cold. But two weeks later it felt like spring.

After a week of warm weather I grabbed onto shovel, pliers, and two posts. I mounted Prince and took off to mend fence. By nine o'clock I was riding along my north line. I dismounted where the wire was dangling at a dry wash, where the winter had loosened the ground.

But before I'd started on the fence I noticed a boot print pointed south. Farther on was another print, only that one was heading north. I could see where someone had attempted to brush out their tracks in the shallow draw, and they were heading for the high ground behind the house.

I felt a shiver go through me. Someone as recently as that morning, by the looks of the tracks, had been spying on the house, and I knew once again my life was in jeopardy. I noticed there were two different prints — two people watching. They must not have been able to get in a good shot, however, and when they saw me riding their way I figured they took off. Lucky for me they missed brushing out a few of their tracks, for it was all the warning I'd needed.

I was almost certain it was Slater. I could see the flattened nest of grass and weeds in the brush where they'd lain in wait. Someone had broken off a few branches of a tree, leaving a clear sight from the crotch of a one-inch trunk — a perfect place to steady a rifle barrel.

The intruders had crossed my north fence, and I followed their tracks onto the next property to the west, which was Joe's place. Their tracks cut through the divide to a canyon of oak trees leading to the Humboldt Road. I hadn't gone far before I found horse tracks everywhere. I could see where they'd tied their mounts, and in the hidden draw they'd made no effort to erase the hoofprints.

One of the horses had a broken shoe. That had to be Slater! I'd had enough of him now, and we needed to have a showdown. In the next few days, one of us was going to leave this world. I was planning to ask Enie to marry me, and I couldn't be dodging Slater's bullets for the rest of my life. Not only that, but Enie'd be in danger too — something I couldn't tolerate.

I rode over to see Joe and told him what I'd found, explaining it as best I could. "I don't get it Joe; he's like one of them ugly bulldogs . . . he just won't give up."

Joe agreed. "And I've known others just like him; they go through life with a chip on their shoulder. I'd hate to spend my days like that myself, each day closer to death without any peace. If you want me to take care of him for you, B.J., I will. After all, he's crossing my property."

"No. . ." — I knew it was something I'd have to do myself. "I'll pray about it tonight, Joe. By mornin' I'll know what path to take."

Joe suggested we work together — set up an ambush for 'em.

I declined again. "Slater's my problem. It's me he wants; but the meetin' I'll set up won't be to his likin'."

The sun came up a bright gold the next morning, a beautiful late-March day that told a body spring was around the corner. I stood back from the window, peering at the high ground northwest of the house. A few minutes later, my fears were confirmed; I saw the gleam of sunlight on metal, no doubt a rifle barrel. They were there waiting for me to walk to the barn. From where the bushwhackers lay was a twenty-foot space between the buildings, where they'd have a clear shot.

I threw on my gunbelt and checked the cartridges in my Smith & Wesson, then stepped out my front door where they could get a glimpse of me. I started toward the barn. But before I reached the open space, I turned around, went back to the house, and walked inside, like I'd forgotten something. I went out the secret door back of the house, slipped down the shallow dry wash, out of sight of the outlaws, and into the back door of the barn.

I mounted up on Dandy, checked my .44 Winchester rifle, and slid it in the boot of my saddle. I rode out the barn doors and galloped by the open space before they had a chance to get in a shot. It must have been a shock to the ambushers when I passed by the clearing, down the lane, and turned east. Out of sight, I reined Dandy around to the west, taking a trail I used at different times. I just turned him loose, and that stallion could run.

I knew they'd be perplexed, but that was what I wanted . . . I wanted 'em to be uncertain and baffled as to what was happening. They'd be wondering how I'd gotten to the barn without them seeing me. It wouldn't be long, and they'd figure out that they'd missed gunning down their quarry. But I had plans for 'em. The outlaws would surely soon leave their lair of ambush and return to their horses.

When I reached the Humboldt Road, I reined Dandy north. Several miles later, I rode past the ravine the gunslingers would exit, and entered a plum thicket. From my hiding place I could see the opening of the gully onto the Humboldt Road.

A short time later, as I expected, the bushwhackers rode out of the ravine and turned north, in my direction. They were probably heading for Junction City. A minute later, I reined Dandy out into the road.

Slow, and in no hurry, I rode my stallion toward the two ruffians. I unlatched the thong holding my six-gun, then checked the chamber; it was full of cartridges. I was soon close enough to where Slater could recognize me. My rifle slid easy in the saddle boot, but in a hundred feet I'd not need it, for the handgun would be my choice.

The bushwhackers stopped their horses when we were thirty feet apart.

I rode Dandy closer, with my reins in my left hand. I wanted my right hand free. After I'd come to within fifteen feet of the gunmen, I reined Dandy to a stop.

"Slater! . . .You murderin' thieves lookin' for me?"

Slater's face was contorted with anger. When I glanced at the other hombre, he was obviously frightened; I could tell he wanted no part of a gunfight. Face to face wasn't the way Slater had planned for a showdown. He'd rather shoot an unsuspecting victim. He was angry to the bone, but wasn't about to be fearful, especially in front of his partner.

He growled, "I been lookin' for ya; now ya got to face a real gunfighter."

As Slater taunted, he was having trouble with his horse. The gelding didn't want to hold still. Dandy wasn't moving a muscle; he was used to doing what I asked of him.

I wanted Slater mad, and prodded back at him, keeping up the taunt. "Is that so? Then ya must be afraid of me, for all you've ever tried to do is shoot me in the back. You're not much of a man, Slater; you're nothin' but a yellow dog tryin' to be mean."

Slater was furious, and that was the way I wanted him. An angry opponent was apt to make a foolish move. His left eye twitched as he went for his gun, shouting his familiar "*Die Ross!*"

But I'd slapped leather when his eye twitched and put two bullets right through his heart. I wanted to make sure it ended then and there, at that time and place.

He got off a shot a fraction behind mine, but his horse flinched from his movement and the bullet didn't even come close. Realizing he'd been fatally hit, Slater peered at me with panicky eyes; he tried to speak, then slowly slumped over and slid off his saddle. He lay there unmoving as the ground turned red beneath him. His horse shied away from the blood, and walked over to the ditch, where he started munching grass.

Slim sat his saddle with his hand away from his gun and called, "Don't shoot! I'm out of it!"

I calmly suggested, "If ya want to try me, I'll put my six-gun back in its holster."

"No . . . no! I'd never make it; and anyway I'm glad Slater's dead. He was a cruel man, and I've been tryin' to get away from him for the past year without bein' killed."

"Well, okay, then we got some talkin' to do. Tell me your name."

"Clyde Dillon . . . they call me Slim."

"And where're ya from, Slim?"

"El Paso, Texas," he replied.

"How would ya like to head for El Paso?" I asked.

"I'd like to go home; only this mornin' I was wishin' I could see my Ma and Pa."

I fixed him in the eye and said, "Tell ya what, Slim, if ya promise to go to your Ma and Pa, ya can leave right now. But I don't ever want to see ya again.

"There's only one thing you'll have to do first, and that's lay Slater across his horse and bury him someplace far south of here. His horse, saddle, and whatever else on his person is yours."

Slim seemed relieved. "I'll do it; ya won't see me again. And I've decided somethin' else, mister. I plan on goin' straight, for it'd break Ma's heart if she ever found out I'd been an outlaw."

"Good for you. Now which direction are ya ridin' from here?"

"South."

"Right answer, Slim . . . and have a good trip."

I watched him leading Slater's horse until he was out of sight, then I rode home. Except for the memory of the killing, it was a wonderful ride, into a mid-morning sun gleaming its ownership of the countryside. For the first time in years I felt like I didn't have a lion by the tail.

The 8th of May was Enie's birthday. She was eighteen. Early that morning I gave her Princess as a gift.

I spent the day at the MacArthurs, and before I left for home that evening I proposed to Enie. She accepted, and told me later it was the happiest day of her life.

Twenty-Six

ONLY A FEW days were left in the month of May when Joe rode into my ranch yard. I'd never really taken the time to realize it before, but Joe was like another father to me. We were not just the best of friends, but right then I felt the love that men can have for each other, a love built on trust and respect. With admiration, I peered at Joe riding tall in the saddle. He was wearing jeans, western boots, blue shirt, red kerchief, and gray flat-crowned hat. Joe was a real honest-to-goodness man of the West.

When I'd first met Joe, he looked the part of a miner, and he was a miner — a Harvard University graduate that, had he stayed East, would have probably been the president of some company by that time. It came to me Joe could have been anything he wanted in life. He had that practical competency some few men achieve; and besides that, there was no greed in the man.

When he dismounted, we shook hands, then he told me he was going to take a few days and ride up the Blue River valley north of Manhattan, an area he'd been through by wagon train way back in the '50s. He'd been impressed with the plush grass bottomland, high-shouldered hills, and erosion-slashed canyons. The Big Blue River meandered throughout the valley and reminded him of a great creek full of long deep holes and flashing riffles. He had me convinced it was one of the most beautiful places in Kansas, and said he wanted to see it again before he died.

I agreed that some time off would be good for him, adding, "But as for dyin', Joe, you've got a lot of years left before you pass on!"

"I don't know, B.J."

I was taken back. "Now wait a minute, Joe, watch your mouth. I come against such talk."

"Well, it's just a feeling I have."

"No matter, cast it out, then have the faith you'll live forever!"

Joe laughed. "Okay, but you're young B.J., and youth ignores the passing of years. I've come to the conclusion that life is really one level after another. When we attain the level we been striving for, we reach for another. What was most important before is not important anymore, and we strive for something different. It's a struggle we have throughout our years, but we need that struggle to make us a better person.

"You know, money was important — essential — to me early in life, but it's not anymore, and hasn't been for a long while. And many times we're devastated by a happening in our life, and we think some evil-doing has occurred, but I've found that things usually happen for a reason, and life turns out for the better. Struggles and disappointments can be a blessing in disguise, though at the time you don't think so. They can also be a stepping stone into a better world that wouldn't be attainable any other way.

"It's only recently, B.J., that I've discovered what's important to me now has nothing to do with my physical senses; it's my spiritual being, to attain righteousness, that I might walk boldly into Heaven to meet my Maker, that moves me."

Silence followed us into the house, for I remained speechless after Joe's words. Later, sitting in the kitchen, we continued our conversation and I could see in Joe's face that he searched for something stored away in what I'd called the archives of his mind. He again recited one of his many recollected poems.

O Death! the poor man's dearest friend
The kindest and the best!
Welcome the hour my aged limbs
Are laid with thee at rest.

The great, the wealthy, fear thy blow
From pomp and pleasure torn;
But O, a blest relief to those
That weary-laden mourn!

I was reluctant to guess Shakespeare this time, and hesitantly asked, "Who was the author of those fine words?"

Joe replied, "One of your fellow countrymen. Robert Burns."

"Ah, Ma's favorite poet, and from Scotland, no less."

"No less," Joe replied, and followed with two more lines of verse.

No one lives equal, or free from fear,
But death lays equal on earth's bier.

"More Burns?" I asked.

"No . . . Joe Woodman," he chortled, and looked at me with a sheepish grin.

"Okay," I said, "I'm gonna quit guessin'. I can't win for losin'."

I thought about what Joe'd said on what was important to him, and it brought to memory an awakening I'd had back in Virginia.

"You know, Joe, when I was about twelve, I had a good lesson in what's important in life. I was with Ma in Leesburg one day, the seat of Loudoun County where we lived. Our farm lay in the foothills of the Blue Ridge Mountains, some twenty miles from town, but Leesburg was where we went to buy our staples.

"I'd spotted a saddle at the leather shop that I thought I had to have . . . handsome brown leather with silver studs. But they were askin' fifty dollars for it, and we didn't have that kind of money.

"I told Ma that I'd prayed to God for the saddle, and she said she figured in that case we'd better save up . . . but to remember that faith must have patience.

"Whenever we went to Leesburg, Ma would take along eggs, cream, and churned butter to sell. After we'd bought our supplies from those sales, Ma would lay aside what she could for the saddle.

"Each time to town, I'd go in the store and in my mind I'd claim the saddle for my own. Though I'd worried someone would take it before we could save up enough, two years later it still waited for a buyer.

"In November of that year, I checked and counted forty-six dollars in the jar where Ma kept the money tucked away. Then early in December, Ma got a letter from her cousin Martha Bentley, in Leesburg. Besides the usual chitchat, the letter contained news about Jessie Craig, one of Ma's school classmates and a close friend. Ma took me aside and told me she was going to town in the mornin'. I'd never thought much about it at the time, but it wasn't like her to go off on her own.

"I had saddled the roan mare for Ma to ride, and when she mounted the horse she gave me last-minute instructions on the care of the children that day — especially Robert, who was only ten months old at the time. By horseback, Leesburg was a four- to five-hour ride, but since Ma had left at seven that mornin', I figured she'd be home before six in the evenin'. At eight, I was gettin' worried; then, finally, around ten she came ridin' up the lane. I met her outside and took the mare to the barn while she went inside to the children. I was the man of the house those days, and had been since Pa went off to fight with Stonewall Jackson in '61.

"That night, when the sun went down, it turned even colder, and when I walked to the house carryin' a bucket of milk, it was already startin' to freeze. Early the next morning after breakfast, Ma told me to harness the two plow horses and hook 'em up to the spring wagon; we were goin' back to Leesburg, and would probably stay the night with her cousin Martha.

"I did as I was told, and maybe a half hour later I reined the horses and wagon up to the house, then set the brake and went inside to fetch Ma and the kids. She and the girls were soon carryin' the eggs, cream, and butter to the wagon. Then they brought out blankets, I figured to keep themselves warm on the trip. Ma had me go to the hillside cellar back of the house and get two big hams and a half of beef. I looked at her, questionin' in my eyes, since that was the biggest share of our perishables laid up for the winter. But she repeated what she wanted, and in short order I had the meat loaded. What else the girls had in the wagon, I didn't know at the time.

"When I walked in the kitchen, Ma was takin' the money out of the jar.

"It was just about daylight when I crawled up into the box beside Ma, who was holdin' James bundled up tight in blankets The three girls in the bed of the wagon were also covered. I scrunched down in my sheepskin coat and shouted . . . *Gee! Haw!* I snapped the reins of the horses, and they jerked into their harness as we thundered and rumbled down our frozen earth lane to where I tooled a right turn on the road to town. A mile later, we stopped at the Thompsons and arranged for them to do our evening chores. That afternoon, we pulled into Leesburg with the temperature still well below freezin'.

"Ma had me stop at the creamery first, to sell our produce. Then she told me to stop at the General Store, where she bought canned goods and unperishables, like sacks of flour and sugar, a large can of coffee, and some other items. What Ma was up to I was uncertain, but she was spendin' quite a bit of money, and when I suspicioned she'd dipped into my saddle money, an ugly feelin' came over me.

"After loading the supplies, Ma told me to take her to James Lofton's place, two miles from town. Lofton was a friend of Pa's. Ma knocked on the door, and I heard only a part of their conversation; but when I saw her payin' him thirty dollars for cord wood to be hauled to Jessie's place, it made me angry. I knew then that Ma was usin' my saddle money. I'd been holdin' James, and after their bargainin' was finished, Ma crawled up in the box beside me and took James from me. She could see I was mad. I felt I deserved the saddle for all the work I'd done the last three years.

"But Ma just put her hand on my arm and said, 'Take me to Jessie's.'

"I'd been there a few times and knew where the place was, but I'd turned stubborn and, what's worse, selfish. I never moved the horses. Ma turned to me and sternly snapped, 'Come on, Bruce Jacob! Let's go!'

"Ten minutes later we pulled into the Craigs' yard. I'd forgotten how run-down the shack of a place had been, and then remembered the Craigs never did have much in the way of niceties. It was comin' onto dark and gettin' colder when Ma softly knocked on their door. A boy about eleven answered, saw us all standin' outside, and shouted, 'Ma! Company's here!'

"I was shocked the boy had no shoes; his feet were wrapped in burlap. Jessie invited us in, and the house was ice cold. The stove had a small fire, but it gave little heat; they had no wood, only small scraps of sticks they'd picked up along the road. There was no food in the house, and I was shaken when I realized they were in truth starvin' to death.

"For many years, since the two had married, Ma and Jessie had only occasionally seen each other. Jessie's husband had been killed at Gettysburg, leavin' her with the four children, aged two to eleven. They were poor to begin with, livin' in that shack about a mile north of Leesburg, and even when George was alive, it'd been a struggle. But now I'd learned, for more than a year times had been even harder for Jessie. Her only means of survival had been doin' laundry for some of the townsfolk.

"Then in August, Ma told me, Jessie became sick and unable to work. She'd been ill for three months and with no income, and things worsened until there was no heat to speak of, nor food in the house. That was the state Ma'd found her in the day before.

"As we were standin' inside the door, Jessie walked into the room, lookin' frail, almost like a ghost. When the girls started haulin' in food, she broke down and cried.

"'Don't you worry none, Jessie,' Ma said, holding Jessie in her arms. 'We're gonna see this through 'til things turn right.'

"The two women standin' there together, both cryin', brought tears to my eyes too, and I fought it as hard as I could without a lot of success. With the staples now inside, the girls started haulin' in clothes and shoes. Ma told Jessie they were clothes we'd outgrown, but I swear I saw some of mine in the batch that I still was wearin', includin' a pair of boots. Yet by that time I didn't care; I'd have given the Craigs the clothes off my back.

"Just then Mr. Lofton pulled up into the yard. I could see his wagon filled to the top with split wood. Ma'd heard it comin', and looked over at Mrs. Craig.

"'Jesse, Mr. Lofton has promised you'll have a year's supply of split wood.' Then Ma said to me, 'B.J., go out and help Lofton unload the wood, and bring in enough to get a good fire goin' so these children can get warm.'

"Ma looked upon the Craig youngsters as children, and for a quick moment I wondered if she ever looked at me in that way. Jessie's oldest boy was only a year or two younger than me. But I knew that Ma had come to depend on me so much over the past three years that I believed she thought I'd outgrown bein' a child.

"When I brought in the wood and built up the fire, Jessie couldn't contain her tears. An hour later, when the old house was warm and cozy, she was feelin' better. Ma even got her to laugh at somethin' that'd happened years before.

"It was midnight by the time we got to cousin Martha's to spend the night. The next day we went home.

"It was close to three in the afternoon when we turned the horses down our lane. Followin' upon us were a few scattered snowflakes.

"It took me an hour to unharness and care for the horses, and when I walked into the kitchen, Ma was puttin' two dollars in the jar. As she turned, I could see the tears that filled her eyes.

"'I'm sorry about the saddle, B.J., . . . we'll save up again.'

"Well, you just know I felt ashamed for any earlier anger I'd had, and I tried to reassure Ma. 'It's okay . . . my old saddle's fine. I don't want the saddle.'

"'You don't *want* it? . . .Why?' Ma asked.

"I remember tellin' her, 'The saddle's just not important anymore.'"

Joe and I sat quiet for a spell in the silence of the room. I was listening to the ticktock of the clock, when he hesitatingly spoke.

"Too bad you didn't get your saddle."

"But, I did," I broke in. "God left it under the Christmas tree two years later, in '66! I'd come to forget about it, but I should have known He'd see to it. I imagine it was settled with Him that first time I prayed.

"I learned later that Ma had gone to Carson, the owner of the General Store, and told him about my prayin' for the saddle; he removed it to the back room, where he'd held it for her. Later, when I was in the store and saw that the saddle was gone, I figured it'd been sold.

"You know, it'll always be my favorite."

Joe nodded. "I knew you sat a handsome saddle; and that's quite a story behind it. . . . But whatever happened to the Craigs?"

"Well," I told him, "it was like a miracle the way things turned out. It's amazin' what God can do if you ask Him.

"By springtime, Jessie was well again. She had so much laundry work from the townsfolk, the girls had to help out; and then Jason, the oldest boy, went to work for Sam Jones at the local livery. With the money Jessie took in, and what Jason made, they were able to live independently again.

"Speakin' of Jason Craig, I remember the time we went to Leesburg in '65. It was May, and Pa was home from the war. We once again stayed the night in town with Ma's cousin Martha.

"There was a school program that evenin', and after cleanin' up a bit, we made our way to the schoolhouse. The room was full of chattin' people when we arrived, but the program soon started, and the visitin' quieted. After several skits and poems, a choir of some twenty students, six to sixteen, filled the stage. Jason, on the back row, was among 'em.

"I'd always loved a group singin', and they were just wonderful; at times you could hear Jason's marvelous voice above the others. Then, at the close of the program, the choristers sang one of my favorites, "Amazin' Grace."

"Ma and Jessie were sittin' next to each other, and toward the end of the song, with the room immersed in the melody, I peered at 'em. Together, as one, tears were flowin' down their cheeks.

"I knew they were tears of joy for where God had brought that family."

Twenty-Seven

WHEN I'D FINISHED my story, Joe continued his description of the Blue River valley as he remembered it from years past, and when he asked me to ride along, I accepted. Before sun-up a week later, he was riding his mahogany gelding and I was on Prince, leading a bay pack horse down the trail from Joe's ranch. Dandy was getting on in years, so I'd decided to take the younger horse on the trip.

It was still dark when we reached the main road leading to McDowell Creek, and along the shoulder of the hill silhouettes of distant trees were fringed against the dark sky. Then slowly the trees began to take on shape as the sun rose above the hills, chasing reluctant shadows with a golden paint brush. From the rimrock we stopped to watch the country put on a primrose mantle moving down vistas of awakening canyons.

The sunlight rode warm upon our shoulders when we crossed the Kansas River at a low-water riffle, in the fading hue of an afternoon light. The cool water hummed around our horses' hocks as they splashed their hooves to the north side of the river. Our tired but eager mounts buck-jumped up the bank, and from there we took a trail meandering beside the wide river-bottom basin of mostly sandbars and driftwood. Young willow trees edged up to the stream of flowing water that twined throughout the riverbed. As we moved down the beaten dark earth of a game trail, songbirds were flittering in and out of verdant plum and gooseberry thickets.

The country was peaceful, and the contentment on Joe's face convinced me I'd done the right thing by coming along. I'd thought for a while that maybe he'd asked me out of courtesy; but now I felt sure he wanted my company.

I thought to myself that most adventures needed to be shared with someone, especially beautiful sights and the wonders of the world. Though there were times when you needed to be by yourself, particularly when you'd fellowship with God. I'd had my best conversations with Jesus when alone in the wilderness. One of those times was when I lay wounded in the Colorado Rockies, healing in the fresh mountain air of the hanging meadow. After hours of conversation, and questioning the finality of death, Jesus had convinced me that my spirit would live forever. I remember that conversation as if it was yesterday.

"*Have you made Me the Lord of your life?*" Jesus asked.

"*Yes,*" I replied.

"*Do you believe Me when My Word says I am in you and you are in Me?*"

"Yes, I do."

"And do you believe I am Love?"

"Yes, it's Your Word."

"Then you are Love, for I am in you."

"*. . . Can Love die?*" He asked.

"*No, Love will live forever,*" I answered.

Then Jesus affirmed, "*There's your proof.*"

We camped in a grove of trees full of walnuts and squirrels. Joe built a fire, and I staked out our horses where they could crop grass and reach water. After supper, I lay back on my groundsheet and watched the squirrels chasing each other among the high branches, leaping ten feet or more onto another limb-bending tree.

Night came to us with the hoot of an owl that sat on a dead branch outlined against the blackened sky. Minutes later he leaned out and swooshed off the limb, on the hunt, soaring down darkened hallways of trees. I listened to the flow of the river singing to my soul, and was soon asleep.

Just past sunrise the next morning, we rode by a farmhouse and listened to a rooster claiming sovereignty over all the country. We found a game trail down the steep bank of Wildcat Creek, where I urged Prince into the stream and felt his feet go out from beneath him. After a short swim, he was on the north bank. Minutes later we rode into Manhattan, a sleepy little village at the business of waking up.

Although I'd been in the town before, I once again peered at a small oasis in a large basin lying between the confluences of the Kansas and the Big Blue Rivers. The peaceful area was surrounded by a ring of hills some two hundred feet high. In reality, the wide Kansas River bottom lay open to the east. You just couldn't see it because of the overlapping hills. Throughout that enormous basin, the Kansas River meandered about with sharp curving bends, and adding to the basin were the confluence valleys of the Big Blue River and Wildcat Creek.

We crossed the Rock Island and Union Pacific tracks, then we rode past the McClusky Hotel and Saloon. The three-story, nondescript frame building at one time had been given a coat of paint, but now wore a weathered gray patina. Just north, the Union Pacific depot could be seen amidst the morning silence, except for the ticking away of the telegraph. Three middle-aged men and a young couple sat on wooden benches between the depot and the tracks, apparently waiting for the train that was blowing its whistle in the distance. To our right, angling across the Kansas River, loomed the newly completed seven-span wooden-trussed bridge of the Manhattan, Alma, Burlington Railroad, its track curving into the depot. The main street of the town was part of the Military Road from Fort Leavenworth, maybe seventy-five crow-fly miles northeast, to Fort Riley, just off to the west.

We reined our horses west onto Main and rode by the General Store. The wind-blown block had a land office, the Wells Fargo station, an apothecary shop, and a cafe, bakery, barber shop, and hardware store.

Back down the street we heard the thunder of hooves and racing wheels crossing the wagon bridge over the Big Blue. Built eleven years earlier, in '71, the bridge replaced the ferry. When we turned, we saw the

Concord stage breaking to a fast stop in front of Wells Fargo to let two passengers step off.

It was early, and few people walked the boardwalks. No more than five wagons were parked on the street. Seven chimes rang from the clock on the courthouse when we pulled into the livery next to King's blacksmith shop. Platt was the hostler's name, and he was an encyclopedia of information. From the livery to the northwest, maybe a mile away, sat a large structure on a low hill. Platt told us it was the Kansas State Agricultural College. From where we stood, a few scattered houses lay between us and the college.

After stabling our horses, Joe and I were hungry, so we walked to the cafe. A dingy, unkempt place met our eyes when we entered, and with some feeling of uncertainty we sat at a table next to the wall. A thin but comely waitress took our order, then shouted it to the cook. She soon returned with our bacon, eggs, and fried potatoes, and we found that despite our concern for how the place looked, the food was delicious.

We walked the town, which didn't take long, and had almost decided to pack up and leave, to camp in the wilds, when we entered the McClusky Saloon. It was afternoon by that time, and we ordered a shot of rye. The bartender, Travis McClusky, was a large man — not tall, but wide — with red thinning hair. His arms and hands were huge, and when greeted, my hand felt lost in his grasp. I'd want no part of a fight with that Irishman, but I soon learned he was a gentle soul, unless you were stupid enough to somehow get crosswise with him.

"Where you boys headin'?" he asked.

I answered for us. "We're goin' up the Big Blue River valley, maybe as far as Randolph."

"Aye," he nodded. "Many a man that travels the valley with eyes to see says there's no prettier place in the universe. Been that way a few times myself. There's nothin' like it around. Past Garrison, on the east side, there's a place above the rimrock called the Little Gobi Desert. I've not seen it, but those that have told me it's an amazin' sight of high desert with a few plum trees and prickly pear in the dunes of sand."

"I've never heard of such a place," Joe responded.

McClusky acknowledged he was certain it was there, he'd just not had the time to witness it for himself.

We spent the rest of the afternoon talking to McClusky. The saloon also served as a cafe, and the south half of the room was full of tables and chairs. Along the south wall was a bench the length of the room. McClusky had said that at times they'd clear out most of the tables and chairs for dances.

Toward evening, we still sipped on our one shot of rye, and McClusky laughed. "You boys sure are heavy drinkers! If everybody took as much as you do, I'd have to close the place! . . .

"But," he continued, "I'm not a heavy drinker myself, and I've never understood the thinkin' of a drunk. They usually end up losin' all the things that were at one time dear to 'em."

I acknowledged he was right. "From what I've seen, liquor's nothin' but trouble. As for myself, I want to know what I'm doin' at all times, and with my senses alert."

By that time, the place began to fill up with railroaders, and we'd decided to stay over for the night. We ordered a supper of steak and potatoes, and after I'd eaten I became sleepy. Joe and I found our room, and by eight o'clock I was in bed.

We stayed in Manhattan another day before heading up the Blue. That last evening, when Joe and I'd stepped into McClusky's saloon, we'd shouldered up to a busy bar to visit a spell, and ordered a cup of coffee. Unable to talk to McClusky, I turned around with my back to the bar and looked at the room full of patrons. At one of the far tables, across from us, a man with a black flat-crowned hat seemed to be looking at me. When I fixed my eye on him, he looked away. A few minutes later, he and his partner were gone.

It could have been an innocent happening, but something told me I needed to be cautious. I didn't recognize the hombre, but there was something familiar about him I couldn't quite grasp.

We'd had Platt get our needed supplies, and he had 'em on our pack horse when we walked into the livery at five o'clock the next morning. When we rode out the livery's double doors, it was still dark, but for a gray ribbon lining the eastern hills. We headed north, west of the Blue River and along the Union Pacific tracks.

After several miles, as we left the basin, the gray ribbon along the hills had turned to gold.

Twenty-Eight

WE RODE A FAIR country in plush bluestem grass, and by mid-morning the valley had narrowed to a couple miles. The river's long pools of deep water and white rapids rushing between high clay banks was a beautiful sight. It became obvious to me, while studying the clear pools of lazy water reflecting a vast sky, how the Big Blue River came by its name — a name that fit the land.

The bluffs moved high above the valley, along the sky, watching our every move as we slowly plodded north. Around noon we neared Stockdale, not much more than a whistle stop on the Union Pacific.

We met four weary cowhands heading south, and they stopped to talk. They were from the Germann Ranch, looking for twenty head of rustled cattle. The day before, one of the cowhands had thought the herd of a hundred head seemed short. They soon found where the fence had been cut, and followed the tracks of the missing animals. They'd been driven to the river, and that was where the cowhands lost the trail. Jim Hedke, the foreman, asked if we'd keep a lookout for the cattle as we traveled north, and I acknowledged we would. Hedke was from the area, and had told me his folks lived on a homestead near Randolph.

But during our conversation, I noticed that one of the cowhands wouldn't look my way. I realized it was the same cowboy I'd seen glancing at us over at McClusky's. And then it hit me; he was Josh Allen, the outlaw that at one time rode with Luke Dillard, and with Slater, when Reggie had been killed. He was the hombre who'd promised me he'd head for Missouri. I hadn't recognized him earlier because he now had a long scar across his jaw, and it had altered his looks. I peered over at him.

"Hello, Josh; how were things in Missouri?"

"Oh, . . . h'llo Ross," he answered, then said no more.

Hedke was surprised we knew each other.

I explained we'd met in Dodge City several years ago. Meanwhile, I could tell Josh was nervous, wondering what I might say to Hedke. He turned to me.

"I went to Missouri like we talked, did some loggin', then I couldn't find work, and when I heard the Germanns were needin' hands, I applied." He hesitated a moment, then continued. "I thought takin' the job as a cowhand was the right thing to do."

There was silence for a moment. The cowhands didn't know what was happening, and you could tell by their expressions that they were puzzled by Josh's remarks. I decided to give him the benefit of any possible doubt.

"Good, Josh, I'm glad ya took this job. I wondered at the time if ya wouldn't be happier in Kansas, where ya could find work as a wrangler."

As I looked around, it seemed the questions in the minds of Josh's comrades were relieved, and he relaxed.

"Yeah, it gets in your blood," Josh replied.

After leaving the cowhands, I told Joe the story about Josh Allen and Luke Dillard. I'd hoped that Josh had nothing to do with the rustling, and that I wasn't making a mistake by not revealing his past to Hedke.

When we'd left the wranglers, we'd headed into Stockdale. Besides the train stop, to load up with water, there was a blacksmith shop, cafe, livery, and General Store. But we continued on into the purple shadows of the looming western hills, as the sunlight gleamed on the river valley and steep shoulders of the rolling eastern landscape.

We camped in a grove of cottonwood where the river made a sharp bend that swung around from the east and back to the south, near the hills on the west. Below our camp flashed a gravel riffle of splashing white water for several hundred feet, and then it widened out into a deep long pool. By that time the sun had dropped below the purple hills and was painting a pink sunset.

That evening we caught four catfish below the riffle, and Joe cooked 'em for our supper. After fussing with the horses, I was soon under cover, and listening to the night sounds. Suddenly a lonely coyote howled to the sky. I could see him through a break in the trees where he'd skylined himself atop the hill, head arched high, as if speaking plaintively to God.

Morning turned from midnight black to gray with almost no visibility. A fog ghosted the trees into uncertain depths, and like thieves in the night they appeared as if waiting for an unsuspecting victim.

After a quick breakfast, we mounted our horses and rode blindly a game trail to higher ground. From the river bottom and above the floodplain in the foothills we rode out of the fog into sunlight. Looking back, the fog followed the river, and its bank of accompanying trees, like a living serpent. This was a fascinating country of abrupt grassy hills and steep promontories, interspersed with tree-infested canyons of twisting creeks making way to the river.

Joe told me we were close to the area where his wagon had crossed the Big Blue in 1854 on his way west.

"I'd partnered up with another man who owned a wagon, and we camped in a grove of walnut not far from here, along with fifteen other wagons. That night I came upon a stranger, and the way he appeared out of nowhere was frightening."

"Who was he?" I asked.

"A hunter, who just came out of the darkness. It was a moonlit night, and I left our campsite, went down the steep bank, and crossed a gravel bar to the river. I sat on a boulder, watching the calm water reflecting moonlight and, in its depths, the shimmering movement of a thousand stars.

From beside me came a voice: "*It's a beautiful night. . . .*" Then he stood before me, a tall man with dark-black hair. I almost jumped out of my skin, and how he'd gotten there without me hearing him I'll never know. There had been no movement or footsteps in the gravel; all at once he was just there. He wore pants and shirt of deerskin, but no hat, and undoubtedly was a trapper and hunter. He had with him a .44 Henry rifle in his right hand and a bowie knife behind his belt.

"I introduced myself and asked, 'To whom might I be speaking?'

"'Jon Drapeau,' he announced. 'And I've been livin' and hidin' in these parts since '48. It's been a chore keepin' my scalp, but I still got my hair. First it was the Wyandotte after me, until they became friendly in the winter of '49–'50. Then it was the Osage, back in '52. Since that time its been fairly peaceful, except for a few renegades tryin' to make a name for themselves. But I've stayed one step ahead of 'em.'"

Joe had me intrigued.

"We must have talked for an hour, when I heard a noise in the bush. Whatever it was captured my attention, and when I looked back, Drapeau was gone. He just simply disappeared, again without making a sound.

"I've wondered the past few days if he's still in these parts. If he is, and wants to show himself, he will. I don't think there was much that went on hereabouts without him knowing of it."

We took our time that day riding north along the base of the western hills, and toward evening we angled a path upward until we breasted the rimrock. We buck-jumped our horses through an eroded split in the ledge, wide enough to take our horses through the rift, then rode over to the rock-topped rim of the promontory cliffs and dismounted.

While Joe and I looked at the panoramic view of the valley, our horses wandered into the deep grass to eat. To the west lay Fancy Creek, and to the northeast meandered the Big Blue River. Fancy Creek rolled out of the far western hills and meandered over to the promontory, where it cut into the hillside bank below our observation point. It was a twisty creek of running riffles and deep holes as far as eyes could see. It reminded me of Mill Creek, a mile below the town of Volland, the cattle-loading rail head, founded when the Rock Island built track from Alma to Alta Vista.

Below Fancy Creek, to the east, along the base of the hill, ran the dirt road from the south. To the right of the road lay the Union Pacific tracks. At the place where the promontory probed out and then curved back west, the road continued north and crossed the Fancy Creek wagon bridge into the town of Randolph.

We mounted our horses and angled back down off the Randolph bluffs to the road. In minutes, and with thundering hooves, our horses crossed the bridge. The town sat on a plateau some ten to fifteen feet above the river bottom to the northeast. The road we traveled went along the east side of a square that was a park with a covered bandstand at its center. Roadway also traversed the other three sides of the park. On the far side of the road were located the town businesses — I recall a General Store, feed store, clothing store, and doctor's, lawyer's, and land offices. East of the main road, across from the park, were a cafe, livery, and blacksmith shop.

We camped out that night and spent the next day looking at the scenery. That evening we checked into a boardinghouse north of the square, and early the next morning we reined our horses south. At noon we stopped, and fixed a bite to eat. We relaxed beneath the limbs of a mulberry tree loaded with the small, deep-purple fruit; it made us a welcome and tasty dessert.

"Mulberries also make good fish bait," said a strange voice.

The tall, patriarchal, gray-haired man that had suddenly appeared gave me a startle and an eerie feeling.

"Well . . . hello, Drapeau." Joe greeted the hunter, who was carrying a rifle and a Bowie knife.

The man looked puzzled at first, then recognition lit his face as he turned back time. "Why, it's been a while . . . let's see, it was '54. Twenty-eight years have passed."

"Yes," Joe responded. "Twenty-eight years and a lot younger. Drapeau, this is my good friend B.J. Ross."

Drapeau asked me to call him Jon. "I been watchin' you men a couple days now and decided ya was all right. Anyone that respects the land the way you have is someone I'd believe friendly. It gets lonely 'round here, and if a man checks out, I'll usually come by to visit and sit a spell."

"Do a lot of people check out?" I asked.

He shook his head. "No . . . you and Joe are the first this year."

Joe added, "I don't blame you, Jon; it pays to be careful around strangers."

"By the way," I asked, "what did ya mean when you said mulberries make good fish bait?"

"Just exactly that. Years past I was fishin' below a mulberry tree, and every so often a berry would fall in the water. It'd no sooner get below the surface and there'd be a wide swirl. Each berry caused the same result. But I couldn't get the berries on my big hook, so I tied on a small one, barbed it through the stem of the berry, then reached out and slowly dropped the bait in the water. I caught a nice one-pound catfish. I could have caught fish all day, but I stopped after ten that size, figurin' it was a school of 'em. Took 'em home, and what I didn't eat I smoked for later.

"If ya want to catch fish, ya have to be aware of what they're feedin' on."

I happened to think of the rustled cattle and asked Jon, "Ya haven't seen anybody driven a herd of cattle in the area? . . . The Germanns up near Stockdale are missin' around twenty head."

Drapeau nodded. "Yeah, I seen 'em a couple days ago. They crossed the river above Garrison and then moved 'em into a canyon several miles north. I thought they acted strange, so I've been keepin' an eye on 'em."

"How many rustlers were pushin' the cattle?"

"Three . . . but yesterday another hombre showed up, so now there's four."

I still wondered if maybe Josh was involved in the rustling and asked, "That fourth one . . . could ya see if he'd had any noticeable features?"

Jon confirmed my fears. "Yeah . . . he's got a scar clear 'cross his right jaw."

I'd hoped Josh wasn't involved; I'd hoped he'd changed his ways. I wondered if maybe I was too forgiving at times, but I'd thought Josh wasn't a hardened outlaw, and I'd tried to help the man. Then I thought of Slim, and wondered if he'd gone the straight and narrow.

When I'd given Josh his break in Dodge City, I'd wondered if it was the right thing to do. It gave me an uneasy feeling, but I'd had no choice; he'd asked for forgiveness.

Now, I felt duty-bound to take on the rustlers.

Twenty-Nine

THE NEXT DAY Joe and I crossed the river to ferret out the cattle thieves. It was three o'clock sun time when we reached the place Jon had described to us. I hadn't wanted Joe to go with me, but he insisted; words can't describe how much I loved that old man.

I injuned up the ravine, leading my horse, until I had 'em spotted camped along the south side of a small meadow. They were in the only open area I'd seen in the box canyon choked with trees. Their horses were picketed to the north in the grass, along a stream of spring water; the cattle were corralled to the east.

I couldn't figure out why the cattle were being held there. The only reason Joe could come up with was they planned to keep 'em there 'til things had settled down.

We'd be able to get close without being seen, as long as we didn't make too much noise, but decided to wait until five that afternoon to hit the rustlers. It'd put the sun to our backs, and hopefully in their eyes.

The hoodlums rested unsuspecting when, with Smith & Wesson in hand, I spurred Prince and yelled a loud battle cry. We hit their camp at full speed. One man was down and not moving. The frightened cattle stampeded up the canyon, but they'd not go far. When Joe and I turned to hit their camp again, two riders were barreling down the ravine, hitting brush and taking half of it with 'em. Josh was trying to mount his horse, which was raring and pulling at the reins.

"Forget it, Josh!" I shouted, as I brought Prince to a fast stop.

He screamed back, pleading, "Don't shoot! My gun's in the holster!"

I believe he thought about drawing, but reconsidered when he saw my gun in hand. I dismounted, walked over to where he stood, reloaded, and put my gun away.

"I should have stayed in Missouri," he added, with a dejected look on his face.

I had no sympathy. "Yeah, you should have; it could have saved you a lot of misery. You might even have had a long life."

Josh looked startled. "You're not goin' to kill me are ya? . . . You can't force me to draw."

"No, I won't force ya to, but I'll turn you over to Germann."

"You can't do that; that old man will hang me!"

"Yeah, Josh, he probably will."

"Don't do it! I promise I'll return to Missouri for good; I'll straighten out. Just give me one more chance."

"No, we did that, Josh. This time you'll face the consequences."

He was crestfallen, and when Joe rode back in from following the other two outlaws, it interrupted my attention for a split second. That was when Josh slapped leather. He tried, but he didn't make it. I dealt him two hot ones where men don't recover.

"The others got away," Joe said as he dismounted and looked over at Josh laying in a pool of blood.

We buried Josh and the other outlaw above the valley floor among the blue-blossomed chicory, where Joe recited the Twenty-third Psalm. It was still light at six o'clock, so Joe and I walked up to the Little Gobi Desert. It was at the top of the canyon where the outlaws had held the cattle, and well worth our time. It made a man scratch his head as to how the sand had got up there on the top of the hills. It wasn't natural, and it matched none of the area soils. Joe thought maybe a titanic storm or cyclone had picked it up off the river bottom and deposited it there. Nothing about it made any sense.

The next day we drove the herd across the Big Blue and were almost to

Stockdale when we met up with Germann and three of his hands. We turned over the cattle and gave Germann the details of what had happened and where the two outlaws were buried. He was pleased, and wanted to give us a hundred dollars for our trouble, but we refused.

Joe and I stayed for a couple more days north of Stockdale, especially after Jon told us about some good fishing spots. While we were camped, the old trapper showed up, and we told him about our trip to the Little Gobi.

He swung his arm to the eastern hills. "I been there many a time — I got away from a band of Osage warriors once by leadin' 'em into the sand."

Jon hesitated like he had more to tell, but thought better of it.

"How do ya think the sand got there?" I asked.

He shrugged. "Don't know. It's a mystery of Nature. But that's not the only oddity in these parts."

Jon could see the interest in my eyes.

"There's the volcanoes . . . I've seen two different sites. One of 'em's not over five miles northwest of Stockdale."

I peered at the old man, trying to discern a half-truth, but he looked sincere. Again he started to say something, then he stopped, and I never questioned him more.

After he'd left our camp in his usual mysterious way, I asked Joe, "Do ya think he's right about the volcanoes?"

Joe nodded. "I don't doubt him for a minute. I don't think the old man would know how to lie."

It was around noon when we rode our horses back into Manhattan, checked in at the livery, and walked to McClusky's. The Irishman was happy to see us, and we ordered coffee and swapped tales the rest of the afternoon.

The next morning, Joe and I were heading for home. Joe peered at the horizons and drawled, "This country grows on you. It hasn't the grandeur of the Rockies, or the mystery of the oceans, but there's something about the prairie that makes a man feel at home."

I knew what he meant. I'd hated leaving Virginia years back, but now I felt like my roots were in Kansas.

Joe looked off in the distance, adding, "And that was the last of the Slater Gang . . . except for one."

"Yeah," I acknowledged. "There may be one left, but this ends it. I believe Slim was sincere when he told me his outlaw days were over. He'd looked me in the eye, and I'd say he meant it."

That evening Joe and I were back home. I was glad I'd gone with him up the Blue, and he seemed happier than I'd seen him for some time.

It was early in July when I rode Prince into Junction City leading a pack horse. I needed staples, for my supplies of flour, sugar, and coffee, along with a few other things, were about depleted. I was at the livery and talking to Spencer when young Jim Brannick stopped to chat. He was riding the grulla I'd seen before. I'd have to say that gray gelding, for beauty and form, was right in there with Dandy and Prince. His mouse coloring, and black mane, tail, and stockings, sure made a pretty horse.

Brannick greeted Spencer and asked about stabling the animal. Then, his business finished with Spencer, he looked over at me.

"Hello, Mr. Ross. Where's Dandy? I see you're ridin' your gelding."

I told him Dandy was at home, taking it easy. "I thought I'd give Prince a little exercise."

I'd almost asked him about his father, but I thought I remembered hearing somewhere that he'd died. After Brannick had left the stable, I asked Spencer if I'd heard right.

Spencer acknowledged it was so. "Back in April . . . the old man was done in by pneumonia."

He didn't know the details, but it turned out the oldest son, the one who hadn't impressed me too much, had inherited all the Brannick property. And word had it, according to Spencer, that the older brother had hated young Jim, and a few days after the old man's death, he had ordered him off the place.

Remembering back, I told Spencer how a little over a year ago Joe and I had taken Dandy to the Brannick's to breed one of their mares, and from what I saw then, Jim was a big help to his father whereas the brother was the same as worthless. "What's Jim been doing to get along?" I asked.

"Well, he came ridin' in here lookin' for work, and I sent him out to the Triple Box B on Clarks Creek to see Pat Boller. He's been a hand there ever since," Spencer added. "I was talkin' to Boller the other day, and he told me the boy's been a good worker. Jim never says much, but I know one thing, somehow he got cut out of his inheritance. Brannick thought too much of the boy to leave him with nothin'."

I asked, "How's old Jim?"

"He's fourteen," Spencer said.

I shook my head. "That's pretty young to be on your own, but I've seen 'em younger, and end up the better for it — that is if they didn't get caught up with the wrong crowd."

Spencer quickly spoke up. "Jim won't go outlaw; he's a good boy. His father taught him well."

On the 15th of July, my life changed. Joe's mahogany bay came plodding down the lane to the house without a rider. I knew something was wrong for Joe's gelding to be coming to my place, even though it was like a second home to the horse. I'd hoped there was some logical excuse for him to show up fully saddled.

I found Joe in the rolling hills of his ranch. He lay dead at the bottom of a dry wash just north of the ranch house. Near as I could tell from the scene, his horse had been spooked and Joe had been thrown from the saddle. From all signs, he'd hit his head on a large rock in the arroyo. I doubted he'd suffered much, from what I could determine. It looked like he'd been knocked out and never awoke. I prayed that his passing had been painless.

We buried Joe in the Upper Humboldt Cemetery. After a short graveside sermon I read one of the poems that I'd found in his journal, in his saddlebags.

With Just My Name

A primrose dawn, gleams light upon,
A budding rose.
From fertile lands, and loving hands,
A blossom grows.

It's off to school, stern golden rule,
Down hallways there,
That, amber days of lilac haze,
Without a care.

From home I flee, mountains to see,
Where nomads roam.
Nothing means more, by land or shore,
Than going home.

Afternoons die, bright suns go by,
And light turns gray.
Loneliness cries, 'neath dimming skies,
Along my way.

Darkness shows face, as cold winds race,
To stake their claim.
They let me know, I too must go,
With just my name.

The choir from the Welcome Church sang "Amazing Grace," and then God brought in a chorus of songbirds singing their heavenly melodies from a nearby clump of verdant dogwood.

Though things never looked brighter for my future, I rode home with a heavy heart.

A week later, riding Dandy, I breasted the Grandview hills, crossed the Smoky River, and rode into Junction City. After a short visit with Spencer at the stable, I walked down to attorney Johnston's office.

I handed him the sealed envelope Joe had given me earlier. Johnston opened it, and read me the will. I was to get all of Joe's property and belongings, and Johnston told me it looked like there would be no problem with the testament. But inside the envelope was another, sealed. Written on the front was "*To Be Opened by B.J. Ross.*" Johnston handed it to me, and I put it in my breast pocket.

It was late when I returned home that day. I finished my chores by lantern, and a halo of golden light on the dark ground led me from the barn to the house. I'd fixed a quick supper, ate, and relaxed a few moments before taking up Joe's letter. I read it in the lamplight of the dark room.

Dear B.J.,

From the time I left the East, I've had no family until I met you. I adopted you by faith when we met in Colorado. You were like a son to me, the son I always wanted.

I hope I wasn't a burden and that you can remember me fondly. Now I have a favor to ask, though before I lay the task upon you, I will need to tell you something more of my earlier life in Boston.

You know that in 1845 I married Jane Thompson. But I didn't tell you that the following year, in July, our daughter Julie was born. However, by the time she was five, my relationship with Jane was in shambles. As I had conveyed earlier, Jane had wanted more than I could give her, and eventually her feelings for me deteriorated to outright anger.

But I had doted on my daughter, and she likewise adored me. She had become, by then, the only reason I stayed in the relationship. Yet Jane's displeasure with me soon became a hatred, which she would often unleash in front of Julie. My pleadings to keep our problems private were to no avail, and it wasn't long, by the time Julie was six, before Jane had placed a wedge between my daughter and me.

I stayed for two more years, until Julie, at her mother's urgings, would have little to do with me. Meanwhile, Jane's tirades had become unbearable; I felt I had no choice but to leave.

And that, my dear friend, leads to the matter at hand. The favor I would like to ask is for you to go to Boston and find my daughter. If, after you talk with her, you feel she is deserving or has the need, I would appreciate it if you would give her $10,000 of the money I have on deposit in the bank.

It might help in your search to know I was living at 817 Spring Street when I left Boston in 1854.

Sincerely, Joe

I pondered Joe's request. It was direct and precise, like everything he did. There was no way I could refuse him.

Thirty

A GOLDEN SUN was pushing purple shadows into the alleyways when I walked down the slope from Washington Street in Junction City to the depot. The ten o'clock was on time, and a whistle blew from out of the western prairies as the train neared town. In five minutes the railcars squeaked to a stop along the wooden platform. The engine puffed deep breaths, as steam drifted out from along the iron wheels, rose upward, then dissipated in the air.

After loading Dandy onto the stockcar, I walked to the passenger car where five other travelers waited to board. I hitched up my gunbelt as I stepped on. "All *aboard!*" came the call. I'd no sooner sat down when the train jerked to a jolting start and then was rolling smoothly down the tracks, leaving the depot shrinking in the distance.

It was the 2nd of August when the passenger train rolled into Boston. Three days later, after a city-wide search, I'd found Julie. She was now Julie Glessner, married, and the mother of three children —

a ten-year-old boy Darrell, the oldest, and daughters Carol, eight, and Shirley, three.

Julie was the eighth out of ten prospects that I'd come up with at the courthouse. On Maple Street I'd stopped at a nondescript dilapidated house in the poor section of town. I knocked at the door twice before a dark-haired young woman answered. She was poorly dressed, but clean, and I could tell, from her demeanor, a nice person.

She looked at me with large brown eyes questioningly. "Yes?" she asked.

"Good day. My name is Bruce Ross. Would you be the daughter of Joe Woodman?"

She had a look of shock on her face, and finally answered "Yes," with hesitation.

"I was a friend of your father's. He died recently, and he'd asked me to come to Boston to find you. If you'd like, I'd be happy to tell you about him and our times together in Colorado and Kansas."

I could see her eyes fill as she again replied "Yes" adding, "I would like to know. Won't you please come in?"

I walked into a small dismal room with a daybed for a couch and two old chairs with tattered upholstery. I settled in a chair across from the couch where Julie had sat down. When I peered at the young woman, the tears were flowing from her sad eyes. My compassion for the lass was overwhelming, and I too became misty-eyed. I sat there fighting against my own tears 'til Julie had calmed her demeanor.

It took three days of visiting before Julie stopped asking questions about her father — where he lived? . . . what the country was like? I explained, the best I could, the endless horizons of prairie grass, rolling hills, vistas of canyon views, and how her father had loved the land.

It was during those talks that her feelings of regret and guilt came to the fore, and she acknowledged how badly her father had been treated. It left no doubt in my mind that she had loved her father deeply. She told me she soon realized, after her father's leaving, how badly she and her mother had treated him, recalling he had always been kind to them. But her mother carried her hostility toward Joe to the grave, even though the allotment Joe had provided her had let her live reasonably comfortable.

Even on her deathbed she had lamented to Julie, "I should have married

Gerald Jensen; he was a gentleman and would have given me all the things I've missed in life."

What Julie's mother didn't know was that Jensen had turned out nothing like she saw him in her imagined world. Julie learned later that Jensen had turned out to be nothing but an alcoholic. Her mother had idolized a man all those years who was worthless and not even close to having the virtues of the man she'd driven from their home.

Julie had married a good man, who worked at the docks when he could, but he made little and they lived poorly from week to week.

After several days in Boston, I had no doubts that Julie was deserving of the money Joe had wanted her to inherit. I felt she deserved more, and decided to do just that. Joe's bank account was nearly $30,000, and I'd decided to give it all to Julie.

On my last evening in Boston, I told her of the inheritance and when she learned the amount, she began to cry.

"Thank you," she earnestly told me through her tears. "I have thought of Father often and loved him dearly, and I have testified so in my prayers as I've asked for forgiveness. To leave me an inheritance after all these years must mean he had loved me too."

I acknowledged that was so, adding, "Otherwise he wouldn't have sent me to find you."

Julie peered over to her husband. "Now we can buy us a place of our own, John. You grew up on a farm and always said you wanted to go West."

"Well, we'll do it Julie! . . . We'll buy us a ranch!" John replied.

It was then I knew they should have Joe's place. "There's no need to buy a ranch," I broke in. "He left Julie his home place of six hundred-forty acres. It has a house, barns, some eighty head of cattle, and a remuda of eight horses. The ranch is fully equipped; all you need to do is move West with the clothes on your back!"

I felt like old Kris Kringle! The Glessners were elated. The children danced around the room, hugging their parents and me. The three-year-old came rushing over and wrapped her arms around my leg, peering up at me. "I love you B.J."

With a lump in my throat, I replied, "I love you too."

I remember little of what transpired the rest of that day, but I must say I'd never seen a happier or more thankful family than on that warm evening in Boston.

When I returned to the hotel, I felt good, and knew in my heart that Joe would have been pleased. My wish was that he could have met Julie as she was now.

I'd determined to keep the place he'd bought on Mill Creek, figuring he'd want me to have something of his own, one hundred-sixty acres of bottom and hill country a few miles north of what would in a few years be the town of Volland.

I telegraphed attorney Johnston in Junction City the next day, explaining that the Glessners were coming West and they were to have Joe's bank account and home ranch, adding he was to tell them nothing about Joe's will, as I would sign the necessary papers when I returned.

Dandy and I breasted the heights outside Boston just as the sun was coming up. I'd decided to see some of the country that my Great-Grandfather John Ross had ridden his troops over during the Revolutionary War. It was a wooded land, and on that morning the sunlight gleamed golden bracelets into the deep purple of long shadows. I loved the region thereabouts, and it came to me that it didn't matter where a person was, America was a land of beauty east to west, Atlantic to Pacific.

"Tread careful on the land," Pa had always told me. "It's God's creation; so treat it kindly, and it will always love you." As I rode that day disturbing little around me, I felt the love Pa had talked about, coursing through my being.

I'd decided to take my time going home, heading by way of Virginia. A week later I rode down the lane that had been so familiar to me, leading to Grandfather's home place. Grandfather had died in '76, and my Uncle William Harrison Ross now lived in the house.

I spent a week riding the Virginia countryside, and even felt like I was going home when I rode into the lane to the farm where I grew up. Virginians are hospitable people, and the Comptons who'd bought the place invited me into the house. After an hour of polite conversation I excused myself, went outside, mounted Dandy, and with their permission rode the site.

The next day I spent at the hidden meadow that was still in Ross hands. When I saw the sanctuary loved by my ancestors, it felt like the twelve years I'd been gone from Virginia had not taken place, and it was all a dream. The rhododendron along the slopes above the waterfall were in full bloom with beautiful pink blossoms. A few petals had fallen in the stream and were slowly floating along my feet from where I stood at the edge of a clear blue pool.

Darkness was painting a purple evening hue upon the countryside when I mounted Dandy and rode the narrow trail out of the mountain retreat. I'd almost left him in Kansas, for he was fifteen now. But I was happy I'd brought him; he remembered the hidden meadow, pawing at the earth gently and then trailing his reins to another part of the basin. He seemed as reluctant to leave as I did when finally we rode away.

The Washingtons still lived on Grandfather's place, as did several other black families. While in Virginia I'd hoped to see Joshua Washington, my boyhood friend for four years after the Civil War, but his father, Isaiah, told me he'd gone West, as we had. The last they'd heard from him, he was working on a ranch in Texas.

It was a few days away from September when the train crossed the Mississippi River into St. Louis. I recalled the trip with Ma and Pa, as we'd passed through the city years back.

I had a layover of three hours in the bustling town, so I decided to take a stroll along the Mississippi. I wanted to see, up close, the waters of the famous river, and walked down to the docks. They were busy, with barges being loaded, and others coming and going. It didn't take me long to figure out there were some tough places along the riverfront that a body should avoid.

The taverns were busy, and in front of one called the Blue Moon, two toughs took an interest in my presence as I walked by to look at a steamboat tied up along the quay. I felt for my holstered gun. It was in place, and the feel of the cold steel gave me comfort, as did the dirk resting comfortably at my back. After looking over the paddlewheel, I checked my watch. I still had an hour, plenty of time to return.

As I started back to the Union Pacific depot, two hundred yards stood between me and the Blue Moon, on an isolated walkway with bales of cotton and bundled goods stacked up on both sides. I soon realized it was a perfect place for an ambush. I looked around and realized the two hoodlums were gone from the bench in front of the tavern.

I'd not gone halfway through the maze of bales when they jumped me. I took a blow to the head that almost knocked me out. Both men were pummeling me, but I managed to get in a few blows myself as I backed into a narrow passage where only one culprit could get to me at a time. Realizing it was now one-on-one, the thief I faced pulled a knife. When he did, I reached for my gun, but it was gone, apparently fallen out of my holster in the scuffle. I pulled my dirk, and the hoodlum seemed shocked I had a blade. In those close quarters, without mobility, we would both get cut to pieces. But he nevertheless moved in slashing, and I parried the best I could, though I still took cuts. When I finally drove the dirk into his midsection, he screamed and fell back into the bloke behind him.

I heard a shout from somewhere ahead, and the two thieves took off running, though one of 'em was having trouble, bent over with his hand covering his belly. I heard feet rushing to where I stood.

The man that had shouted was the Captain of the paddlewheel I'd just looked at. He and several of the crew were returning to the boat when they heard the commotion. The Captain stayed with me, and the rest took out after the thieves. I wasn't seriously hurt, mostly bruises and a couple of nasty cuts.

I'd found my Smith & Wesson partly beneath a bale, then the Captain took me to the boat and cleaned me up a bit. From there he had two men accompany me to the depot, and just in time I stepped up into the railcar.

The following day the train pulled into Junction City. I spent the next two days there healing up and visiting with Spencer.

When I finally saddled Dandy, heading for home, golden sunlight was streaming through the opened doorway of the dark stable. I reached the top of the Grandview hills, then stopped, took in the view, and realized I couldn't be living in a better place. It mattered not in what part of the country a body lived, for wherever home was it became the most beautiful place in the world.

But I thought of Joe, and my heart ached. I'd miss him as much as if I'd lost my right arm. Late that September, the Glessners moved into Joe's ranch. They were wonderful neighbors. Julie told me on one of her visits that she felt close to her father again by living in his home.

On October 25, 1882, my watch showed six o'clock when I rolled out of bed. It was my thirtieth birthday, and I felt like the luckiest man in the world.

When I walked to the barn, my feet waded in darkness below the circle of light from my swinging lantern. By the time I'd finished my chores, a radiant sun was glowing brightly above the eastern hills. It had turned cold overnight, and a deep frost covered the bluestem; in the morning sunlight the grass glistened like diamonds along the purple canyons.

I stood by the house and thought of Pa when I looked at the far horizon. It had been a family belief passed on, he'd explained when we prepared to leave Virginia, that a man lived in three worlds in his lifetime. And the third was the best.

I thought I was now entering my third world. The first had been Virginia. The second my adventures in the West.

At half past two in the afternoon I hitched up the black mare to the buckboard and stepped into the buggy. With a snap of the reins, the mare trotted down the lane. At the main road, I tooled a familiar left turn. The Welcome Church was but three miles away. I'd be there in plenty of time for the four o'clock service.

The sun had disappeared into a gray overcast covering the sky, and something cold and wet touched my cheek. My eyes followed large snowflakes drifting in the atmosphere that settled down onto the tawny prairie and disappeared. I peered beneath my hat into the restless flurries of cold winds bending the long grass and attempting to rock the buggy, but I smiled at the elements that might try to discourage my state of mind.

Surely no inclement weather could shake my buoyant mood. . . . This was the day of my wedding to Enie, and ahead of us lay a new beginning.

Epilogue

ON DECEMBER 1, 1940, my Grandfather Bruce Jacob Ross died. He had lived a full Christian life, and had told Enie on his deathbed, "I've always believed in a merciful Father, and know in my heart that faith in God is the only way to live, and die."

I was a young lad that cold blustery day of the funeral, and from an overcast gray sky occasional snowflakes drifted down only to be carried away by a stiff wind moaning in the bluestem grass. In some way, the day seemed fitting; the weather was not unlike the elements the day of Grandpa's wedding.

You could feel the winter air away from the potbelly stove that glowed red in the corner, next to the altar and pews. A heavy frost had coated the windows, and the room, for comfort, required a coat.

At ten o'clock the minister opened with a benediction, and toward the end of the service, Lucy Poole sang Grandpa's favorite:

Carry me back to old Virginny,
There's where the cotton and the corn and tatoes grow,
There's where the birds warble sweet in the springtime,
There's where the old darke'ys heart am long'd to go,
There's where I labored so hard for old massa,
Day after day in the fields of yellow corn,
No place on earth do I love more sincerely
Than old Virginny, the state where I was born. . . .

From the church, my father drove to the Welcome Cemetery in his 1938 Pontiac, and after parking along the gravel roadway, my mother and father and I slowly walked to the opened gravesite, covered with a tent, beside a throng of relatives and friends.

While standing listening to the minister's prayer at the grave, my father for a moment held my hand in his warm clasp. I'd seen other young boys hold their father's hand, but it was the first time my father had taken mine. He was from an era when it wasn't the manly thing for fathers to do, but I think on this sad occasion he let his guard down and figured it was acceptable. His lifting that veil of manliness, ingrained from childhood, that solemn day at the cemetery, made it something special . . . a kind of love that a young boy never forgets.

Cover artist . . . Tom Bookwalter, a nationally known illustrator and graphic artist, is currently a graphic design instructor at Kansas State University, Manhattan. Bookwalter's work appears in national magazines, annual reports, calendars, posters, and brochures. He has been honored by the National Geographic Society, the East and West Coast Society of Illustrators, the International Society of Business Communicators, and the Greater Jackson (Mississippi) Advertising Club. His clients include Rockwell International, 3M Company, Hewlett Packard, Ford Motor Company, VISA, IBM, United Technologies, Honeywell, Levi Strauss, AT&T, the National Football League, *The Washington Post*, and Miller Brewing, as well as the Department of the Navy, the Federal Reserve Bank of Kansas City, and the United States Information Agency.

Bookwalter attended Peru State University in Nebraska and earned his B.A. from Emporia State University, Emporia, Kansas. He attended the prestigious Art Center College of Design in Pasadena, California.

Bookwalter is represented nationally by the Neis Group, of Grand Rapids, Michigan; Munro Goodman Artists Representatives, in Chicago and New York; and the Image Mill, Des Moines, Iowa.

Also by Harold G. Ross

Throughout My Passing Day

Where Eagles Fly

Along Golden Hills

Homage to the Gods

Brannick and the Untamed West

Horizons West